W9-CUQ-045

The New Country

Judaic Traditions in Literature, Music, and Art

Ken Frieden and Harold Bloom, *Series Editors*

The New Country

STORIES FROM THE YIDDISH ABOUT LIFE IN AMERICA

Translated and Edited by Henry Goodman

With a Foreword by Elie Wiesel
Drawings by Dana Craft

A Dora Teitelboim Center for Yiddish Culture Publication

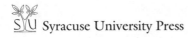 Syracuse University Press

Copyright © 2001 by The Dora Teitelboim Center for Yiddish Culture, Inc.
All Rights Reserved

First Syracuse University Press Edition 2001

01 02 03 04 05   5 4 3 2 1

This edition is an abridged version of *The New Country: Stories from the Yiddish about Life in America,* originally published in 1961 by YKUF Publishers, New York

The paper used in this publication meets the minimum requirements of American National Standard for Information Sciences—Permanence of Paper for Printed Library Materials, ANSI Z39.48–1984.∞™

Library of Congress Cataloging-in-Publication Data
New Country. Selections.
     The new country : stories from the Yiddish about life in America / translated and edited by Henry Goodman ; with a foreword by Elie Wiesel ; drawings by Dana Craft.
        p. cm. — (Judaic traditions in literature, music, and art)
     "This edition is an abridged version of The new country . . . originally published in 1961 by YKUF Publishers, New York"—CIP t.p. verso.
     ISBN 0-8156-0669-9 (alk. paper)
     1. Short stories, Yiddish—Translations into English. 2. Jews—United States—Fiction. 3. Immigrants—United States—Fiction. I. Goodman, Henry, 1893–1990. II. Title. III. Series.
PJ5191.E8 N482 2000
839'.1301083273—dc21   00-034430

Manufactured in the United States of America

To Rebecca and Rachel

In the hope that you and your generation will come to know and love those who came before and will create a legacy in your own way for those yet to arrive.

HENRY GOODMAN was born in Romania in 1893. He came to the United States in 1900, residing in Philadelphia and eventually in New York. He graduated from Columbia University School of Journalism in 1915. While still a student at Columbia, Mr. Goodman contributed translations of Yiddish stories and poetry to the esteemed publication *East and West,* including translations of David Einhorn, M. Rosenblat, Mendele, Dovid Pinski, I. L. Peretz, and Abraham Raisin. Upon graduation he worked as a reporter for the *World* and as a copyreader for the *Tribune,* and also contributed short stories to *The Seven Arts* and *Pictorial Review.*

From journalism, Mr. Goodman turned to teaching. He taught in the English Department of Thomas Jefferson High School for thirty-four years and also taught courses at Hunter College. Goodman was a prodigious translator of Yiddish poetry and prose into English, publishing *Creating the Short Story* in 1929; *Stories of the City* in 1931; *Three Gifts and Other Stories,* a translation of Peretz's stories, in 1947; the original *The New Country* in 1961; and *Clinton Street and Other Stories,* the works of Chaver Paver, in 1974. He also compiled and edited *The Selected Writings of Lafcadio Hearn.* In addition to literature, Goodman published a highly regarded two-volume historical opus, *Our People in the Middle Ages,* in 1962. Goodman was also an avid contributor to *Jewish Currents* and the *Yiddish Forward* for over twenty years, to which he submitted dozens of book reviews, articles, stories, and translations. He died in New York in 1990.

Contents

Imprisoned

His Trip to America

We Strike

The Greenhorns

PART TWO

Making a Living

Chaim Becomes a Real-Estatenik

Chaim and Chaye

We Work in a Shop

Point of a Needle

Chaim Thanks God for Deliverance

PART THREE

And What of the Children?

PART SIX

Not All Greenhorns Are Jewish!

Foreword

ELIE WIESEL ————————————————————————————

THIS ANTHOLOGY DOES NOT NEED an introduction; its authors speak for themselves. They represent the best of Yiddish literature in America. Poets and essayists, social commentators and humorists, journalists and novelists: all had things to say about the new country that offered them and their fellow Jews a haven with its possibilities to build new homes and new lives.

You read these pages, many of them brilliantly translated, and you wonder: why aren't their authors, with the exception of Sholem Aleichem and Sholem Asch, better known? Many of them belong to the category of great writers.

Take Joseph Opatoshu or Peretz Hirschbein—one day their novels about Eastern Europe will be discovered by a daring publisher or literary critic. That day will be a celebration not only in Yiddish circles, but also in the world of letters.

But in this volume, the general theme is America and its newly arrived Jewish immigrants. You read their stories with laughter and tears. Sholem Aleichem's scenes of New York life in the streets; Moishe Nadir's satire about job hunting; reminiscences and observations by Jacob Gordin, Isaac Raboy, Abraham Raisin, Chone Gottesfeld, and so many others. Some episodes are funny, others moving; many deal with social issues, others with psychological ones; some are imbued with a quest for dignity, others are preoccupied with identity.

Read this remarkable book and you will come closer to its gifted and often inspired protagonists and their enchanted universe.

The Dora Teitelboim Center
for Yiddish Culture

DORA TEITELBOIM was an internationally renowned Yiddish poet, whose fiery social motifs sang and wept joys and sorrows and, above all, the love of mankind. Teitelboim, the poet for whom "the wind itself speaks Yiddish," as she asserts in one of her poems, had a dream of establishing an organization that would promote Yiddish poetry and prose to a new generation of Americans by making Yiddish works more accessible to the American public, thereby cultivating a new harvest of Yiddish educators, writers, speakers, and performers.

The Dora Teitelboim Center for Yiddish Culture continues the dream of its namesake by publishing high-quality translations of Yiddish literature. It runs an annual cultural writing contest, promotes the rich texture and beauty of Jewish culture through lectures and cultural events, and produces documentary film and radio programming.

For one thousand years, Yiddish has been the language of the troubadour, poet, sweatshop toiler, revolutionary, and dreamer. Yiddish became the vehicle of secular Jewish life, giving solid footing to a people without a territory of their own. Although Yiddish fell victim to an unnatural death as a result of the Holocaust, it is now experiencing a renaissance not seen for many years. *The New Country,* a republication and refurbishment of the original 1961 YKUF classic about greenhorns coming to America, is a testament to the beauty and endurance of the *mame-loshn* (mother tongue) through the trials and tribulations of Americanization. It retains an enduring view of the fear, wonder, estrangement, labor struggles, humor, and endurance of Jewish immigration in the first third of the twentieth century that forever changed the face of Jewish life. Yet through it all, so much remains. It is up to new generations to move through this new millennium, with our feet firmly resting on the values, scholarship, and humor of our forefathers and foremothers.

January 2000   David Weintraub
                                                       Executive Director

Preface to the Original Edition

WITHIN THE LAST YEAR or two I saw an exhibition, arranged by the Yiddish Scientific Institute, called Dos Shtetl. By means of photographs of homes, markets and market stalls, synagogues, individual men and women and children, groups of people, the town pump, the streets; by means of communal posters, announcements, workbooks of school-children, letters and scraps of writing, the agendas and minutes of community organizations, family albums and other items, the exhibition sought to rebuild, as a memorial to a life wiped out, the shtetl, which has been the seedbed of almost everything we treasure in the past of the East European Jew. That the exhibition did its work effectively I can testify from the impact it made on me. I returned to it again and again. And I must confess, I returned with a more intense interest that I had ever felt when sauntering through the ruins of Pompeii or the Forum in Rome.

That my memory was at work, there can be no doubt. Over the pictured degradation of what had been the villages and small towns of the old Pale, habitations mean and miserable against even some of the habitations of the African American in backward areas of the South, there floated figures out of Chagall; snatches of talk out of Kasrielevka, Glupsk, Kabtzansk; Tevye and the Rebbe of Nemirov and the unforgettable Rebbetzin of Skul came to life before my eyes. And though a feeling of unplumbed despair was in my heart that this had been the setting of life for millions of my people, overriding the despair was an assertive pride. For out of this mean and unsightly and horribly demeaning landscape had come none other than those Yiddish writers whom we honor, and many of whom are included in this book, *The New Country*.

I want briefly to substantiate my pride. It rests on the uncompromising honesty of Libin, the unsentimental gentleness of Raisin, the complex and revealing analyses of Zalmon Libin, the raillery and pointed probing of Moishe Nadir. And then there are the sensitiveness and precision of Tashrak, the power in Opatoshu, to say nothing of the engaging, exhilarating, and dramatic qualities of Raboy, Chaver Paver, Sheen Miller, and the many others who appear in this book of translations. Now that the work is done, I may publicly confess that reading the works of these writers, feeling the flow of their Yiddish, with its idiom and tradition, its burden and glory of historic and Biblical allusion, its flexibility of structure, its responsiveness to every emotion, was one of the most pleasurable experiences I have had.

Like the exhibition Dos Shtetl, *The New Country* is a re-creation, too, a re-creation of the America to which our fathers, grandfathers, and great-grandfathers came in the eighties and nineties of the nineteenth century and the earlier years of the twentieth. It is more than that, too. It is a re-creation of the ways of life of the immigrants and their children, and of the transformations in American life which they experienced and helped to bring about. It is a testimonial to the spirit with which they faced the problems of their new setting.

But this book is more than a record. It is the living reality of the East European Jew getting settled in an environment so utterly unlike anything he had known in the shtetl; it pictures his getting into stride in the America which had promised so much and which, though it pressed on his soul, gave him only what he was strong enough and courageous enough to take. It gives us the domestic scene, the life within the homes, the relations between the old and the younger generations. It reveals those moments of lightheartedness and laughter (through tears) and occasions of self-mockery so characteristic of our people. It singles out individual lives and experiences, telling of them with sensitiveness and revealing insight. And it brings the Jew into meaningful relationships with the non-Jewish world.

The arrangement of the sections gives us, finally, an interesting view in a chronological sense. In each section of the book, the order proceeds, for the most part, from earlier writers to those closer to our own time. This permits us to see not only the changing, living experience of the culture, but also the responsiveness which has marked the growth of Yiddish literature in the new country.

I am happy to acknowledge my gratitude to Nachman Maizel and Itche Goldberg for helpful suggestions in the planning of this book.

1961

Henry Goodman

Introduction

IT IS NO MERE MATTER of social form that the Jew, raising his glass in a toast, drinks a *l'chaim*, a toast to life. In that gesture, he celebrates and extols life itself. He affirms the conviction that living here and now is the central concern of humanity's interests, that improving the human condition is the dearest wish of most people. Life is sacred, the individual's own as well as that of his fellow man. Life is sacred, as is every effort to safeguard it and every action to enrich it. Describing the Jewish people against a background of outrage and murder more fiendish than anything they had ever experienced in their history before our own day, Zalmon Shneur reminds us that they are:

> A people pledged to life.
> Pledged to uprooting the evil within life.

And it was a sentiment distilled from an ever-living ethos that Emma Lazarus voiced and that generous American thoughtfulness inscribed on the base of the Statue of Liberty. Do we not recognize a counterpoise to Hillel's words: "Do not do unto others what you would not have them do to you" in her lines:

> Give me your tired, your poor
> Your huddled masses yearning to breathe free?

Immigrants were coming to America from many parts of Europe for decades before the arrival of the Jewish masses from Eastern European lands. In the latter part of the nineteenth century, the immigration included increasing numbers of Jews from Eastern Europe who fled before mounting waves of persecution and pogroms. Among these Jews would be the founders of Yiddish literature in America.

Who, seeing them in their outlandish garb as they came into the ports of the Atlantic seaboard, could have imagined that their children and grandchildren, and they themselves, would gain distinction in all the fields of American life: industry, philosophy, commerce, science, the arts, the professions, social service, politics—yes, and even gangsterism and rascality, the great American game of taking the public for an expensive ride? But at that time, certainly, they looked tired, and poor, and terribly bewildered.

To what were they coming? To what conditions of life, to what prospects for themselves and their children, to what environmental and cultural influences, and what new horizons?

Vernon L. Parrington, discussing American life and literature of that time, suggests what the answers would have been had the questions been asked. And, of course, some of the individual writers themselves would have subscribed to those answers. The Yiddish writers, many of them represented in this book, *The New Country,* answer the questions in moving and, very often, beautiful stories.

Parrington shows that it was a time of questioning, of large-scale grumbling, a time of measuring the actualities of need and hunger for many against the expectations which expanding industry held out to all but, with calculated cunning, turned into ever-increasing profits for the few. Those expectations proved as pretty as soap bubbles, and as empty. Farmers and workers came to question the ways of capitalism, as they took stock of what was actually happening to them in the course of industrial and financial expansion. Actualities of daily living disillusioned and embittered men and women on the farms, in the shops, and in the factories of the country.

The spreading discontent, wedded to growing knowledge of European social philosophy, gave impetus to protest and action, an impetus that found its counterpart in the work of many American writers.

Thus, Stephen Crane exposed the dreadful slums and tenements of New York, the degradation to which their inhabitants were reduced, and the stupefaction in which they endured conditions they had neither strength nor will to alter.

Edwin Markham, stirred by the dehumanization he found in the camps of labor, farm, mine, and factory, voiced his warning to masters and lords of this world in "Man with the Hoe."

Hamlin Garland, himself a refugee from farm life in the Midwest, wrote of the brutalizing toil on the land and the exploitation of the farmers by the holders of mortgages.

Frank Norris exulted: "By God! I told them the Truth," writing the crucial word with a capital *T* to show he would have no truck with those who softened in any way the suffering and failures in American life.

William Dean Howells, a Socialist, was outraged by what he saw in the upper middle-class circles he knew. He let a tycoon lay down first principles: "If [the businessman] looks about him at all, he sees that no man gets rich simply by his own labor, no matter how mighty a genius he is, and that if you want to get rich, you must make other men work for you, and pay you for the privilege of doing it."

Upton Sinclair could not accept in silence what he learned about the foreign-born workers in the slaughterhouses in Chicago.

And, even that seemingly light-minded jongleur, O. Henry, pointed with bitter scorn to the employer who paid his girls just enough to make them easy prey for the Piggies who lay in wait.

But all of these writers, with the exception of Garland, escaped from the farm, were outsiders, sympathetic outsiders to be sure, who were moved to set down what they observed. They wrote firmly, sharply, clearly, with the objectivity that distance encouraged.

The Yiddish writers, however, the pioneers of the literature just coming into being, were a different case. The noise and the heavy atmosphere of the sweatshop were in their ears and lungs. The stench of the tenements was in their nostrils because the tenements were home and atelier at the same time. Poets and writers of tales, journalists and pamphleteers, they were setting down, in the heat of their own passionate reaction to confinement in the cellars and grim lofts of the little subcontractors, the intense realities of their own experience. Bovshover, Edelstat, Winchevsky, Morris Rosenfeld, Libin, and Kobrin, no less than Abraham Cahan, Jacob Gordin, B. Gorin, Krantz, Feigenbaum, and others, were united in one enterprise: teaching the newly made proletarians, their fellow immigrants, the need and the virtue of protest, the value of joint action of all for the benefit of each. These writers were a generation tried in battle, who had known the struggle against the czar and, in a few cases, against evil labor conditions in England.

The fiction that came from these lives and experiences, the stories reflecting bewilderment, despair, simple joy, hopefulness, and struggle, were set down by the pioneer writers in bold, dramatic strokes. The writers, formed by the struggles in which they took part, were impatient of literary artifice or subtlety or were, indeed, incapable of them. They had stories to tell, human experiences, sufferings, and triumphs to impart; they would not stop to embroider, to beguile the reader with skills that entertain, to ease boredom with tricks of linguistic refinement and intellectual surprise. The commonplace for them, the simple, the *poshetus* (plain), for, like Sholem Aleichem, whose epitaph written by himself declares that his "tales in Yiddish were written for common men and women," these earliest of the American Yiddish writers were intent on sharing with their readers, most of them unsophisticated in literary taste, observations and interpretations which would steel their will to resist social wrong, to recognize injustice, to act for the betterment of life for the many whose lives can stand betterment. The commonplace for them, but with what poignancy it becomes invested, what tenderness comes through, what values ethical, humane, take shape!

But there were themes other than battle cries. There was the awareness of American spaciousness; the frequent looking back to what, in retrospect, seemed to have been an idyllic life "at home" but to which very few desired to return; the meetings of fellow townspeople, gathered often for purposes of aiding someone more unfortunate than themselves. There was the critical examination of some who, having preceded them to "Columbus's land," had ostentatiously liberated themselves from the behavior patterns of the places of their origin. There were the new and unexpected difficulties with children who were responding in unlooked-for ways to the environment of freedom and independence; the fitting into a machine-controlled existence after a life of piety and small-town calm; the conflicts and emotional crises nothing in their lives had prepared them for.

Aesthetic considerations would come consciously to take their part in the rapid evolution of American Yiddish writing. There would be imagists and impressionists, symbolists and romanticists, among the writers coming to notice in the world of Yiddish culture. New writers would grope their way to recognition in a literary world with next to no publishing apparatus outside the few newspapers and the magazines: *Zukunft* and, much later, *Yiddishe Kultur*. The early years of the new century would see the arrival, from Europe, of Sholem Asch, Abraham Raisin, L. Shapiro, and the rise of new Yiddish writers in America.

The latter, the "Americans," would proclaim new intentions, artistic and experimental, as was befitting an appreciation of the turbulent metropolis which they were taking in stride. They were reaching out, in proud discovery and delight, to the unexampled splendors of American nature and space. American rivers and landscapes come into Yiddish poetry and prose. It is true they come in by way of the Palisades, the Hudson River, and the Catskills. But the reach of interest and imagination soon extends to Kentucky, the Dakotas, the Rockies, the western shore. Yiddish writers were becoming enchanted wanderers over the face of America, intoxicated with the ease and excitement of movement, weaving a living web of Jewish culture from city to city across the land. New themes, new insights, and nuances come into the widening stream of Yiddish literature through such writers as Ignatov, Glassman, Raboy, Chaver Paver, Opatoshu, and others.

But all of the writers show, in their various ways, that the best of Yiddish writing retains a moral seriousness, a critical yet compassionate interest in the strivings, achievements, and failings of fellow beings. Their stories are not stories alone; they are experiences to be shared, to be consumed by the reader so that his life may be enlarged, his horizon extended, his humanity deepened and made more sensitive, his emotions enriched. Realistic as some of these writers become, the tight-lipped coldness, the clinical aloofness admired in some American and other non-Yiddish writing, are utterly out of keeping with the feeling, approach, attitude, and practice of the Yiddish writer. And there never is a Jewish aesthete who, like the glorious young Mussolini, is moved to ecstasy by the flowering of a firebomb over the habitations of human beings.

By the time Di Yunge and the Insichists (Introspectionists) are ready to execute their aesthetic and experimental designs in poetry and prose, the language has been completely freed of a stiff Germanism that accompanied it from the other side. It is now ready for the subtle uses to which it will be put by M. L. Halpern, Rolnick, Eisland, Leivick, Nadir, Chaimowitz, Glatstein, and others.

Of equal importance is the growth of a reading public with an increasingly subtle responsiveness to the best that its literary artists can provide. The process had begun far back.

The more the life of the Jewish masses in Europe was becoming secularized in the nineteenth century, the more surely Yiddish literature became the means of ready communication and understanding among them in their different centers of settlement—Russia, Poland, Galicia, and Romania. In thus becoming the vehicle of secularized Jewish life, Yiddish literature, along with a growing flexibility of language and image-making plasticity, took over, in increasing measure, a role hitherto held by Torah: the role of giving solid footing to a people without territory of its own. Yiddish literature became that pseudo territory so ardently discussed by the splendid Yiddish critic, Boruch Rivkin. On this soil, this territory, the Jewish reader could move with whatever sense of security his nerves and the literature could fashion for him.

These writings, at first in Europe, then later in this country, created an atmosphere of moral sensitiveness, spiritual refreshment, and cohesive Jewishness among growing numbers for whom the Jewish religion no longer served as a bond. Yiddish poetry, stories, novels, and plays deepened the will to endure as Jews. They strengthened the resolution to face the world with the inner certainty that there is a *menschlichkeit,* a humanness, in all humankind. They reasserted the faith that we can set flowing the fountains of goodness in others by making accessible to others this source in ourselves.

Thus, Yiddish, both language and literature, became the common ground on which an increasingly secularized Jewishness, though segmented through dispersion, could achieve a cohesion that has seemed anomalous to the non-Jewish world. A Russian Jew, stopping off in Paris, London, New York, Mexico City, Buenos Aires, and even in Shanghai of a few years ago, could get along well on Yiddish. And if he were a person of intellectual interests he could find those with whom he might discuss the varying phases of Sholem Asch's genius, the criticism of Samuel Niger, the essays of Dr. Zhitlovsky, the plays of Peretz Hirschbein, the novels of Dovid Bergelson, Joseph Opatoshu, etc.

The extent to which Jewishness, the sense of oneness, had become identified with the Yiddish language may be seen in a statement made in Poland, in 1937, by a religious group, Bnoth Agudath Israel:

> Yiddish is a language which the Jews have created in the Diaspora. This language became the expression of the Jewish soul, of Jewish longing and aspiration, of Jewish joy and suffering.

To take lightly this language of the people is to take lightly our entire past in which our Jewishness took form. This language is the only means by which the large masses of Jews can give expression to their thoughts and feelings. We must guard and protect this precious vessel and certainly not be ashamed of it but, rather, take pride in it and show it on every occasion and in every situation.

Pride in the language and in what has been wrought in it is not unwarranted.

Leaders of the Haskalah—the Enlightenment—used it as the language of instruction in worldly subjects. In the hands of Mendele, Sholem Aleichem, and Peretz it became as sweetly pliant as a withe: It could sing, sting, bite, burn, cool, and hearten. Unforgettable Tevye could express total helplessness and immovable resolution at one and the same time, as when he says: "It's become a custom with our people, God be praised, that as soon as there is a rumor of a pogrom, we begin flying from one town to another."

Raisin, Asch, Liessin, and, later in the twentieth century, Moishe Nadir, M. J. Chaimowitz, Leivick, Moishe Leib Halpern, and many others, cultivated the language, refined it, made it playful, delicate, powerful, full-toned, as their individual purposes required. In the hands of L. Shapiro and Yona Rosenfeld it became deftly searching, while it retained a lucid and lyrical flow.

But the fact that a great deal of Yiddish writing, flexible, well nuanced, and translated into English of nearly comparable qualities, is something totally strange to the non-Jewish reader argues the presence of some elements of uniqueness. The Jewishness of "H*Y*M*A*N* K*A*P*L*A*N" is at home everywhere. Arthur Kober's witticisms find ready takers. An explanation offered by some, in relation to the difficult writings, is that the specific piece is too recherché, too deeply enmeshed in a complex of Jewish allusion and cross-reference to which the uninitiated can find no key. It is an explanation that fails to explain.

Consider the case of the late John Erskine, professor of English at Columbia University, a competent judge of writing, and himself a known critic and writer.

Many years ago, the short-lived magazine *East and West*, sponsored by Harry Rogoff and Henry Greenfield, undertook the work of presenting Yiddish literature in translation. A new venture, the magazine invited John Erskine to pass critical judgment on its first number. That criticism revealed such difficulties of comprehension, such failure to grasp the points of view of the writers analyzed, as to show the existence of a chasm between the world of Jewish experience and perception, and that in which Erskine was at home.

Raisin, Peretz, and Libin, represented in that issue by stories of poverty, painful tenderness, and deprivation, all but cry aloud for a social order that will make impossible the situations they present. Erskine acknowledged the success of the translators and the skill of the writers, but said of Libin: "A suspicion taunts the reader that he may be grieving more deeply for the evicted family and the frustrated boarder than the author of the story grieves," and of Raisin: "Even here the suspicion follows that the writer may be laughing at his characters, that the pettiness he has exhibited may be intended for the satiric rather than the kindly heart."

One might as well see satire in Van Gogh's "Potato Eaters," or Max Weber's "Adoration of the Moon," or read Raisin's "Five Potatoes" for its satirical intention.

Well, what was wrong? Erskine could not see that these grim pictures were made by writers who were using contemporary terms to urge a justice about which they and their readers had learned, in childhood, as students of the prophets. The realism of these writers might derive from the Russian or the French, but the intention and the passion, given impetus by new, organized social thinking and social effort, came from another source. It welled up in them as it had in Mendele and Sholem Aleichem, from a deep-rooted faith that humankind can be made worthy of a better world, that humanity's will can be shaped toward worthy ends. The emphasis is always on human beings, on their will, on their responsibility.

This social idealism has made for the unity, the continuity in spirit and feeling, of Yiddish literature from its beginning down to our own day. The reader of Yiddish was and is at home in the presence of the Yiddish novelist, story writer, poet, and essayist, whatever the land of origin of the work may be. Outward differences exist, of course, owing to locale and environmental circumstance. Underneath those differences, however, there is an unswerving loyalty to the belief that a person has the duty and power to build the good life on Earth. That the faith and belief, and even the ideal, have been betrayed is no deterrent. That humanity builds in the face of death, this is the daily miraculous redemption of life.

These qualities and characteristics are part of the heritage to which Jewish thinkers, religious and secular, have clung since Biblical times. Yiddish writers are in this tradition.

In a penetrating glance at Nietzsche, Thomas Mann cites the philosopher as saying, disdainfully: "When Socrates and Plato began to speak of truth and justice, they were no longer Greeks, but Jews or I do not know what."

Mann comments: "Well, the Jews, thanks to their morality, have proved themselves *good and preserving children of life* [my italics]. They have, along with their religion, their belief in a just God, survived millennia, while the profligate little nation of aesthetes and artists, the Greeks, vanished very quickly from the stage of history."

It is worth observing that Bernard Berenson's insistence that a work of art must be "life-enhancing" stands foursquare on the ground of humane purpose underlying every enduring structure raised by Yiddish writers.

PART ONE

Getting Settled

The Tenement House

(By Way of a Backdrop)

LEON KOBRIN ⸻

A TENEMENT HOUSE on Suffolk Street. Like most tenement houses in the Jewish quarter of New York. A dark gray, monstrously large six-story building. In some windows pillows are being aired. From other windows there are suspended thick, colored winter blankets or white sheets, a man's suit, a woman's flashing silk petticoat, or children's swaddling clothes. The house stands among others like itself, with stores, cellars, and peddlers' stands, with a drugstore on one side of the street and another on the other side . . . seeming as gray and unfriendly as a prison, as if some deep melancholy were immured within it . . .

It blocks the path of the sun and the sun rays cannot break through its high stone walls. It restrains the movement of the air and only infrequently does a fresh breeze steal into the windows. Only when a storm breaks out, when a dark cloud sweeps over the roof, and lightning zig-zags, thunders crash, rain roars and whips the windows through which hands appear and quickly disappear with the pillows, blankets, and other articles that were being aired; when the storm whips the windows and the stony walls and the tin signs of the stores tremble and rattle; only then can the tenement house no longer withstand the mighty pressure and streams of fresh air that break through doors and windows into the hallways and rooms, for a while.

Otherwise, it is stifling in the hallways and rooms of the tenement house, even in winter. An eternal half darkness lowers there, as if a cloud had lost its way, spread into all the nooks and corners, and remained

3

there forever. And a special odor, a particular tenement house odor, floats in the semidarkness of the corridors.

It makes no difference—sunshine, pouring rain, falling snow—the monster tenement house does not change its congealed, unfriendly, gray, stone, blind appearance. Around it no spring sprouts green, no summer blooms and withers, no autumn decays, no winter freezes . . .

Its stony surroundings do not blossom, do not turn green, and do not grow. Nor is there a trace of tree or blade of grass anywhere. Life boils there, wells up, and makes itself heard. Its voice is ever to be heard, its laughter and song, its sigh and groan. In even the latest hour of night, the voice of life is still to be heard there. A child begins to cry. A boarder has returned from a ball, at dawn, and his echoing steps on the stairs and the shutting of a door are heard. A young woman, returning from a love tryst, is frightened by the scraping of her stealthy, timorous footfalls on the bare, stone stairs and the grating of the carefully opened door . . . A young man runs through; he is also a tenant, the shame and misfortune of the Jews of New York, a gangster who lives by theft and murder, and his steps echo with impudence through the entire house. And sometimes in the middle of the night a woman gives birth there and her cries are heard. And sometimes in the middle of the night someone dies there amid wails of mourning. A doctor mounts the stairs. A doctor descends the stairs. Doors bang on one floor, then on another. Sounds of whispering, bare feet, a cough, a sleepy yawn . . . A young man steals on tiptoe up the stairs and to a door and knocks quietly. A pair of naked arms opens the door and admits him to a half-dark room where a young woman sells her body secretly, and to whom buyers may come from ten at night to five at dawn . . . And from the door opposite comes the hoarse whirring of a machine. There a pale woman, the mother of several small children, is at work because her husband, the provider, is in the hospital. She has obtained children's garments to sew from a shop and works at night, because in the daytime she is busy with household duties and the children. And on the floor above, into the hallway, there float from one door deep snores and nervous steps, back and forth, back and forth . . . That is where a young Jewish poet lives with a family of working people. The husband, a workingman, after a day of hard work in a shop, is now asleep, whistling and snoring. The young poet, seated in his room, was dreaming and thinking until the snoring broke upon his dreams, put to rout the exaltation of his thoughts, and now he strides across the room in a state of confusion . . .

And very high above, on the sixth floor, under the roof, other steps are heard through the door, slow, measured steps, as if someone were measuring the floor foot by foot . . . a young man preparing for college . . . working by day, he has no time for studying and is now walking up and down the room, slowly, slowly, step by step, book in hand, eyes red with fatigue, and repeating and repeating, draws out the words in a sleepy voice.

And on hot summer nights, when the tenants, hundreds of souls, feel as though the stony walls of the house would smother them with their great heaviness, there is even more commotion in the house. Doors bang more frequently. There is the constant sound of footsteps in the hallways and rooms, of feet shod and bare . . . Groans and cries carry from above and below, cursing and mocking . . . Everyone seeks air and sleep on the roof, on the fire escape, downstairs, out-of-doors, near the house opposite the garbage cans, ranged in front of the tenement houses for the garbage trucks . . . Men sit by the windows, in their underwear; their wives likewise, and sometimes their grown sons and daughters, and sometimes even their roomers, male and female. The suffocation stifles even the sense of shame! Everyone is seeking to catch a breath, a drop of air, to cool the burning body, to escape being choked . . . The little ones, poor creatures, cry in torment. Their exhausted mothers are helpless; the wearied fathers grow cross . . .

Twenty-four families live in the house, four families on a floor, and with their male and female boarders they number a total of two hundred beings . . . The rooms are small, hemmed-in boxes, oblong and four-cornered, four and five to a family. The wallpaper in the rooms is stained; it may be with grease, with sweat, or even with tears . . . the same crowdedness and semidarkness in all the rooms. The same blind, gray wall of a neighboring tenement house in the windows of the rooms to the rear . . .

Jewish immigrants live here, Jews from Lithuania, Poland, southern Russia, Galicia, and Romania. Most of them workingmen and workingwomen, most of them not working people in the old country . . . On every floor, behind every door, a different past, a separate present, a different life experience, an isolated existence, one sorrowful, beaten, wounded, hopeless, and another cheerful, sunny, triumphant, filled with hope and expectation . . . here, an old woman who will soon sink into the past; there a young-blooded girl who is just beginning to weave the multicolored threads of her future . . . Here and there, people of various ages, characters, and types. From one door comes the sound of Lithuanian Yiddish, from another Polish Yiddish; in one hallway a man and a woman are conversing in the Yiddish of Volhinia and, in another, a woman is cursing in the Yiddish of Galicia . . . More often American-ized Yiddish is heard, and very frequently Yiddishized English, sea-soned with the coarse language of the streets, and not infrequently the noble diction of Shakespeare and Byron and, sometimes, even the beautiful literary Russian of Turgenev.

The tall, gray, stone walls of this tenement house hide people of var-ious lands and cities, the proud and wealthy, common people and pau-pers from the old homelands. Refined folk and coarse, scholars and ignoramuses, parents of children who are a source of joy, and of chil-dren who might better not have been born . . . Children who have left their parents in the old homes, and yearned for them, and parents whose American children have deserted them . . . Parents who are ashamed of their offspring and children who are ashamed of their par-ents. Old and young, ugly and beautiful. Sunny faces of girls that are drenched with the magic of springtime, and the pale, withered faces of women on which lie the shadows of a wearisome life . . . The dreamy eyes of the young, illumined by thought, and dull eyes of exhausted workers in which thought has been quenched for a long time. The im-pudent animalism in the face of a young gangster, and the refined, med-itative face of a college man, all these are hidden by the high, gray, stone walls of the tenement house . . .

A girl steps out of the dark hall, and remains standing outside on the stone stairway. Her throat is white, her hair black and shiny. Her cheeks are rosy. She stands and looks about. The long, slightly downcast lids scarcely quiver. What magic is spread on the pure white brow under the black hair! What charm in her lovely, innocent smile!

You stand and marvel: How does she come to be here? How could she have grown up there, behind those gray walls, in this stony world, without a green sprout, without sunlight, and without air? How has the shop not withered her by now?

When the eyelids lift, a pair of eyes look out, so black and shiny that all the stony, gray environs are illumined and brightened . . .

Oh, young Jewish beauty, you bloom and grow by the light within you, which tenement house and shop have been unable to extinguish!

A young man, a dude, comes out of the dark hallway, and remains standing on the stone stairway. His face is marked by lustfulness, his eyes bear the veiled, undefined look of a criminal . . .

He beholds her and his eyes turn to her with a friendly, gracious smile.

He does not know her, but is trying to become acquainted. At times he has succeeded in such attempts; at other times, he has failed.

Before six in the morning. The entire tenement house has awakened with a roar . . . Doors bang, footsteps and voices are heard on every floor . . . People from the tenement house emerge into the streets, slumber still on their faces, bundles under their arms. Singly, in pairs, and in groups of a few, old and young, men and women, boys and girls, they go out and mingle with the others who are streaming from all doors, all ends of the streets . . . And the living streams mount and raise a turmoil in the early morning air, overflow the sidewalks and the streets, move amidst horses and wagons, among automobiles, flow into the dark, thick, living streams set in motion earlier, fill the streetcars, mount the stairways to the elevated railroad, drive onto the subways, and lose themselves with a dulled tumult in the white tiled caverns . . .

Packed with tenement house inhabitants, the streetcars keep up an incessant ringing of gongs. Overhead, the elevated trains are packed with similar occupants. Underground, filled with the same kind of passengers, the subway trains fly and roar.

A little later, the streetcars and elevated trains expel great waves of passengers at street corners and stations . . . And these people flow into the streets where the factories are waiting, mingle with the flowing streams of other people, from different regions and of different nationalities . . .

The factories are still silent, their black doors opened wide for the living waves that sweep toward them, sweep on and on and subside within.

When the streets are finally emptied, the doors close and the mighty angry roaring of the factories is soon heard. From all the windows comes this roaring, from every floor, from above and under the ground . . .

This is the roaring of the energies of the tenement house dwellers, this is the roaring of their labors.

Half past eight in the morning. Children pour into the open from the tenement house, mingle with the children from other tenement houses, and the air echoes with their screams and playful laughter . . . They move on to the great, bright buildings which await them with wide open doors. The children pour and pour through the bright doorways and soon their footfalls are lost behind the walls of the city schools.

But even then, there is no quiet in the tenement house. The street yells up to it. An infant weeps because it has tumbled from a chair, and the mother, on top of that, beats and shrieks at the child, with tears in her voice. Two women, neighbors, are quarreling over something. Now each of them stands by her open door, one disheveled head thrust toward the other, hands gesticulating as the women hurl the wildest curses at each other! A woman trudges up the stairs carrying a heavy bucket which thumps against each stony step. Here a woman rushes hurriedly down the stairs in need of something at a store, while a pot is cooking on her gas stove . . . Elsewhere, an unemployed male boarder is singing a snatch from the High Holiday service, singing in cantorial manner, so that the echoes fill the whole tenement house with their sadness . . .

Thus, until nightfall . . .

At nightfall, the human tide sweeps back over the streets, sweeps down from above, from the elevated stations, up from the white tiled caverns under the ground, out of the streetcars, sweeps from all sides directly toward the half-dark doorways of the tenement houses . . . The street cries with its thousand voices. Automobiles fly by with their great, fiery eyes. There is a movement of trucks and carts, pulled by horses and by men. There is the ringing of streetcar bells . . . and the human stream pours on, unceasingly, without a stop, does not look about, does not heed anything, and hundreds of thousands of feet move on and on into the half-darkened doors of the tenement houses.

Electric lights flare up in the streets. Little lights are already twinkling in stores and restaurants and the human stream still flows on . . .

Now, our tenement house is all echo. On every floor a gaslight is burning in the hallway. Through every door some sound is heard: here the clatter of dishes, there the shouting of children, here a burst of laughter, there a gush of weeping . . . Behind each door an isolated world.

We shall try to look through the doors on the first floor.

Here is a gray door with a large black number "1" upon it . . . Who lives there? What kind of existence goes on behind it? What sort of past? What kind of hopes and disappointments? What kind of joy and what kind of bewilderment?

Alone in a Strange World

SHOLEM ASCH _____

LIKE AN ANCHORITE IN A DESERT, Meyer lived on the third floor of one of the tenement houses on Essex Street, in New York, on the shore of the other side of the ocean in the midst of a population of five million and among nine hundred thousand of his co-religionists. He did not belong to any fraternal group or society of either secular or religious affiliation, and had nothing to do with anyone. His fellow townsmen on Third Street, whose address he had carried with him and who had received him when he left the ship, had found him a Jewish "place," a shop that did not work Saturdays.

For more than seven months Meyer had occupied a seat beside a window, opening on a high wall, and had been sewing seams of shirts on a machine. How he ever got there in the first place he does not know to this day. His fellow townsman, a cousin, the son of his Aunt Malka (his father's sister), had led him into a deep cellar, and they had traveled here by train. Since then, he had ridden to work and back every day. He did not even wonder at the train, which raced like some fearful beast underground; on his way to America he had seen so many things, and his mind was so confused, that he would not have been surprised by anything any more. He did not even think it strange when his relative proposed to him that he take to sewing shirts and then he found himself seated before a machine . . .

That he, Meyer, son of Reb Yossele Sochatshover, who was famed throughout the city for his learning and piety and who had been a merchant of parts, should become a shirtmaker like Senderil, the ladies' tailor of their town! Everything is possible here, and that's why this is

America. It was nothing to be ashamed of, and the important thing was he was making a living, giving him a livelihood to support his wife and children at home where they waited for his letter and a ruble or two. He accustomed himself to the idea quickly, put his mind to it, and said to himself: "This is my sustenance," and he sat there a whole day, the others with uncovered heads, he with a skullcap.

There were girls in the place. He did not see them but worked diligently without speaking a word to anyone. To himself he would repeat a passage from the Mishnah, but for the most part, his thoughts were centered on his home: on how the children were getting along and, especially, on Yossele.

Vividly he could see Yossele seated in the cheder, studying the portion of the Law for the week, and he could actually hear the boy interpret the passage. A receptive mind, that! The little fellow undoubtedly went to the Beth Medrish between afternoon and evening services in pious devotion. "What a fine child," Meyer said to himself, and felt his heart languish with yearning for the boy. And when the day came that he was able to send Chana Leah the first ten rubles (it was only five dollars, there), no one in the world could come up to him, his heart was filled with joy. He felt that he was there, with them; he saw the postman deliver the letter and his brother-in-law, Leibish, read it to Chana Leah; she so pious and righteous, a veritable saint to think of what that woman endures bringing up the children, everything depending on her, and the children themselves, providing their tuition. And there is Yossele, close to his mother, pulling at her skirt: "Show me father's letter."

It is said that America is a country where Jewish ways cannot be observed as they should be. That is really not so. The one who desires to observe Judaism can do so anywhere. The proof is that Meyer would get up while it was still dark so that he might study the portion for the week before saying the morning prayers. This was his habit from childhood on and he had brought with him a set of the books of the Mishnah. At first, the other boarder, the young man who slept in the same room with him, complained that Meyer did not let him sleep. After a while he got used to Meyer. But Meyer retired to his corner of the room where his bed and chest stood, and that was his home. There, at a small table, he studied in the morning and said his morning prayers before going to work. There, in his corner, he lighted his two Sabbath candles every Friday night and by their light said "Sholem Aleichem";

he was not concerned with what happened around him. He did not see anything.

Often, when on Friday nights he would be seated at his little table greeting the Sabbath, his neighbor would be seated over a weekday task or would be playing cards with a friend. Meyer never rebuked them, knowing well it would be of little use. He did not go to look for any other lodging; he knew that it would be like this elsewhere as well. He did not look and did not see what was going on in other parts of the room—the Holy Sabbath reigned in his corner.

He did not worship with any fraternal society. On his first Friday night in this country, his fellow townsmen on Third Street had taken him to the Congregation Anshei Lenshne, a society of townsmen. The society met on the same street where he lived, on Essex Street. When he went to the place of worship, Friday evening, the street was filled with people and, as if to spite the Sabbath, the biggest trading was done on Friday night. As night fell, the tables multiplied in the middle of the street and blocked the passageway, and there were crowds at every table. These were Jewish workers, homebound from the shops. They listened to the loud cries of the merchants who extolled their wares with the greatest noisiness. Jewish boys—he could tell from their faces—played ball in the street into the Sabbath, set fire to the piled-up debris and paper without anyone's admonishing them it was the Sabbath. Weekday haggling pursued him to the very door of the congregation, and, even on the stairway leading to the place of worship, Jewish women were seated, trading and bargaining with those on their way to prayer. He fled to the congregation from the profane world of the street, but the Sabbath which prevailed in that congregation, itself in the very midst of the workday world, was so impoverished, so commonplace, that it left the impression it was about to be completely submerged in the vast everydayness in which it stood. He looked about and saw, in the middle of the room, a reading desk and holy ark, which someone had rolled out of a corner.

Another man, also a Jew, began to light candles, although the Sabbath had already begun. The congregants began to gather, one by one. For the most part, they were artisans from his town whom he had known at home. Some of them he had known many, many years ago when he had seen them as a child; they made the impression upon him that they were appearing in a dream. Others he did not know at all. The beadle had been an inept tailor at home. He was nicknamed "Billy Goat" because of his yellowish beard. He had been sent up to Brisk for a robbery one time, and from that time disappeared completely . . . and here he was in full command of the shul; he greeted Meyer with an effusive "Sholem Aleichem" and now looked at him pityingly. Meyer looked about for someone familiar from his hometown, with whom he might exchange a word; he saw among them only tradesmen, not his kind at all. They greeted him and questioned him.

Now a man went to the reading stand and began the services. Meyer knew him . . . a onetime smith in their village.

Meyer recalled the Sabbath at home, in their tiny village, where all stores were closed, where the town itself was closed, and the welcoming of the Queen of the Sabbath by the chazan, Reb Laibel Bear, and he was engulfed in longing for his home, wife, family, his children. Sabbath! His Yossele, head covered with the round cap he had bought him for the last Simchas Torah (Meyer always visualized Yossele in that cap), is now standing and swaying over his prayer book. And at home the table is set. The candles are lighted, and Chana Leah, his clever and active wife, is wearing her new cowl—and he is so far away—but he would not indulge in grief for this was the Sabbath and a public welcoming of the Queen of the Sabbath, so he accompanied these tailors and tradesmen in their singing "Come My Beloved."

After services, he sat down in a corner as had been his habit at home: not to leave right after the services but to remain behind for a bit of study—besides to whom should he hurry home? And he did have a feeling of Sabbath, despite his clothes. But, seated and in the act of rocking, as he recited the closing prayer, he saw that the reading stand and the ark were being rolled back into a corner, where they were curtained over with something, and now there began to appear a different kind of congregation—musicians of some sort followed by young women and young men. Meyer stopped reciting the prayer and gazed about wonderingly. The man who had lighted the candles came over to him, in his Galician style cap, and said to him in his Galitzianer accent:

"Sorry, Uncle, you'll have to leave; tables must be put in place because the dancing master will soon be here."

"What! In a place of worship on Friday night!" Meyer cried out.

"Congregation Anshei Lenshne holds its services here from six to

eight every Friday night in the fall and from seven to nine in the summer. It is already after eight, and it is now time for the dancing master."

"Here, in this place of worship!" Meyer still wondered.

"Now it is no longer a place of worship; it is now a dance hall."

Meyer seized his prayer book and fled. From that time on he did not
worship with any group and did not eat meat prepared by an American
Jewish slaughterer; by himself alone, in his own niche between his bed
and chest, Meyer welcomed the Sabbath, sang all the melodies learned
from his rabbi, longed for the Jewishness he missed, longed for his wife
and children, particularly for his youngest child—for Yossele.

For Yossele, Meyer's love was beyond all measure, and as distant a
father as he had been at home so devoted a father he had become now
that he did not see his children. It is true that even at home, if a child
was sick he would watch entire nights by the bedside and pawn everything, to the last stick, to pay the doctor and the druggist. And now, in
this alien world so far from his own, he was pining away for his children
and especially for Yossele. At times he would be seized by a desire to talk
about Yossele, to boast of his merits and learning. He would recall
many instances of his wise remarks and, when he was taken with the
need to speak about Yossele, he would walk to Third Street, to his compatriots. On Third Street, his fellow townsmen, members of the Anshei
Lenshne, would come together at the home of the widow of Chaim
Cohen and her seven sons and three daughters. Chaim Cohen had been
one of the most reputable householders of their town, and his family
had constituted half the town. It had been a very large family (his father
and his father's father, natives of Lenshne, had had many children—no
evil befall them), and every other householder in town was an in-law or
an uncle, or merely a cousin.

After Chaim's death, the children, one by one, wandered off to the
distant land. At first a younger son, a tradesman, went away and he
began to draw the entire family after him, until they brought the widow
over. And since then, the house on Third Street was the address for all
who were going to America from Lenshne, until half the town was
transported. From the ship a telegram would be sent to "Auntie," and
some young fellow would hurry off to meet the newcomer from
Lenshne. There, at Auntie's, he would be put up for the first few days
until he had discarded some of his "greenness" and found work. And
there, in Auntie's house, all the *landsleit* would gather every Saturday

night and talk of home, of their native town. When a newcomer from Lenshne arrived, he would bring greetings and letters for his compatriots who came to Auntie's to receive them.

A large house, where all the unattached sons lived with their mother because the family remained close-knit. And Chaye, Chaim's widow, was a woman who knew, from her own experience, the meaning of needing to seek out the land of Columbus. The youngsters, of course, argued with her, protesting they did not see what she had lost in coming to America: At home she could look out only on the town pump, while here she went to the various theaters. But she insisted that Columbus was hateful to her (she called America "Columbus") as were his theaters. And, all things considered, her Columbus had brought her only misfortune.

If a son did not bring home all of his pay, she would again exhume Columbus, and she threatened several times to go back home, although she had no one in Lenshne to whom to go since all her family was in America. More than once her sons would find her, at the most unexpected times, seated with folded arms, and with weeping eyes, saying she wanted to go home. And it occurred, one time, that they had to buy her a ticket to send her home, but no sooner did she come down to the ship and look about and behold the children and grandchildren she would be leaving behind, than she exclaimed: "To whom, alas, would I be going since Columbus has taken all my children from me?" She took her parcels and went back to Third Street.

Thus, the Widow Chaye's place on Third Street was the meeting place for the natives of Lenshne. The young people called on the sons because they had their own organization called the Lenshne Young Men's Society, at the head of which stood the sons who carried on the behind-the-scenes politics every Saturday night. The older men belonged to the Congregation Anshei Lenshne, and the women simply came to Chaye because it was known that if you wanted to meet a fellow townsman or merely wanted to talk of home, it could be done on Third Street.

Saturday night. Meyer, having performed the ritual dividing Sabbath from the workday week, in the space between his chest and bed, dressed in his coat and, as was his habit, went to his townsmen. He was very sorrowful for it was eight months that he had been away from home, without wife and children—and what sense was there in his being alone? He remembered his Sabbaths and his lonely Passover, and the youngsters at home without a father—who was looking after them? It was true that from the moment of his coming here he had begun thinking of some goal, and though he had been sending money to Chana Leah, at home, he had also been setting aside small sums from his earnings for some practical purposes. But how would it end: Would he return to them or bring them here? What he had saved was too little for him to go home on or to bring them over. And now there was talk of a slack, when times would be bad. Others belonged to some kinds of organizations that gave them money when times were bad. His kinsman on Third Street had persuaded him to enter a society, something called a "union," where all workers were joined together. But he was nevertheless annoyed that this kinsman took him for a worker. What kind of worker was he? He, a Jew at home in books.

But it was not of this he was thinking now, walking to Third Street. To return home—what would be the sense? The same pauper as before. And how would he earn a living? Now that he was here, he was earning and maintaining two homes (Meyer considered himself an establishment) and even saving something, and people said that Rochelle, his oldest daughter, would also be able to earn money here, quickly, and if folks came here with children, then parents were really lucky, as witness Chaim's widow on Third Street. However, how does one simply transport Chana Leah and the children? And what about their Jewishness, their studies? Well, as for most of the gang—they'd never come to anything as scholars—they don't want to study, as it is. But Yossele? And, thinking of Yossele, he was engulfed in such a feeling of fatherly compassion that he began to pity himself. He always imagined Yossele, standing in the house, in Meyer's very spot, prayer book in hand, praying piously. Or he imagined seeing him on a Saturday afternoon (Yossele had begun to study the Bible and had already memorized the portion for the week) with the Bible opened to the section, and seeking someone to hear him out. He approaches his mother to listen as he repeats the section. But the mother looks into the book and does not know what Yossele is saying.

With thoughts like these, Meyer came to his townsmen. In the house, he found their wives and the baby carriages in which they had brought their children. Again he remembered Chana Leah and thought to himself: "Have no one with whom to leave the children so they must take them along."

The house was full—men, women, older children, and nurslings—all seated on the beds, on small benches and stools, and on the floor. The women held the nursing children, while the other ones were playing in the middle of the room. The room was filled with cigarette smoke. At the head of the table was seated Joel, the wadding maker of Lenshne, and around him their townsfolk to whom he was talking about the town.

Joel had just arrived from Lenshne and, at once, all his townsmen in New York knew that a new townsman had come, and now they had gathered at the home of the Widow Chaye to question Joel about their kindred.

"And what about old Chaye-Roshe, is she still alive?" asked someone in the crowd, about an old woman known to all of them.

"No, one day during Passover she was going down into the cellar, broke a leg, and died."

"Died!" They all shook their heads. "She was an old woman."

And, instantly, they all recalled stories and anecdotes about Chaye-Roshe.

"Do you remember that Chanukah night when she was rendering fats in our house, and telling us stories about a lively pullet?" one of Chaye's sons asked another.

"And what a cook she was! What dishes she prepared! You know, she did all the baking for my wedding party. What delicacies, what cookies—that was some baking!" called out a woman who was seated way in back.

"And how is my aunt?" asked a man in the center of the crowd.

"Who is the aunt?" Chaye looked around in the group to discover the questioner—till she caught sight of a small man—"Oh, Beila Genendel?"

Meyer also wanted to ask about his family, but the crowd had surrounded the wadding maker so completely that he could not move close to him. Everyone asked not only about near ones, but about acquaintances, and there were those who were eager to know what had happened to certain streets, houses, cattle, and other animals in Lenshne. One person, an elderly man with a large paunch and many ornaments of gold, whom Meyer barely recalled as if in a dream and who was known to the rest as "the Allrightnik," was talking about observing the anniversary of someone's death and about returning home after that anniversary. Then he told about his former sweethearts, whom he had left in the town. He asked about each of them as if he thought they had remained unmarried.

The wadding maker observed that the whole company listened politely to the Allrightnik and, for that reason, answered his questions before any others. And now it turned out that all the girls he had left behind were old women, all parents of married children. He seemed struck with amazement, as if it were something unnatural. After that the Allrightnik related that all of his onetime sweethearts had sent him their grown-up sons and that for every kiss he had given the mother, in his youth, he gave the son ten dollars. The company broke into laughter, but Meyer felt embarrassed, blushed, and withdrew to a corner.

The Allrightnik's stories enlivened the company and he sent out for beer for the whole crowd. Then they began to recall happenings which had occurred in the town, in their childhood, and they named people who had already been lying in their graves for a long time, and names of houses and streets, of which not even a trace was left. At this moment, Moishele Kozak, who, in their native town, was known as a madcap and trickster and had, supposedly, played in some theater, and was now a hairdresser and active in the theater, arose and began to imitate Shloime Suknik, with his squeaky voice, praying at the cantor's desk; he did a takeoff of Chaye-Roshe, dancing before a bride about to be conducted to the restroom, and of Genendel Breina being taken with cramps after the Sabbath pudding, and of Itzille, the doctor's assistant, coming on the run with his bottle of smelling salts. These were all folks resting, these many years, in their graves somewhere on a little hill on the other side, of whom no one living had ever known or ever heard, save these few natives of Lenshne who had wandered off on that side of the ocean and had now assembled in this small room to recall Lenshne, their old dwelling place.

While Moishele Kozak was thrilling the crowd with a glimpse of these rarities, Meyer quietly approached Joel and inquired about his dear ones. Joel turned around and beheld Meyer.

"Oh, it's you. Sholem Aleichem. Your young son—what's his name—Yossele, I think, who is known throughout the town, kept running after my carriage and begged me to give you his assurance that he is studying and is waiting for you to examine him. Wait, he gave me some kind of note."

Joel searched his pockets.

"Yes, he asked me to tell you," he continued, "that the rebbe is teaching him to write, and he sends you a page written all by himself."

Joel found and drew from his pocket a wrinkled piece of paper.

"That little fellow begged so hard that I could not refuse him."

Meyer went off to a side and opened the wrinkled paper. It was a page from a writing pad, on which, line after line, were scrawled some syllables in a childish hand.

"I want to see Daddy-dear. I want to see Daddy-dear." Thus, one line after another.

Meyer studied his son's handwriting for a long while. For a moment he became thoughtful—spread open the piece of paper in his hand, then with measured steps and thoughts went over to Chaye's oldest son, Moishe Dovid, who had already become a thorough American and spoke English and was constantly teaching the newcomers how to deport themselves, and asked him cautiously:

"They say that one can get boat tickets here on installments—is that so?"

"What, do you want to bring your folks over?" his kinsman asked him.

"I hardly know." And then, as if in consultation: "What do you say to that?"

On the Streets of New York

SHOLEM ALEICHEM ⎯⎯⎯⎯⎯⎯⎯⎯⎯⎯⎯⎯⎯⎯⎯⎯⎯⎯⎯⎯⎯⎯⎯

COMING INTO NEW YORK IS FRIGHTFUL. The trip itself is not so terrible as the changing from one train to another. You have just taken your place—pop! You're flying in the air like an eagle, over a long, narrow trestle fit to kill you. This, they call the "Elevator." You think you are through? Wait a minute. You crawl out of the "Elevator" and you transfer to another train and you go down steps as if into a cellar, and you dash under the earth with such speed that your eyes become dazzled. This, they call the "Subway."

Why is one called "Elevator" and the other "Subway"?

My brother Eli says that "Elevator" comes from the word "ladder" (*laiter* in Yiddish). And "Subway" is the word used by our peasants when they drive a yoke of oxen.

Our friend Pinney laughs at him, fit to burst. "That's as fine an explanation as a bag of sticks. Oxen," he says, "crawl and this flies!"

"That's why this is America," Eli answers. "Everything flies."

My sister-in-law Bruche butts in and says that this very America would be lots better if people didn't rush as they do. She swears she will never ride again, and that's that! Neither by "Elevator" nor by "Subway," even if she knew her fortune depended on it. She would sooner, she says, go on foot rather than fly, helter-skelter, insanely above the clouds or rush under the ground. Then she winds up with a proverb: "Don't lift me up and don't dash me down" . . . a strange woman, my sister-in-law. You could easily get me, on the other hand, to go riding

From *Motel Pessie in America.*

20

around on the "Elevator" and on the "Subway," all day and all night long. And my friend Mendel, likewise.

It seems to me we've already been everywhere in the world. It seems to me we've already seen enough of trolley cars in Lemberg, Cracow, Vienna, Antwerp, and London. But such crowding and such shoving and such crushing together as here, in this Gehenna, we have never seen anywhere! Head touching head. One goes out, two come in. No place to sit. You must stand. You toss about. You must hold on to rings. They call it "strap hanging." You become stiff in the joints. With God's help, one seat is free, but there are a dozen claimants. Finally, after no end of trouble, you grab a seat.

You look around you. You are sitting between two goyim, powerful creatures. They sit and chew the cud, like oxen. Much later I learned that what they are chewing is called "chewing gum." This is a kind of sweet with gum in it. You keep it in your mouth and chew. It must not be swallowed. Young boys, that is, little fellows, old people, and cripples make a living selling it.

Our friend Pinney, you may remember as I once told you, is a sweet tooth by nature. He took to this confection and steadily swallowed a whole boxful. The end was he got a violent attack of stomachache and was nearly poisoned. Doctors pumped the gum up from his stomach. They saved his life. But I'm getting ahead of the story. Now let us return to our arrival into New York City.

All the time we were traveling on and in the "Subway," our people, men and women, were talking continuously. I say talking, but that's not true. Who can talk on the "Elevator"? Or in the "Subway"? The noise and the tumult, the grinding of wheels, the screeching of rails, and the shuddering of windows deafen you. You can't hear your own voice. You must shout to one another as to a deaf-mute. Our people became hoarse from shouting. Several times, Mother pleaded with Pessie:

"Pessiniu, my little soul, my darling heart, my little love! Leave the talk for later."

For a moment they become quiet but soon they begin again to shout at the top of their voices. After all, they are alive, good friends, former neighbors. How can they restrain themselves and not pour out their hearts to one another? Such a long time they had not seen one another. And there is so much to tell! So much!

Having spoken and shouted about incidental matters, they turned their talk to the question of where to go and with whom to stay. After much debate and wrangling it was decided that Mother and I and our friend Pinney and his wife, Teibele, should stay with our old neighbor, Pessie the Stout. And Eli and his wife, Bruche, were to go on to their in-laws, Yoneh, the baker, and his wife, Rivele. Well, and Mendel? Pessie said she would take Mendel with her. Rivele, the baker's wife, said no. At Pessie's she said there were enough mouths even without him. This offended Pessie. She said there are no superfluous teeth in the mouth and no superfluous children in a mother's brood.

"Quiet! Do you know what? Let's ask the one we're speaking about himself." That's what Moishe, the bookbinder, Pessie's husband, said, and asked Mendel: Where would he rather go—to him or to the baker? Mendel answered that he wanted to go where his friend Motel is going. I myself had thought nothing other than that Mendel should say just that.

"Very soon, only one more station, and we'll stop!" Yoneh, the baker, now spoke in American. We didn't understand the meaning of "station" or the meaning of "stop." He translated the words: "Station" is *stanzia* and "stop" means that we are to get off, to leave the train.

"*Michuten* [male in-law], when did you begin to talk this language?" Mother asked him, and Rivele, his wife, answered for her husband:

"I assure you, *Michutainesta* [female in-law], that in a week from now you, too, will begin to speak this language, for if you will go out to ask 'Where is the *kutzev*?,' you'll go around *kutzeven* and *kutzeven* till doomsday and no one will answer you."

Mother asked: "Then what shall I say?"

Pessie answered: "You will have to say 'the butcher.' "

"Let them sicken first!" my sister-in-law Bruche interrupted. "Even if they were all to say '*kutzev, kutzev,* and *kutzev.*'"

Suddenly we came to a stop. Our in-law Yoneh, the baker, grabbed his wife, Rivele, my brother Eli, and my sister-in-law Bruche, and made for the exit. Mother, too, got up. She wanted to accompany her children, to see them off. Pinney, too, got up, went to see his friend Eli off, and, at the same time, to decide with him when and where they should meet. But how decide? Discuss what? Before you could wink an eye, Yoneh, the baker, and his wife and my brother Eli and his wife, Bruche, were off, the conductor shut the door, the train gave a jolt. As Pinney was standing, thoughtful and confused, the jolt threw him off his feet.

In a moment, he was lying in a woman's lap. She gave him such a shove with both hands that he flew to the opposite side of the car and his little hat flew to the door. And as if that wasn't enough, there was laughter besides. Everybody in the car laughed. I and my friend Mendel laughed too. We caught it from Mother and from Pinney's wife, Teibele, for laughing. But try to restrain yourself!

Everything in the world comes to an end. There was an end, too, to our coming into New York. Now we were in the street. If I did not know that we were in America, I would surely have thought we were in Brod, or in Lemberg. The same men, the same women, the same cries, the same dirt as there! Only the tumult and commotion are much greater here. The noise is more intense, louder. And the houses are taller—much taller. Six stories is something to smile at. There are twelve-story houses, and some of twenty, thirty, forty, and even higher than that. But more about that later.

In the meantime, there we were, in the street with our bundles. We had a distance to go, on foot. Here, they call that "walking." And we started walking. At the head walked Moishe, the bookbinder, with his short legs. After him, walked Pessie the Stout, his wife. Her feet could hardly carry her, she was so fat and heavy. After Pessie walked Pinney and his wife, Teibele.

Pinney's walking was enough to split your sides for laughter. When Pinney walks, he hops on his thin, long legs, which trip over one another. One trouser leg is up, the other down; his hat is shoved back on his head; his neckerchief is all awry. What a queer figure he is—if only I could draw him!

I and my friend Mendel walked in the rear, behind all of them. We stopped at almost every window. We were pleased that the inscriptions were in Yiddish and that there were so many Jewish objects on display: prayer books, ritual vests with fringes in the four corners, skullcaps, mezuzahs, and matzohs—imagine that! In the midst of everything, at the beginning of winter—matzohs! Undoubtedly, a Jewish city. But we were not permitted to tarry long. Mother called: "Come here!" We had to go.

He who has not seen a New York street has never seen anything beautiful. What is not to be found on that street? Men are trading. Women are sitting and talking. Children are sleeping in their little wagons. Here, these are called "carriages." All carriages look alike. Here, on this street, infants are fed milk from small bottles. Larger children are at play. And they play with a thousand different playthings: buttons, hoops, balls, wagons, sleds, and on skates. That's something on four wheels, fastened to the feet, on which you ride. You can be deafened by the shouting of the children in the street. The street belongs to the children. No one would dare to drive them away from there. Come to think of it, America is a country that was created for the sake of children. And that's why I love this country. Just let anyone try to lay a finger on a child!

My brother Eli once learned—on his own skin. He will warn ten others not to try it. This is what happened:

One time I and Mendel were in the street, playing checkers. This is a game with round, wooden buttons, which you pitch. In the midst of our game my brother Eli came up. He grabbed me by the ear, with one hand, and prepared to slap me with the other, as was his wont in the old country. Suddenly, a ragamuffin shot up as if out of the ground. He rushed up to my brother and tore me out of his hands. Then he rolled up his sleeves and said something to Eli in American. But as my brother did not understand English, the boy planted a fist right under my brother's nose. Immediately a crowd of people gathered. And my brother defended himself in Yiddish, saying that since we are brothers he can teach me how to behave. But the crowd told him that in America, things aren't done that way. Brother or no brother—you can't hit anyone under your size.

Go and dislike such a country!

A Wall

ZALMON LIBIN ─────────────────────────────────

IT IS NOT THE DREADFUL BASTILLE that has fallen; it is not an army
of revolutionaries that has greeted its fall with echoing cheers of joy—
this is America, New York, a free city in a free land; we have no Bastille,
we have no revolutionaries . . . It is the wrecking of a large, dark, five-
story ruin of a tenement house. The building has been torn down by
paid workers, hired by the owner of the house; and it has been torn
down because it had already become too weary to stand and would not
have needed much coaxing to collapse of itself, if a helping hand had
not been offered betimes; and also because the landlord has already ex-
torted so much in rents that he is now empowered to erect a new ruin,
a larger one, a deeper one, a taller one with many, many more tenement
caves than the older one had possessed, and will thereafter rake in more
rent, more and more dollars . . . Rent! Rent!

In the meantime, the dilapidated tenement house has been razed
and the rear wall, which rested on the very nose of the tenement house
opposite, and which robbed many, very many weak and pale poor folk
of air and light—this terrible wall has been demolished . . . God's light
has suddenly looked into many dark chambers. A bit of air has breathed
into the airless, damp tombs through the open windows . . . Embittered men, pale, despondent women, and languishing children have
looked out of the windows and, with amazement but with joy and satisfaction, regarded the bit of open space, have half closed their eyes so
unused to light, and have inhaled the air. What joy! What delight! Air in
the windows!

This is in midsummer. The weather is fiery hot, boiling, and there is a stir of wind through the windows—a pleasure! The poor are drinking in this joy and their children are frantic with delight.

"Oh, Mother, look at the light," a child rejoices.

"Oh, the street! See, there's a street!"

"The light! The light! Look at those uncles and aunties," a young child, entranced, babbles to its mother.

"There's a wind, a little wind," another child exclaims.

And Hershman, the presser, says that he will not sleep on the roof this night, that his own rooms are good enough now. And Abraham, the peddler, believes he will not need to steal up to the roof to catch his breath. He will sit here by the open window and breathe and cough quietly and comfortably . . . The wife of Morris, the suspender maker, is busy: She is moving the bed in the front room close to the windows, and everything is topsy-turvy . . . The poor are rejoicing . . . the children are dancing with glee . . . The wall of a tenement house has been razed . . . Suddenly there is light . . . there is a bit of air . . . Good! Oh, how very good!

Among the impoverished folk who have been visited with this sudden stroke of luck is Mr. Chaim Garber.

Chaim Garber has been living in this house for almost three years and how that wall has served to annoy him!

Chaim Garber is a paper-box maker. When work is to be had, he makes his seven dollars a week, working regular sweatshop hours: from 4 a.m. to 10 p.m., and when he is out of work, naturally, he does not earn even that. Bosses do not pay wages for nothing.

Chaim has a wife—a tall, lean, stern, consumptive woman—and, in addition, now has five youngsters. The youngest is three months old.

Because of the wall which makes his rooms pitch dark, his rent is low. He occupies three rooms and pays six and a half dollars a month. Chaim Garber knows that you cannot find rooms at such a low rental anywhere; he treasures his home and is very respectful to the landlord. Nevertheless, when the first of the month arrives and it is time to pay the six and a half dollars, you would suppose there had been a death in the family. Chaim himself becomes dizzy and altogether confused, has frightful dreams at night and cries out, and his wife, Goldie, becomes a total wreck. She is seized with coughing spells, hears bells ringing in her ears, and seems to become slightly deranged—in short, life itself seems to come to an end. Thus, Chaim knows very well that he cannot afford to pay more than six and a half dollars for rent, and for that reason he actually trembles over his home.

But the wall, that wall right before his window. Ay, that wall annoys him to death . . . darkness! Always, always, the darkness. It spreads such gloom and sadness that, at times, you are seized with the desire to fling yourself from the window, as you gaze at that wall of darkness. The children's eyes are weak because of this constant gloom . . . and maybe Goldie, too, is so sick and angry because of it. But what can he do about it? Chaim understands very plainly that the wall saves him a few dollars every month and he regards the wall as a necessity in his life and is not ungrateful; in fact, at times he is very thankful for the wall. Naturally, if the rent would remain the same, Chaim would not mind if the wall sank ten fathoms into the earth. But he knows this is impossible. Sunny rooms are expensive in America; sunlight costs a great deal. And that's that. Both Chaim and Goldie are already so accustomed to the wall, that even when they are outdoors they have the feeling that the wall is hovering before their eyes.

And suddenly, altogether unexpectedly, men come and tear down the wall, light pours in, and when the windows are opened there is a breeze. The joy of it!

The Garbers cannot become accustomed to it and simply cannot believe their own eyes. Nevertheless, the wall is no longer there and Garber and his ailing Goldie and the children, including the infant, are like people born anew.

And, although the first of the month is speeding close on its fearful black wings, Garber does not become dizzy. Goldie has become much milder and does not scold as she used to, and does not beat and pinch the youngsters . . . She breathes more easily and the children, too, have been transformed . . . more cheerful, more animated.

As soon as light comes into the rooms, the filth that has accumulated thrusts itself on their attention and Goldie and Chaim work with all their strength and clean them thoroughly.

Goldie scrubs the floors and Chaim drags hundreds of pounds of rags and rubbish, and just plain dirt, into the street.

"It's become roomier in the house," Goldie says as she finishes cleaning.

"No wonder," Chaim responds. "So much rubbish, so much filth thrown out."

"How did it ever accumulate? We never even noticed it, it seems," Goldie says musingly.

"It was so dark we couldn't see," Chaim explains.

"Altogether different rooms." Goldie looks happily around her.

"Brightness, that's all. Brightness!" Chaim exclaims.

It was Saturday morning, the third day of light. Chaim did not work Saturdays, so he did not need to hurry to the shop, and was now seated beside the open window, contemplating God's world with great satisfaction.

The children were all asleep on the floor, near the window, and Goldie was preparing tea.

"Chaim, come have your tea!" Goldie called to her thoughtful husband.

Chaim did not hear his wife and did not answer.

In the days of "darkness," he would never have escaped a few of Goldie's choice curses in a situation of this kind. Now, however, she walked over to him and said, good-naturedly: "Chaim, come drink your tea."

"What?" Chaim spoke up.

"What are you thinking about?" Goldie asked with a smile.

"I'm thinking," Chaim said, "how good it is to be wealthy."

"What makes you say that?" Goldie asked, looking at her husband and smiling.

"Just see what a pleasure it is!" Chaim spoke, his eyes still looking out of the window. "What a joy it is to live without a wall right against your windows."

"Who doesn't know that?" Goldie nodded in agreement as Chaim continued to speak.

"Just look, look out . . . A world to see . . . You know you're alive . . . Human beings . . . Horses . . . Walking, riding . . . People talking . . . A world of life."

"Go on, lunatic, have a glass of tea," Goldie said good-humoredly and also began to look out of the window.

"What a pleasure!" Chaim could not contain his delight.

"But who knows for how long?" Goldie spoke with a sigh. "Probably they will soon erect another building."

"Nonsense! The whole summer may go by this way," Chaim consoled his wife. "And we'll thank God for anything beyond that. And it's not costing us anything extra, at that."

"Will you have something with your tea?" Goldie asked.

"Yes," Chaim said. "Give me a piece of bread; I feel like eating."

"Ever since the rooms became light, we eat more," Goldie said as she handed her husband a glass of tea and a piece of bread, at the window.

She took a glass of tea for herself and also sat down near the window.

The two drank their tea, ate bread, looked out, and found great satisfaction in doing so.

The children began to rise and rushed to the windows with shouts of enthusiasm.

"They don't even ask for food," Goldie said as she looked lovingly at her brood of undernourished, naked, pale children.

"The light," Chaim said philosophically. "That is, apparently, more precious than food."

There was a knock at the door and Mrs. Hershman, a tenant from the fourth floor, came in.

"Good morning," Mrs. Hershman said.

"Good morning, good morning," Chaim and Goldie said, as one. "Take a seat."

"You enjoy looking at the street?" Mrs. Hershman said and smiled strangely as she spoke.

"Well, who can deny it?" Goldie responded. "What do you say, isn't this light a joy to the eye?"

"Yes, of course," Mrs. Hershman answered, "but this light won't be for long."

"Are they going to build soon?" Chaim asked, and both Chaim and Goldie looked with fear at Mrs. Hershman.

"No, they won't build so soon; it may be a good many months, but . . ."

"But what?" Chaim and Goldie interrupted together and looked at Mrs. Hershman with wide open eyes.

"But they're going to increase the rent a dollar and a half a month for all the rear apartments, on account of the light."

Chaim and Goldie did not say a word, but a shadow darkened their faces and both of them sat still for a while as if numbed . . .

"We are destined to die with a wall before our eyes." Chaim was the first to break the unhappy silence.

"Bells are ringing in my ears again," Goldie answered. "May the bells toll the landlord's passing."

"Go! Gorge yourselves, rascals!" The tall, lean woman shouted suddenly to her children.

"Let them look out . . ." Chaim smiled bitterly. "In a little while we will have another wall; we will have to move from here. We cannot pay eight dollars a month."

On Sunday the Garbers learned, officially, from the housekeeper, the sorrowful news about an increase in rent and, on the next day, Chaim and his wife went to look for other rooms. After searching for half a day, the Garbers found rooms for the same rent they were paying in their old quarters.

Again, three dark rooms with a wall right before the windows, perhaps even a little closer than the other wall.

"What did I need to wrench my insides for, cleaning those rooms?" Goldie said ruefully on the way back.

"And I dragged out so much filth!" Chaim added regretfully.

Imprisoned

ISAAC RABOY _____

MANIS AND HIS WIFE, SHEBA, were lonely on Delancey Street. They had neither relatives nor acquaintances, and they had exhausted the small sum of money they had brought to America. They had no one from whom to borrow money and, on top of that, Manis disliked to borrow. He could not get himself to approach anyone for a loan. Manis was a quiet and strange kind of man. For the trifling reason that he had not wanted to spend two weeks in jail, he fled to America. And here he was always on guard against strangers. It seemed to him that he was surely being sought here, that he would be drawn into a trap and clapped into prison.

Naturally, Manis could not just sit with folded arms in America, and therefore he was learning how to fold shirts in a factory. He was now well into the sixth week of this learning process and was already proficient in the art. But the owner of the factory had not even acknowledged Manis's presence there, and this embittered Manis. He knew, and did, the work and it hurt that he was not being paid for it. He looked about him in the factory and thought to himself that he had been trapped in a prison, after all. The low windows protected by iron bars, and the heavy doors sheathed in iron, and the dirty walls covered with cobwebs—all of these gave Manis the feeling he was in prison.

Manis was deeply distressed that he had come to America. He might just as well have served those two weeks in Podolia and been done with it! Here he was sentenced to a lifetime of folding shirts.

From *Iz Gekumen a Yid Kein Amerika.*

That was the thing that troubled him. "Why won't they admit that I already know the work?" he asked his wife.

"You probably can't do it yet," she said, pouring oil on the fire.

"What nonsense! If I tell you I know it, I know it."

"Learned it at your father's, eh?"

"That's not . . . But I know—."

"Then the time will probably come when they will see that you do."

"May I live to see that time."

"What luck for you!"

"Well, you know what I mean . . ."

"Don't I, though! . . . I don't want to go to the grocer's anymore . . . I'm ashamed to ask for more credit."

"I believe that by next week I'll bring some money home." Manis tried to soothe his wife.

"You merely believe—."

"That's what I think . . . I can't say for sure when I'm not sure. But I believe that I will."

"Why don't you talk to the boss?"

"He's a sullen man and a German Jew to boot."

"A German Jew?"

"Yes."

"Then better keep quiet."

"And if I do keep quiet?"

"Maybe he will soften of himself."

"And if he doesn't?"

"You will speak up then."

"Perhaps I ought to speak to him now? What do you say, Sheba, speak to him now?"

"Do I know? You yourself say he's a German Jew. And who knows what these German Jews are like."

"He's a German, all right, and a sour one, at that."

"You'd better wait, then."

"If you say wait, I'll wait . . . And the grocer gives you mean looks?"

"Like this," and Sheba fixed her eyes to show him how the grocer looked at her.

"What's he afraid about? I'll go down to him myself," Manis spoke lightheartedly, "and have a talk with him."

"He'll certainly have more respect for a man."

"I'll go down at once." Manis put on his hat and combed his beard with his fingers. "Tell me what you need and I'll bring it right up."

"Let me see—we need sugar, bread, a good herring, grits, and half a dozen eggs."

"Good. Down I go and I'll be right back." And Manis left and descended the wooden, squeaking steps, thinking how old the steps were, and how they had been worn out by the feet of those who had trodden on them. How long, actually, should steps serve? And these might very well collapse just as someone was walking on them . . . Some staircase, he thought as he walked outside.

Ever since he arrived in America, his nose had been stopped up because, Manis thought, of the strange air and atmosphere of the rooms in which he lived. There was the smell of burnt wood, of food fried in vinegar, of salted fish, and thousands of other smells which choked one's breath and turned one's stomach. On top of that there was the human stink of what they called the "toilet." In addition there was the stench of the illuminating gas—a stench sour and strangely unpleasant. In a word, Manis's nose had been clogged from his first day in America.

As he came out into the street, he stopped and tried to catch a breath of fresh air. This is the way he did it: He shut his mouth, gritted his teeth, and tried to clear his nostrils by blowing them both at once. Since he couldn't clear them both at the same time, he blew through one nostril. That one was clear, he thought, and blew through the other. And as he cleared the second, the first nostril became clogged once more. Manis stood there blowing his nostrils, and passersby stopped to watch and looked at him as if he were insane.

On he went, blowing, blowing, until he realized that he would achieve nothing and decided to let his nose go hang. And thus he had been walking about for weeks with a stopped-up nose.

Now he came out of the house, tried to clear his nostrils to fill his lungs with fresh air, tried and failed and again cursed his nose, then went to the grocery store to which his wife, Sheba, had directed him.

Arriving at the grocer's, he stopped at the door in a fit of uneasiness, turned back, and went, instead, to the window of the store. The window was dirty with flyspecks and dust. Behind the window there were all kinds of containers with all kinds of goodies: dried prunes, lumps of sugar, raisins and figs in wreaths suspended by strings, and a small sack of coffee, a small sack of rice, and a small sack of beans. Lying in the sack of rice was a large, fat cat, asleep.

At first Manis thought the cat was a paper cutout. Because it could not enter his mind that a live cat would be permitted to sleep in a sack of rice. After all, America, too, has a sense of what is fitting. Who would permit any such thing? It must be a cutout. Manis stood there, looking closely, and saw the cat move its tail, open its mouth, and lick its paws carefully with its tongue. "No," Manis said to himself and felt nauseous and spat out the bitter spittle that flowed into his mouth.

He looked into the store but could see nothing, because the window was so dirty. Meanwhile he recalled what he had come for and started once more toward the store and again remained standing at the open door. Women, buried with packages, came through the door and almost bumped into him. They threw him angry looks as they went on their way. Tall women, fat women. Manis looked after them and wondered what they could be thinking, and what, in the devil's name, they needed all of their fat for. And wanting to go into the store, he still lacked the courage to do it.

For, what would he say to the storekeeper?

"I am Manis of this-and-this address, my wife has been buying on credit and doesn't have the nerve to pile on more credit; that's why I have come myself to tell you you may trust her because, with God's help, I shall pay you."

In this way, Manis put words into his own mouth and then even provided himself with the grocer's responses: "And if you don't pay?"

How would he answer if the storekeeper asked that question? Surely he would freeze and remain speechless.

Better not go in. Manis went back to the window and stared at the cat in the sack of rice. He became incensed and knocked on the glass. The cat took fright, leaped out of the sack, and fled. "What wantonness," Manis thought to himself and did not notice that someone, in an apron, had come out of the store and stationed himself beside him, hands hidden under the apron.

"What do you want, Mister?" asked the man in the apron.

"I?" Manis spoke fearfully. "I don't want anything. There was a cat sleeping in the sack of rice—right there." Manis pointed to the sack.

The storekeeper's burst of laughter exploded in Manis's face. Manis remained glued to the window and was overcome by a feeling of shame which, try as hard as he might, he could not possibly suppress.

Going back from the store to his house, Manis took count of the numerous times he had been insulted in America and arrived at the resolution that Sheba must not learn anything about this. He would tell her only about cheerful things.

He walked up to his home, deploring, as he did so, the condition of the stairway, and entering his rooms he stood still for a while and exchanged looks with his wife. She understood everything and said nothing. She merely turned the gas up a little higher, seated herself, and rested her angular face on her arm.

Manis wanted to seat himself and could not summon the will to do so, or felt it would not be proper to seat himself now. His will was like a rope of sand. It was fortunate that he disliked tears. He therefore walked back and forth in the room, stopping each time, in the course of his walk, at the window for a glance outside. The sky was near enough but the stars were far away. The Earth, too, was far away—in fact, there was no Earth. America?—He did not like America. An abomination . . . although in truth, he could not have said what he expected to find in America. There was just one thing he wanted: to begin talking with Sheba. But he did not know how. Dear God, surely you might show a person how to do so simple a thing as open a conversation with his own wife . . .

"Whatever are you thinking about?" Manis asked Sheba and felt that this was not what he truly wanted to say.

"Just so, Manis," Sheba seized on his words. "Listen, Manis, aren't you very hungry?"

"Not very, on my word," Manis said so childishly as almost to offend Sheba. "Really not. Very likely you are."

"Neither am I." Sheba smiled bravely. "What hard work have I done today?"

"Neither have I done any hard work," Manis eagerly took up this thread of talk. "Believe me, I would willingly work ten times as hard to have what we need in the house."

"Did you go into the store?"

"No."

"What an idea, my sending you."

"I didn't dare risk it."

"That's right."

"Rather do without, than be put to shame."

"True."

"In this way, no one will know about us."

"Better this way."

"When you're a stranger, you must pay for it."

"I know that."

"All because I didn't want a term in jail."

"Why bring that up?" She stared at him with puzzled eyes. "I thought we agreed never to speak of it."

"Just a slip of the tongue."

"Never speak of it again!" Sheba pointed a warning finger. "And now I'll show you that I can get anything I want at the grocer's. I just feel I can do it, you'll see."

Sheba went down and into the store with the lively cheerfulness of one who has just come into a fortune. The shopkeeper welcomed her with his fixed smile while his bald head turned red. He was certain that Sheba had indeed come into money. She asked for everything she needed and haggled over everything she bought.

"My husband works hard and I must look after every cent," Sheba said, and her eyes and lips smiled coquettishly. The grocer approved this sentiment. He wrapped everything carefully and asked whether she needed anything more. He liked doing business with women who appreciated the labor of others. He talked and talked and almost bored Sheba to death with the flow of his troubles. Finally, Sheba told him to charge it to her account and watched him make the entry in his book.

Sheba entered the house gaily and strewed on the bare table all the things that were packed in the paper bag.

"You see all this, Manis. He never even made a wry face," Sheba announced happily.

"Silly. What's he to be afraid of?"

"That's true. What's he to be afraid of?" Sheba prattled on. "And you should have seen with what deference he served me. And he told me all his own worries."

"Is there anyone else who has troubles?" Manis asked in a mocking tone.

"There is, yes there is."

How good the bread was, the well-baked bread from which Manis cut generous slices, and how tasty the herring, fleshy, fat, and white. And good, too, were the glasses of tea which they sipped in pleasant contentment. Their faces flushed with the genuine satisfaction of those who enjoy life and who feel that there is hope for a future of serene and sunny days.

His Trip to America

ABRAHAM RAISIN _____

AFTER MY FRIEND HYMAN had been in New York for five years and had worked at various trades from box making to paperhanging, from paperhanging to serving as a "hand" in a newspaper plant—he felt the pull of the larger world around him.

"I can't stay here any longer. I'm stifling here!" he complained to me and spread his hands as if he were about to fly.

"Where to—back to Europe?" I clipped his wings.

"No," he sighed, "I want to go to America!" And his eyes began to glow with a strange fire. "I want to travel to America!"

"You're crazy!" I was frightened. "That's just where you are—New York is its principal city . . ."

"No, brother," he groaned. "New York is certainly not America; New York is Brisk, Kovno, Berdichev, Lemberg, Yehupetz—anything you please—but I want to go to America. Even when I was a child I was already dreaming of America."

"Then where is America?" I asked him, greatly disquieted about his mental condition.

"At least California," he boomed, and his face became radiant. "At least California, brother! That's where it begins, although the genuine America is Brazil."

"You'll soon land in Japan!" I mocked him.

"Not Japan," he would not yield. "Although, if it comes to that, you may be sure Japan is more American than New York. But I mean the true America—California."

And my friend began his preparations for the trip to America—that is, to California.

The misfortune was—my friend Hyman could not under any circumstances save up the large sum of money which the trip to California involved.

Two years passed and the good fellow groaned once more, spread his hands like wings, and pleaded:

"Help! I want to go to America!" and he cut the trip from California to Chicago! "But I must go to Chicago!"

Certainly the fare to Chicago was cheaper—eighteen dollars, and my friend could get there! But times became more difficult for him: unemployment, shiftlessness, and other circumstances.

No! Chicago was too distant. He could not undertake such a journey!

Another year passed. My friend Hyman now begged: "Brother, give me some advice. How do you shake the dust of New York, and how do you transport yourself, despite everything, to a corner of America?"

I was genuinely concerned about his affairs, wanted to aid him with advice, and we took the railroad schedules to find cities in America. We discovered that Detroit was thirteen dollars away. My friend slapped his hand on Detroit in the schedule and sang out: "Yes—I'm going to Detroit!" He spread out his hands—he was already in flight.

But soon he rubbed his forehead, searched in his pockets, and found that, though thirteen dollars was no money at all, he did not have it now. In other words, he would again have to begin scrimping and saving for the next few months.

The few months fled. When I met Hyman he was languishing.

"Well?" I asked.

He had only seven dollars and, with outspread hands, he wailed:

"I could not save more than seven dollars. I am dwindling like a candle, here in New York. I want America!"

"Go to Boston," I advised him. "Boston is a real American city, even though they have a Yiddish paper there, but no one knows about it or even notices it. Yes, brother, on seven dollars you can get to Boston."

My friend was contented. Sure Boston is an American city. As to the only Yiddish newspaper there, he scorned it—he would certainly not glance at it. And if any lecturer from New York came there, he, my friend, would play possum—he was in America, at last, and no more greenhorn lecturers for him. They could do nothing to him there—he would be in America!

But, by the time his preparations were made, the seven dollars became three and a half; and he had to pay a dollar to the laundry—how do you make such a trip without laundry?

"Brother!" he wailed once more, "Boston is out—I have exactly two and a half dollars—but I've got to get to someplace in America. If I don't I'll get sick here, die, and be buried somewhere in a cemetery, by my fellow countrymen, and I will never get a peep at America."

"If you really still have two and a half dollars," I condoled with him, "then you're not in such hard luck. For that sum you can travel to Philadelphia. There, too, there is a Yiddish newspaper and, unfortunately, a daily at that, but it's the same as in Boston—no one knows about it. On the other hand, however, Philadelphia possesses that famous bell which declared freedom to America. I really think that, for that alone, you ought to go to Philadelphia."

My friend Hyman became strangely elated. He began to count his capital until he discovered he had only a dollar and a half.

And thanks to my counsel he decided to go to Paterson, New Jersey—so much closer to California—and he would have nearly a dollar left for living expenses the first few days.

And, finally, he started off on his distant ways—to Paterson.

However, as it turned out, he did not get to Paterson, either. I met him a few months later, walking along on Pitkin Avenue in Brownsville. "Haven't you gone to Paterson yet?" I asked him in wonderment.

"No, brother, I could not go. Just before I was to start out an unexpected expense turned up and I was left with only half a dollar. Out of longing, I fled to Brownsville."

As he spoke, he threw a glance of hopelessness at me, as if to say: "Hard, it's hard, brother, to reach America, once you fall into New York."

We Strike

SHOLEM ALEICHEM ——————————————————————

IT SEEMS TO ME that there is no better thing in the world than a strike. When you are studying with a rebbe who beats you too hard, you are taken away and sent to another *melamed*. In the meantime you quit going to cheder (Hebrew school). That's what a strike is like.

My brother Eli and our friend Pinney quit going to the shop. Now that they are at home, the house has taken on a different appearance. As it was, we saw them only once a week—Sunday. Because, as I've already told you, when you work in a shop you must get up at dawn so that you should not, Heaven forbid, be late. And when they used to come home I was already asleep. Why? Because they worked "overtime." That meant that when all the other workers went home, our folks stayed at their work in the shop. Not because anyone compelled them to, but that they should earn more. Although when it came to paying them, whole days were deducted from their pay. How were they to blame?

"Let us suppose we were attacked by thieves," was the way my brother Eli put it.

"Let us suppose you are a lummox!" my sister-in-law Bruche said to him. "If I were working in a shop," she said, "I wouldn't let them put anything over on me. All the foremen and all the bosses would get it from me, first." And you may take her word for it. She'd do it, too.

That's why she cooled off when all the shops declared a strike. That meant that all tailors, as many of them as there were in New York, laid down shears and irons and—good-bye. What a to-do there was—in homes, on the streets, and in the halls! A "hall" is a meeting room or a theater. All the tailors in New York gather together for a meeting and

43

they talk and talk and talk. You hear words there which you have never heard before: "General strike," "union," "organized," "forty-eight hours," "higher wages," "better treatment," "scabs," "strikebreakers," "pickets" . . . and other such words which you don't understand. My friend Mendel says he does understand them. But he cannot explain them to me. "When you grow up," he says to me, "you will understand them yourself." Maybe so. In the meantime I look on and watch them all get excited and my fingers itch. How I would like to set them down on paper, draw each one of them separately, the way he looks, what he is doing, the way he stands, and the way he talks.

Take my brother Eli, for instance. He himself did not say a word. He went over to each crowd and stuck in his nose, or put a hand up to an ear. At the same time, he was biting his nails and was greatly excited. It was fun watching my brother shake his head in agreement with everybody who was talking. He agreed with every speaker, no matter what he was saying. At one point, a tailor with a tumor on the left side of his head came over to him. The tailor grabbed him by the lapel and shook him and spoke right into his face, saying that the whole fuss was in vain. The tailors would gain nothing through the strike because the "association" of the "manufacturers" was too strong for us! My brother nodded his head in agreement. And I am very much afraid that my brother Eli knows as much about the meaning of "association" and "manufacturers" as I did. As proof, here is another example. Another tailor came over to Eli. This man had a face like a duck's and when he spoke he slapped his lips. This tailor took hold of one of Eli's buttons, spoke to him, and slapped his lips together. Every minute he shouted: "No! We must fight, fight to the end!" My brother listened to him and again nodded his head. A pity my sister-in-law wasn't here. She would have given him a mouthful . . .

But our friend Pinney looked altogether different. If you haven't seen him and heard him talk at a meeting, you've missed the prettiest sight in your life. Our Pinney's figure must surely be familiar to you from my earlier accounts (you also probably remember).

His myopic eyes and long nose look right into his mouth. And you've certainly not forgotten his long, narrow trousers, one trouser leg down, the other up, and his tie across the unbuttoned shirt. And his talking—that frothing outburst of his, and the beautiful, lofty words, and the names of the great which pour as if out of his sleeve? Now just picture Pinney's getting warmed up and talking to a crowd of thousands who just don't want to listen to him. He began way back with Columbus and his discovery of America, and was soon on the topic of the United States of America and was all set to talk and talk. The crowd wouldn't let him go on.

"Who is the speaker?" one tailor asked another.

"A greenhorn!" the second said.

"What does he want?"

"What's he bothering us for?" . . . "What is he batting about?"

"Sharrap!" one man shouted and many others took up the cry: "Sharrap!"

"Sharrap" is a rather ugly word. Its real meaning is "Beat it!" But our friend Pinney is never frightened by words. When Pinney gets going, he's like a cask of water with the bung loosened and lost. You may try to shut off the flow with your hand or a wad of rags—but there's no help for it. It's a waste of effort, until the water has run out to the last drop. Pinney must talk himself out. Unless, of course, he is pulled off the platform. Here, it is called the "stage." And this time that was exactly what had to be done. Two tailors, pressers they were, took him by both hands and did him the honor of conducting him off the stage. That did not prevent him, however, from attaining what he had set out to attain. The remainder of his speech he delivered to us on the way home. And when we came home he continued his talk to my mother, my sister-in-law Bruche, and to his wife, Teibele. I and my chum Mendel were also among his audience. And it seemed to me as Pinney talked that he was right. But tell that to women! When Pinney had talked his fill, my sister-in-law Bruche spoke up in a parable, as was her habit:

"What's the difference to the turkey whether he is slaughtered for the Purim feast or the Passover seder?"

Maybe you know what Bruche meant by that?

In the meantime the days were going by. The strike was a strike. The workers were as firm as steel and iron. Meetings took place every day, at a different place each time. The manufacturers, I heard, were equally firm. They would not yield. But they would have to yield, everyone said. There is nothing the workers cannot achieve. This is America! They had come to their last resort. If that didn't work, it was all over! That's what our men said. What was the last resort? All the strikers in

New York would gather together and march through the streets. That meant thousands upon thousands of tailors would march through the city with their banners. This pleased me and my friend Mendel a great deal. We would be the first in line.

However, talk to a woman like my sister-in-law Bruche! She said it looked to her like children playing at soldiers. She said: "A pity to wear out your shoes!" You should have seen our Pinney and heard what he said to that! By now preparations for the parade had gone pretty far. I and my chum Mendel were all set, as you get set for the Fourth of July. That's a holiday in America when you shoot firecrackers in the streets and occasionally, they say, someone is killed. That's no small matter— the Fourth of July! That's the very day when the United States threw off the yoke of its oppressors . . .

I and Mendel were already very festive. Just then our pleasure was ruined. A man had been killed on Canal Street. Pinney brought us the news and he had been at the very spot and seen the murdered man. Pinney said the man deserved to be killed. He had been a gangster, Pinney said. Mother asked him what a gangster is. "A thief?"

Pinney said: "Worse than a thief!"

Mother then asked: "A murderer?"

"Even worse than a murderer," Pinney answered.

Mother asked: "What can be worse than a murderer?"

"A gangster is worse than a murderer," said Pinney, "because a murderer is a murderer and a gangster is a hired murderer. This man had been hired to beat the strikers. He seized a girl striker and tried to beat her. She raised a rumpus and people gathered and a fight broke out." We couldn't get another word out of Pinney. He strode back and forth on his long legs. We could see he was frothing with rage. He flashed fire. He tore his hair and poured a flow of words and names:

"Ay-ay, Columbus! Ay-ay, Washington! Ay-ay, Lincoln!"

The upshot was Pinney picked himself up and fled!

Whatever else would happen, we were the ones most affected in the meantime—I and my chum Mendel. Mother vowed on her health and life that she would not let us out on the street for all the money in the world—neither me, nor Mendel, nor Eli, nor Bruche, nor Teibele. Because, she maintained, if it had come to the point where people were killed in the streets, then the world was coming to an end. She threw us into such a state of terror that Teibele burst into tears like a child. God knows where her Pinney is now! Whereupon, mother forgot all about us and turned to ease Teibele of her fears: Our God is a mighty God; nothing would go amiss with Pinney; with God's help Pinney would come home unharmed, and he would continue to be a good husband to his wife and a father to his children who, God willing, would come in time. Teibele, at this time, had neither kith nor kin and was doctoring, in the hope that she would have children someday.

"And many children," Mother assured her.

"Oh, that it may be so!" I said and got a slap from my brother Eli, who told me not to be fresh and not to shove my tongue where it didn't belong.

Thanks to God, Pinney came back. And he returned festive and joyful. That man—the gangster who had been killed—was alive and would live. But he would be crippled for life. He was not killed to death. He had only been thoroughly beaten up. They had knocked out one eye and broken his hand. "Good for him! Let him not be a gangster!"

But Mother pitied him. "Let him be," she said, "whatever he is. There is a God in Heaven. Let Him deal with him. Why," she wanted to know, "does he deserve to have a hand broken and an eye knocked out? Are his wife and child to blame, that they should have a crippled father?"

The strike went on and on and we went about without a stitch of work. My brother Eli was entirely dispirited. Mother began to console him. She said that the God who had brought us safely to America surely would not forsake us. Our in-law, Yoneh, the baker, and our good friend Pessie the Stout and her husband, Moishe, the bookbinder, and the other acquaintances and friends came daily to comfort us with words of good cheer. They said the sky had not fallen. Where was it decreed that you should make a living in America only from tailoring?

The Greenhorns

CHAVER PAVER _____

"AND THESE ARE THE PEOPLE of New York?" Moishe asked Uncle Laib, who had welcomed him at Ellis Island.

"Yes, these are the people of New York," his uncle smiled.

"Why is it they have no time at all, these people of New York?" Moishe set his big, shabby bag down in the middle of the street, the better to look about.

Automobiles headed straight at this greenhorn with his bag and his uncle tugged him by the hand: "Quickly, Moishe, quickly, quickly, don't you see?"

Moishe became alarmed at the sight of the machines heading straight for him. He grabbed his bag and dashed, in fear, to the other side of the street.

"What's this rush? What's their hurry?" he demanded angrily.

"Each of them, poor fellows, is being rushed—pushed. He may not even stand still on the sidewalk. This is not Tcheremaiyev, Moishe." Uncle Laib instructed him in the customs of the country. "In Tcheremaiyev, they walk at ease, come to rest in the middle of the street to consider some matter, to give thought to something. Here, there is no time for thought. If you are going somewhere, keep going or you'll be run down or crushed."

But Moishe no longer heard what Uncle Laib was saying. Moishe's hat fell off his head as he stood craning his neck at the gigantically tall houses across the way.

"Well, come on now." Laib picked up Moishe's hat and put it on

48

Moishe's head. "Come quickly, Tanta and the family are waiting for you."

Moishe wondered at his uncle's use of the word "Tanta." He knew that *Tante* was a German word. In Tcheremaiyev no one said *Tante*. They would have laughed at anyone using the word. His uncle had also said "family," seemingly distorting the word *famillye*.

"Come on, hurry up." His uncle ran up the steps to the elevator.

Moishe was offended that his uncle had spoken this strange word to him. "Hurry up" certainly had a sound of mockery in it.

His uncle dropped a coin in a slot, pushed a kind of railing, and was on the other side. Many people were dropping coins in the slots; the railings kept turning with the clack of abrupt blows, exactly like the chopping of wood.

But Moishe was not permitted to observe the way the railings worked. He was rushed along with his bag, which he now feared to leave out of his hand. He was pushed and shoved through the open door of a car. Before he could see or gather what was happening, the door closed of itself and they were rushing past houses and rooftops.

By now Moishe's head ached. He could comprehend nothing. It was as if he saw everything through darkened glasses. He did not even observe that the shining outdoors had disappeared, with its buildings and windows and rooftops, and that small lamps had lighted themselves within the car.

"Now, Moishe, we are traveling underground."

"Underground? How is that possible?"

"Just to make sure, take a look out of the window," his uncle laughed.

Moishe peered through the window. Nothing but stone walls running by at lightning speed.

"You see, Moishe, we are traveling through a tunnel, a long ditch deep underground."

"And what's up there, above us?"

"Up there is the city of New York."

"And there are people going about?" Moishe asked wonderingly.

"People are going about, houses stand firm, and automobiles are running."

Moishe's mind refused to think any more, his eyes refused to take in any more, his ears would not listen. Moishe was confused, lost, suddenly wearied.

Therefore he could not recall how he was led into the house or whether he was sleeping as he walked. He did see something of the outdoors and streets, but it seemed to him that this was long ago, before they went underground. But, however it had been, now he found himself in a house. A strange woman embraced and kissed him. Children looked at him with mocking, laughing eyes, reached their hands out to him, and spoke to him in a strange language. It seemed to him that they were ridiculing him.

Someone told him to sit down. He sat down. They began to ask him about Tcheremaiyev. He spoke, but his lips did not feel that he was speaking. They told him to eat. He ate, but there was no taste on his tongue.

People came in—Jews. Jews in disguise, like actors in the theater in Bucharest. Middle-aged Jews and older Jews without beards or earlocks, with collars and ties. Their speech neither Yiddish nor German, with a strange sing-song. Their laughter was strange. Their names were strange: Harry, Max, Sam, and Morris and Louis. They called his uncle Louis.

Later it turned dark. Someone pulled a string and there was light. And Moishe felt the call of nature. He felt ashamed to tell anyone. He had such cramps that he wanted to cry. His aunt observed that the greenhorn was in distress. She whispered to his uncle. His uncle led him into an alcove but he could not understand why he was conducted to this alcove. Then he observed water taps, a mirror, and a toilet seat. He understood immediately, because he had seen similar objects on board the ship. But it was hard to understand that a toilet would be set right in the middle of a house.

His uncle walked out after explaining how to pull the chain to release the flow of water. Moishe remained alone, ashamed, for there were people on the other side of the door and they would hear him.

Moishe walked out, ashamed and humiliated.

They all laughed and slapped him on the back.

"You'll be all right in America, Morris, you'll be all right."

So they had converted his name "Moishe" to "Morris" and he had not even put up a struggle. Just had no more strength to fight.

On the way from Ellis Island to his brother Herschel's house on Prospect Avenue in the Bronx, Berele Pickpocket learned a few English words: "Hello, how are you, thanks, all right." He picked these words right off the lips of people around him. In the subway he saw two men greet each other. One said: "Hello" and the other answered: "How are you?" A little later he saw a young man rise and give his seat to a lady. The lady said: "Thanks."

Then he did the same thing—rose hastily from his place, and tugged at the peak of his bicycle cap. The lady said: "Thanks."

His brother laughed. He had left Berele a young pup in Tcheremaiyev and now he was so handsome, lithe, and clever—so quick to pick up American ways. How charmingly he had dressed in his Russian blouse, its high collar buttoned on a side.

"Berele, I see you'll be all right in America."

"What's the meaning of 'all right'?"

"That means 'good.' "

"In that case, it's all right," Berele responded, his white teeth smiling.

People in the car looked at Berele's strange dress with ridicule in their glance. But he was not embarrassed. On the contrary, he felt free and altogether uninhibited, smiling to all, completely at home.

After a while, at a large station, the doors of the car opened and many passengers crowded in. Now Berele stood squeezed amid the crowd, greatly pleased to be crowded so. How delightful to push among these people. You could hardly feel your own hands. You wouldn't even feel it if anyone were to pinch you.

Later, in his brother's house, Berele took from his pocket a gold cigar case, which he showed to Herschel. Herschel could not stop marveling at the cigar case.

"That must cost a fortune. Where did you get it?"

"Found it," Berele said, with an innocent look.

"You don't mean to tell me you found it in Tcheremaiyev?" Herschel said with a shadow of suspicion.

"Why not in Tcheremaiyev?" Berele asked jocularly.

"Because the name, engraved right here, is an American name."

"Read me the name," Berele said eagerly.

" 'Jay Borden,' says the inscription."

"Huh, huh," Berele muttered.

"What do you mean—huh, huh?" Herschel found it hard to understand.

"Very likely the man who lost it was named Jay Borden," Berele said with compassion for Mister Jay Borden. "I found it when I was leaving the ship." He spoke with simple innocence.

"What a lucky greenhorn," his sister-in-law laughed. "His first step on American soil and he strikes gold. You'll be all right in America, Berele."

ף

When the automobile reached Boro Park and Boris saw the fine houses and streets, the attractive stores with signs in Yiddish above them, he was overjoyed. "Bosher-Kosher" and "Talmud Torah" and "Rabbi Gaon so-and-so" and "Mohel Umsadur Kdushin" and "Mikveh Koshere L'bnus Yisrael"—a truly Jewish country, America. How delightful!

Uncle Shlomo actually lived on one of these fine streets. He had his own house, with a white, glass-encased balcony, a flower garden, and a lovely red tile walk leading to the entrance.

What a chubby family! Uncle Shlomo, called Solomon in America, was the father-fatty, tall and corpulent. Aunt Clara was the mother-fatty. A tower of a woman. Her thick black hair was braided in thick, heavy braids, which wound about her head several times. A strong, healthy aunt of great weight and proportions.

His uncle's two boys, nice little fatties, both. Cheeks bursting with good health and blood; shining eyes, rounded heads. Dressed like little aristocrats, in knee pants, in fine tan shoes, in costly striped shirts, they bore themselves with dignity and respect toward their greenhorn cousin.

Beatrice, the sixteen-year-old daughter, was pretty chubby, too. Plump and rounded, with thick curly hair and cheeks that were peaches and cream, she had small, fleshy hands and lively, well-turned legs and little feet.

A fortunate family. They regarded Boris with goodwill and friendliness. Goodwill and friendliness beamed from every corner. What elegant furniture in the house! Never in his life had he seen such furniture, such beautifully carved chairs with silken cushions, such thick white rugs, such ornamented lampshades, and such a beautiful black grand piano. Uncle Shlomo must be very wealthy, indeed. Boris sighed in self-pity at the thought that he had come to America, such a poor man himself.

"Why do you sigh, Boris?"

"For sheer delight, Uncle Shlomo and Aunt Clara. I am so thankful to you for bringing me to America."

Aunt Clara realized immediately that he was a fine boy. She even said to her husband, in English, that his nephew was a fine boy. Uncle Shlomo was greatly pleased that his wife was so taken with the greenhorn. He slapped his nephew on the back and said: "Just be a decent fellow and you'll have the best of everything."

There was a maid in the house, a dark-skinned maid. But the striking thing was her name—Sarah—a Jewish name. She probably stemmed from one of the ten tribes—one of the lost tribes.

Sarah was setting the table while Beatrice played the piano. Her mother had asked her to play in honor of their guest.

"Sweeter than honey. *Msukmidvosh*—well, well." Boris expressed his expert judgment of the performance.

Uncle Shlomo was delighted that his nephew was not only sensitive but capable of injecting a Hebrew phrase on occasion. Shlomo would certainly not be embarrassed by this greenhorn at the Congregation Anshei Bessarabia, of which he, Shlomo, was president.

Uncle Shlomo's house was a pious house. Four skullcaps were brought in, on a silver tray, by Sarah after she had set the table. Uncle Shlomo donned a skullcap, the two chubby boys put on skullcaps, and Boris also put on a skullcap.

The older boy was named Seymour. "Derived from Simcha," Uncle Shlomo explained, "named after Simcha, my grandfather and your great-grandfather, may he rest in peace. My youngest is named Haskel, after my wife's father, Chatzkel, peace be to him, and Beatrice is named after my mother, your grandmother Breina, peace to her memory. What a fine woman she was, your grandmother." Uncle Shlomo was moved to tears. "Why, she said her prayers every morning—never, never missed a morning."

By now Boris was not listening to what his uncle was saying. He was watching with growing eagerness all the movements of the black maid, Sarah. Never in all his life had he seen a person of such ebony color, and particularly such a young girl and one so beautiful to boot. How she moved about, carrying the heavy trays, with dancing step and a song on her lips! And what a fire was burning in her flashing eyes!

"Well, well," Boris sighed once more.

"Why do you sigh again, Boris?" Uncle Shlomo laughed.

"Just so, Uncle Shlomo, for no special reason."

ত

Oh, so this was sister Yetta! Zlatte did not recognize her sister Yetta when the latter came to welcome her off the ship.

At home Yetta had been a glowing girl with thick, long, reddish braids. As Zlatte remembered her in Tcheremaiyev, she had been plump and cheerful, with a ringing voice and ready laughter. Now, in America, she found a caricature, a takeoff, of her sister Yetta: an emaciated girl, with hair cut short, with glasses, pallid skin, and a faded voice.

"My sister Zlatte, my sister Zlatte." The American sister embraced the newcomer from Tcheremaiyev, her little sister who was still wreathed in the precious fragrance of their native village.

Zlatte wept along the entire way her sister took to Williamsburg. Life had been hard in America for sister Yetta. Life had been hard for all the members of her family back in Tcheremaiyev: Father, a beggar at strange doors; Mother and little brothers and sisters, poor, ill clothed, and hungering for a piece of bread.

Sister Yetta! Sister Yetta!

Sister Yetta brought Zlatte to the room where Mrs. Klein had installed another bed for the greenhorn.

However, the sisters slept together in one bed, the first night. The American sister held her sister from Tcheremaiyev in her arms, clinging close to her fragrant young body, fingering her fresh young body with loving tenderness.

How cold were sister Yetta's hands! Bloodless. How cold were sister Yetta's fleshless feet! How thin her breasts, how bony her hips. She had aged and was sickly. How good that she had brought her little sister to this country. She would not be so lonely now. She would have someone to cling to.

"And what's Father doing, and Mother, Zlatte? And how are the youngsters—the little brothers and sisters, Zlatte? And what is Tcheremaiyev like, now? Tell me everything, everything, Zlatte."

The sisters talked to each other. They talked late into the night—talked and wept and kissed one another.

"Are you asleep, child, are you asleep?"

Although Zlatte was now twenty years old, Yetta still addressed her as "child." Zlatte really had been a child when Yetta went away. Now her child Zlatte was asleep. She was sleeping and had forgotten that she was in America. Instead, she was still on the ship. Waves were lifting the vessel, up, up. The waves reached to the sky, great mountains of water were rushing onward . . .

Zlatte fell into the water but did not drown. She began to swim. She swam well, she swam with strong strokes. There was another swimmer near her—it was Moishe. She was ashamed that Moishe was swimming near her . . .

With her little sister asleep, Yetta lay awake beside her. She thought and thought of her lost years, of her sad years. If only her little sister might be spared what had happened to her. May she find the comfort and happiness of this land. May her youth not be wasted upon the dismal machines. May her sister, at least, come to know some joy.

Yetta cried. Inwardly and quietly she cried, Yetta the exhausted and tormented older sister, Yetta the shop girl . . .

ত

At home her sister-in-law had been called Kathie. She was still called that here. At home her brother had been called Misha. He was still called Misha. And they still spoke Russian in the house; spoke Russian even with the children.

They lived on St. Mark's Place. Not far from Second Avenue. A large part of the Russian colony lived in this neighborhood. In close vicinity were to be found a few Russian churches, a Russian bookstore, a few Russian cafes.

Her brother Misha had nothing to do with Jews in America. At home, too, Misha had had little to do with Jews, her elegant, heroic brother Misha.

But in America, she found him with a bald head and a big paunch—this heroic brother Misha who used to ride horseback in Tcheremaiyev, dressed like an aristocrat, in yellow riding boots and a short student jacket.

In America Misha sold candies to the youngsters off the street. At home it would have been said that he had a stall in the market. Here it was called a "candy store"—selling soda water, ice cream, and stationery.

He had fled to America from his father's wealthy home because of a love affair. His father would not consent to the match. It was beneath him to be brought, by means of the match, into a relationship with Meyer, the doctor's assistant, of Tcheremaiyev.

Both young people had disappeared suddenly—Balaban's bright son and Kathie, the male nurse's daughter.

"My dear brother, my dear brother." Manya Balaban wept and could not be comforted.

"Now don't cry, sister mine, don't cry." The brother kissed lovely Manya. "Rest after your trip, pull yourself together."

Rest after the trip? In these four cells, on the fourth floor, suffocating, crowded, and noisy? A house in such disorder—her sister-in-law, Kathie, in a filthy dress, disheveled, unkempt, as if the house were too much for her.

Her brother Misha had two little girls—eight and twelve years old—two little girls, noisy, smeary, dirty, and always shrieking.

There was also a dog in the house, its paws muddy, its muzzle filthy. Its flabby coat was stained with ashes—obviously it had been chasing the cats near the ashcans. The dog kept barking at Manya, enraged by the stranger, bared its teeth while the sister-in-law laughed and the children laughed at Caesar's cleverness.

Caesar was the dog's name and he was a spoiled dog, the only male child. He crawled on the table, stuck his muzzle into the dishes, leaped on the bed with his muddy paws, and the family gushed with joy over Caesar's clever antics.

The single window in the stuffy bedroom opened on a blank wall. The room was dark as night. Manya lay on the bed. She had stretched to rest up after her trip. But she could not rest. Her limbs trembled as if in panic.

At home, servants had waited on her in her father's house. She had grown up in luxury and comfort, fondled and indulged in all things by those around her. She had read in their spacious garden—had rowed about the lake in her own boat, gone driving in her own carriage. An aristocrat at home.

She wept and could find no consolation.

"Now, no more, sister mine—*nie platsh sestritzania platsh,* don't cry." Her brother Misha stood beside her and tried to calm her.

Her brother Misha with the bald head and big paunch—not a trace left of his former brilliance and glory. A sorrowful, helpless little man who must don his apron and go to the candy store to relieve his wife, Kathie, who was so unskilled and awkward with the customers.

ভ

There was no one at home, anyway, so they took Freuke to their restaurant. His sister Malka owned a restaurant on one of the noisiest streets in the Bronx, not far from a subway station. The restaurant was open from daybreak until late into the night.

So Freuke sat in the restaurant all through the day. He was seated at the last table in the rear, looked on, and was silent.

His sister Malka (called Molly in America) was busy in the kitchen. His brother-in-law was busy serving the customers. His two nephews, two unusually tall boys, were also busy. The three men were constantly carrying cooked dishes out of the kitchen.

Close to the ceiling of the restaurant a fan was revolving, cooling the air. A large number of electric lights were burning and there were many mirrors on the walls.

His flat-footed brother-in-law kept running into the kitchen. His two nephews also kept running into the kitchen. And outside, the street was clamoring, banging, and roaring. And Freuke was mute, chained, and bound. He could not stir from the table. He must sit there. He could not make a move by himself, alone, because everything around him was strange. He would have to sit here until they told him to rise. And when he rose, they would conduct him to a house. He would have to follow. No matter where they took him, he would have to follow.

Hour after hour he sat there, and never once did his sister emerge from the kitchen if only to say: "Brother Freukela, how are things with you, brother?" And neither his brother-in-law nor his nephews called to him or as much as threw a glance his way. All of them were terribly occupied with business. People came in, people went out, and his brother-in-law squeezed the cash register. A numeral appeared, a little drawer jutted out to the sound: "Tzick, tzick."

The electric fan hummed and revolved so rapidly that it was hard to see whether it was going at all.

"Zhe, zhe, zhe," the fan ground on. And this sound, "Zhe, zhe," ground itself deep into his hearing. Many years later, at the mere sound of that "zhe-zhe," he would become moody, downhearted. It reminded him of that feeling of being lost, helpless, and fettered.

Freuke slept. He slept with his head on the restaurant table. Nobody saw that he was asleep—neither his sister, nor brother-in-law, nor tall nephews. The latter kept running in and out of the kitchen.

The sound of the fan, "zhe, zhe," kept humming in his ears. His closed eyes were heavy with misery and loneliness.

Who would then have thought, looking at this lonely young greenhorn, sleeping there so wretchedly, that he would, in time, turn out to be a man of wealth, one of New York's millionaires. . . ?

PART TWO

Making a Living

Chaim Becomes a Real-Estatenik

TASHRAK _____

ONE EVENING I WAS SEATED at home when a young fop, wearing a colored vest, came in. I knew at once that he was in the real estate business for who, other than a real-estatenik, can indulge in the luxury of a figured vest, in the middle of the week?

He introduced himself: James Pussy. I said: "I am plizzed to mit you, Mr. Puzzy," and thought to myself that his Jewish name probably was Zushe Katz. Mr. Pussy seated himself confidently and soon pulled a pencil from behind his ear, a sheet of paper from his pocket, and, without a by your leave, began to talk business to me.

"I have heard," he said, "that you are having lots of trouble about a home. You keep moving—from one house to another and can't 'tzettle' in any one place. What I have come to see you about is to give you helpful advice, that is, counsel, so you can 'tzettle' in your own home. Stop paying the landlord money, become a landlord yourself, the owner of your own house. Tell me, how much money can you invest?"

"How many houses have you to sell?" I asked him.

"Never mind," he said. "You don't need to get so steamed up if I want to know something, that is, ask a 'question.' I have come to you with a business proposition. This week I sold a house on Madison Avenue for fifty thousand dollars, a double tenement house on 103rd Street for sixty-five thousands dollars, a 'partzel' in Brooklyn, and some sixteen or seventeen lots and thirteen houses here in the Bronx."

"You must make a lot of money, then," I said with great admiration.

"What do you suppose?" my wife butted in. "Some people make money, work themselves up while you remain a customer-peddler.

What's the matter? Couldn't you have taken to real estate? Why does everybody have a 'chantze' and not you? Eh?"

"Keep cool," Mr. Pussy said and smiled. "You don't need to quarrel over it. Let's rather talk business. If you can invest a few thousand dollars, I have a house for you that's a peach, a beauty! If you have more to invest, I have thirty houses for you from which to choose the one you want."

"Listen to that, Chaim," my wife interrupted him. "He's got thirty houses, and what have you got?"

"She-goat! Those houses are not his. He is just a real estate agent. He deals in houses. The one who owns them is the landlord."

"And I want to make you a landlord," Mr. Pussy said. "Tell me, how much do you want to invest?"

"How do I know?" I said. "First tell me what kind of merchandise you have for me."

He began to write with his pencil and listed them: Bargain One, Bargain Two, Bargain Three—some eight bargains in all, all of them investments on which you made a down payment of a couple of thousand dollars, and then got mortgages on the balance. You could live in the house yourself and rent a floor or two to tenants.

My wife became deeply interested, moved over to the table, asked questions, bargained vigorously, and in the course of half an hour spoke like a born Realtor. The real estate agent spent about two hours with us, drank tea, and had a pleasant time. He left us his card and the list of bargains. We promised to notify him when we had come to any decision.

When he went out, my wife said to me: "Do you know, Chaim, what has just occurred to me? Guess!"

"How do I know what can occur to the mind of a woman? Maybe that the cow flew over the roof and laid a crate of eggs."

"Don't be silly!" my wife said. "You men all like to laugh at us women. A very simple idea came to me, just now: Why shouldn't you become a real-estatenik yourself? You've learned something about the business today and I can help you a bit. I understand it fairly well, already."

I felt the blood run into my face, for what can be more embarrassing to a man than to have his wife hit on a sensible idea that did not even occur to him?

"Yes, yes," I said to her. "You are very wise! I've been thinking about it without you. And I don't need your help, you understand?"

And I began to cough. To tell the truth, I am not accustomed to lying and if I ever tell a falsehood it sticks in my throat.

By the next day, my wife had noised it about all over the block that I had gone into the real estate business and that I was buying and selling houses.

On the very next morning three real estate men came at the same time to offer me new bargains. I listed their bargains in my notebook, one after the other, the number of floors, the size of the lot, the amount of the first mortgage, the second, the size of the cash payment, in addition to other details about taxes, repairs and other expenses, income from rents, and, in particular, the address of the house.

After that, I offered them my bargains. They listened and made entries in their notebooks.

In the evening of the third day, six real estate dealers came to see me. But I got rid of them quickly because that evening I intended to call on a prospective buyer of houses.

I went to the home of a fellow countryman, a pushcart-peddler, whom I suspected of having saved a pretty sum of money. I showed him my bargains and demonstrated how he could make a fortune. He heard me out and wrote it all down on a sheet of paper. I saw I would not make a customer of him and asked: "Why do you set this all down in writing?" He said: "Well, maybe I'll find a customer for these houses and if it's a deal, I'll give you a share of the commission."

I went from him to another fellow countryman who has a grocery store. I no sooner began to tell him of my bargains than he called out: "So that's what you call bargains! Just sit down a while and I'll list you some bargains. I have greater bargains than yours. I've been in real estate half a year." He detailed five distinct bargains and I entered them in my book.

I made my way home weary and hoarse from talking. I was sunk in thought: What strange people we Jews are! Whatever one trades in, all trade in. 'Twas ever so. At one time Jews dealt in old clothes, rags. Later, the style was running to newspaper stands. And now, it's houses. The logic is sound: Out of rags they make paper and out of paper they make houses. Take a look at tenement houses and see how they are built. Thin walls with tiny rooms, as if they were actually made of paper, and it seems that a strong wind could blow them away. And that reminded me of the story of the elders who appeared before King David and said: "King of Israel, Jews need a livelihood." David answered: "Let them take in one another's washing."

Well! Didn't he mean the real estate business?

When I came home, I found—guess whom? Mr. Pussy himself, the very first real estate agent through whom I came to the idea of going into realty! I saw that he and my wife were hitting it off at a great rate: rattling on about "partzels" and lots.

The real estate man showed me a list of new bargains. I said: "Let me have them" and he spoke and I wrote in my notebook.

He said: "Oh, I see you've become a real bookkeeper. What's up?"

"I, too, have gone into the real estate business," I said with pride.

"Have you made a sale already?" he asked and smiled.

"No," I answered. "It seems that I am not yet skilled in the business. However, I realize that there are many who are ready to sell houses, but there are very few who want to buy them. Whoever I talk to is ready to sell, but if you propose that he should buy anything, he skips."

"If you know that," the young man said to me, "then you are a real real-estatenik. You are now an expert. It is as you say: All Jews are real estate agents, but only to sell. Good-bye, and have a pleasant night."

He went away.

Dear reader, maybe you'd like to do a little trading in real estate? I can sell you anything you like—even half of New York!

Chaim and Chaye

ZALMON LIBIN _____

CHAIM AND CHAYE—these are their names. They are a married couple. It is ten years since they were married, and it can almost be said with certainty that in the ten years of their married life there has not been one day when they were separated from one another. They have always, always been together; all their lives they have been close to one another, eye to eye.

Chaim had been a bachelor who could not earn a livelihood, not an old bachelor, mind you—in fact healthy and not bad-looking—but he could never earn his keep.

Chaye had been an old maid, quite a few years older than Chaim, and not at all good-looking, to boot. To make up for it, she was hard-working, and having spent fifteen years in shops, she had accumulated about eight hundred dollars in cash, articles of clothing, some jewelry, and kidney trouble.

Therefore, mutual acquaintances and fellow countrymen took them in hand and brought about the engagement of these two.

At first sight, Chaim promptly fell out of love with his bride-to-be. But since he had always had a torturous existence, had never had a decent meal on his own, had always dragged about without a settled lodging, and now he beheld a bride with a sizable sum of money and an explicit plan to open a small business that would yield a livelihood for life, without any headaches, he agreed to the betrothal.

Chaye, on the other hand, fell for her young, handsome bridegroom the moment he was introduced to her. True, she knew about his greatest weakness—that he could not earn a living—but she did not care about that. She had her few hundred dollars in mind and deep in her heart she was really contented that the situation was such that it was she who would be the provider here, and not her future husband. This circumstance filled her soul with peaceful certainty about the future; it gave her a sort of guarantee that she would be secure in her husband.

A few friendly tongues had even tried to intervene, and warned the old maid:

"Look out! Be watchful." They quietly murmured their secret to Chaye. "He's just a snip of a youngster, that choice of yours; guard your few hard-earned dollars; one like him can snatch them up and—away! Go, catch him!"

Such prophecies would cut the heart of the old maid, but she would take hold of herself and answer, with simulated calm: "Never mind, leave it to me; everything will be all right!"

That's what she would answer, but in her heart she was planning to arrange her future married life so that, as far as possible, she would be secured against desertion and also against fears of losing her little money.

So the two were married, and soon after the wedding they bought a small business: a candy and cigar store.

The business was of a kind which demanded the attention of two people and neither of the two could leave it for a minute. The young wife had taken good care to obtain just such a business. Similarly, she had taken care to see that it was established in her name, and these were her thoughts about her husband: "You will stay with me now, my little duck, like a prisoner."

And it turned out as Chaye had thought. Her "little duck" stayed put like a prisoner.

It was now ten years since they had bought the candy store; business was lively and they were making a good living. Both of them were occupied a whole day, seven days a week, twelve months a year.

They lived in a few rooms in back of the store, and that was very convenient: Here was their store, here was their dwelling, here they ate, here they slept, and there never was an occasion for being away from one another, even for one day. Always, always together.

And the wife looked after her husband—almost spoon-fed him with the best foods obtainable. And it was she who looked after his clothing; she bought him a suit when the proper time for doing so had come; she took his trousers to the tailor for cleaning and pressing when these were necessary; she took his things to the laundry—everything . . . so that even his shaving became her affair. Immediately after the wedding she had bought him a "safety razor" with all the trimmings, and he shaved at home. She would have his soap handy, see to it that he always had bay rum and powder—in a word, she provided every convenience for him so he would have no occasion to rush off to a barber . . .

It might be supposed that, for a haircut, Chaim would have needed to go to a barber, but it turned out to his "good fortune" that Chaye was an artist of a hair cutter and when her husband needed to have his hair trimmed, she took him in hand and left him looking like a well-pruned tree.

So Chaim was provided for, in all directions, and his whole life was so ordered that he did not need to make a superfluous move. He sat behind the counter, took money, and put it into the till. That was all!

Chaim's life might truly have been paradisal had it not been for the fact that his corpulent body was diabetic as a result of his eating too much. This made his peaceful manner of living somewhat uncomfortable. But even in this situation, Chaye again took a hand and looked after him as carefully as she could so that her Chaim would suffer as little discomfort as possible. The doctor who came from time to time to treat Chaye's kidney trouble killed two birds with one stone by also treating Chaim's diabetes. And everything would have been all right except that Chaim's soul suffered from a deep, hidden wound and, in this trouble, Chaye could be only of little help.

In the depths of his soul, Chaim carried about a dream that could never be realized. The desire of his life was to be left alone, whenever that might happen, without his Chaye—if only for the briefest time, if only for one day in his life.

He would, perhaps, have been willing to give half of his life, if the opportunity came to live in the great world, alone, without Chaye. It seemed to him that such a chance would be a miracle, a very great fortune for him. And this desire became the sweetest dream of his existence.

And it seemed to Chaim that if such a miracle, such good fortune, came to him, he would go out of his mind for joy . . . His very soul would be renewed, wings would sprout on him, he would fly in the air, he would turn the world upside down. But no miracles occurred. Chaye was always in the store, never, for even a second, took a step away from her husband, and when Chaim wished to imagine himself alone, without her, he had to close his eyes. That was all he could do.

But one time in Chaim's life a piece of good luck came to him. It was truly a miracle. Chaye's kidney trouble flared up; she was on the point of passing away. The poor woman needed an immediate operation. An ambulance came from a nearby hospital and Chaye was carried out of her candy store.

The top of Chaim's head almost flew off for joy. As if crazed, Chaim ran about the candy store and the rooms in the rear . . . what pleasure—no Chaye! Now Chaim's imagination ran riot . . . and he began to lay plans for the spending of the finally arrived "vacation" of his life.

What spirited plans they were! And for great joy, Chaim forgot that he himself was not altogether well. He forgot his diabetes; he forgot that he was a man who needed to look after himself with great care. He forgot everything. He rushed into a saloon and took a hearty drink—something which, because of his diabetes, he should not, under any circumstances, have done. And if this was not enough, he gave himself a little party, fetched a pint of beer, and had a gay time.

In a few hours, his diabetes acted up. He became unconscious. Friendly neighbors came in and again an ambulance came from the hospital to which Chaye had been taken, and out of the candy store poor Chaim, too, was carried.

The candy store was closed for the time being.

Three days after her operation, as soon as Chaye opened her eyes and came to herself, she asked the nurse that her husband should be notified not to worry about the business, that he should close the store and come to be beside her. The nurse informed Chaye that her husband had been spared the need of coming to her because he was there, in the hospital, in a bed close by, in the men's ward.

For the moment Chaye was frightened, but when the nurse told her how her husband happened to be in the hospital, and, in addition, assured the sick woman that he would recover soon and both of them would be able to leave the hospital at the same time, Chaye rejoiced and felt as if newborn.

On that very day, Chaim was already sitting beside his wife's bed.

Husband and wife left the hospital at the same time and the candy store, which had been closed, opened on an auspicious day.

We Work in a Shop

SHOLEM ALEICHEM _____

I CANNOT TELL YOU precisely how they work in the shop, because I don't know myself. They won't let me into it yet, because I've not yet been confirmed. I only know what I hear from my brother Eli and our friend Pinney. Every evening when they come home from the shop, they tell us marvels beyond belief. They are always exhausted and famished. And we sit down to the evening meal. Here, it is called "supper." Bruche hates this word as a pious Jew hates pork.

There's another word my sister-in-law can't bear. That's the word "window." Bruche says about it: "Wind and woe, Let our enemies know." Then again, she cannot stand the word "stockings." It would never occur to you that "stockings" are *zocken*. Or, to take another example—what will you say about the word "dishes"? Bruche says: "It seems to me that *posudeh* is a much prettier word." Or, what could be simpler than *lefel*? No! They can't bear it. They insist that a *lefel* is a "spoon." Not for nothing does Bruche say (she has her own pat sayings): "America is a country, steak is a choice morsel, "fork" is a *gopel*, and English is a language!"

My brother Eli and our friend Pinney work in two different shops. One is an operator, that is, he is a tailor by trade. The other is a presser. An operator does not need to sew by hand. He stitches at a machine. But you must know how to do even this, the machine doesn't stitch by itself. Then how does my brother Eli come by this knowledge when neither our father, nor our father's father, nor our father's father's father had been a tailor in his life, nor had he ever even seen a machine?

We descend, Mother says, from a line of nothing but cantors, rabbis, and beadles. That's the rub!

However, this is America. In America, there's nothing a person cannot do. In America you get the know-how. As proof, take a rabbi. You certainly must know what it takes to be a rabbi. A rabbi must at least be able to pass on religious law. Nevertheless, there are rabbis in America—they are called "reverend"—who were butchers in the old country. My brother Eli became acquainted here with a mohel, a "reverend" who officiates at the ceremony of circumcision. At home, he had been a tailor, and a ladies' tailor, at that!

Eli asked him: "How come?"

He answered: "America!"

How did my brother Eli learn to stitch? Let me ask you, how did that botch of a tailor become a mohel? Eli really sweated it out, poor fellow. They gave him small pieces that were left over, to run through the machine. So he ran them through, back and forth, and became "all right." By the next day, he was stitching away. You can imagine yourself the kind of sewing that it was! But it must have been good enough, because Pinney could not even do as well. Not that he was too lazy to work—Heaven forbid! Pinney would turn to any kind of work, if only to make a living in America.

The trouble is he is nearsighted and, at the same time, does everything in a hurry. They also sat him down at a machine, like my brother Eli. They also gave him some small leftovers to run through the machine. That was when the misfortune happened. Here, it is called "an accident." In his haste, our friend Pinney caught the left sleeve of his jacket under the needle. Lucky it wasn't his hand. Well, well, the way the whole shop laughed at him. Fellow tailors shouted: "Hurrah!" They called him "greenhorn," that is to say, a green hand. A greenhorn is one who has just arrived from the old country and doesn't know how to open a door. To be a greenhorn is more embarrassing than being a thief. But that wouldn't have been half-bad, as Bruche says, if something else didn't have to happen. Just listen to this:

In this very shop where my brother Eli was working at a machine and where our friend Pinney came to learn the trade, there happened to be an old acquaintance of ours and an enemy of Pinney's—the tailor from Haiseen. If you still remember, this tailor from Haiseen traveled with us on the same boat—Prince Albert. You probably also remember that our friend Pinney and this tailor were at dagger points. So God must bring it about that Pinney should meet him in this shop. And what a meeting!

In this shop, the tailor from Haiseen is a big shot. He is no machine operator, but a "cutter." He cuts the materials for the operators to sew. But that's not enough for him. He says he will not remain in this business for long. He is expecting to become a designer in a short time. And that's certainly a feather in his cap. A designer is the man who makes the fashions. A designer earns fifty dollars a week, seventy-five dollars a week, and even a hundred. If a man's in luck, he doesn't care where it comes from! As Bruche says: "God gives everything to one, and nothing to another!"

When Pinney walked into the shop, the tailor from Haiseen came toward him. He focused his glasses, and stuck his hand out to Pinney, and said to him: "Hello, landsman! How do you do?" In other words: "Sholem Aleichem, how are you, kinsman?" Our friend Pinney looked at him with his nearsighted eyes: "Who is this clown?" He did not begin to recognize him. Only when the other reminded him of the Prince Albert did Pinney remember him. And Pinney says he got three stabs in the heart! Actually, what did this tailor ever do to him? But Pinney says he simply cannot look the man in the face. He says that, even if he knew he could earn a thousand dollars an hour, he would not stay in that shop for a minute! On top of that, the "accident" with the sleeve caught in the machine!

In short, Pinney didn't want to be an operator any more. He went off to another shop and hired himself out as a presser—an apprentice, to begin with. When he learns the trade, he will go higher and higher. How far?

"Who can tell?" says Pinney. "No one knows when his day will come. Neither Carnegie," he says, "nor Vanderbilt, nor Rockefeller knew that they would become what they are today."

In the meantime, Pinney is doing it the hard way. And all because of that habit of his—doing things in a hurry. To top it off, there's his shortsightedness. Every day he comes home with new burns.

One time he came home with a sore nose. What happened? He burned his nose while pressing. How does the pressing iron get at your nose? Pinney says that his nose did not wait for the pressing iron to be courteous enough to come to it. He can afford, he says, to have his nose go to the iron. Nevertheless, how did his nose get to the iron? It turned out that Pinney was looking for a piece of cloth that needed pressing and because of his nearsightedness he had bent close to the table and brought his nose, point down, on the hot iron.

"When a *shlim-mazl* falls in the snow, he invariably hits a stone."

I don't think I need to tell you who made that crack; you yourself will guess that Bruche said it. My sister-in-law has a pointed tongue.

Bruche is not satisfied. Neither is Mother. Nor Teibele. Have you ever known women to be satisfied? They bemoan us menfolk, because we must toil so, in America, to make a living. No trifle, this working in a shop! At half past seven in the morning you must already be at work. It takes an hour to get there. You must have a bite to eat. Certainly, you must also say your morning prayers.

Now figure out when does one get up? And you mustn't be a minute late, because if you are they deduct half a day's pay for every five minutes. How can they tell whether you are late or not? Leave it to America. In America every shop has a kind of clock. The first thing you do when you come into the shop is to go over and press the clock. In their language, this is "punching the clock." "Clock" *(zaiger)* is a timepiece and the word comes, my brother Eli says, from *glock* (bell). A "glock" rings, and a clock rings, he says. But only a wall clock.

As proof, he says, there is a *zaigeral* (pocket timepiece). It doesn't ring, so it is called "watch." I asked Eli: "Why 'watch?' " He said: "What then should it be called?" I said: "Watchlet." Elihu asked me: "Why 'watchlet'?" I answered: "If a *zaiger* is a *zaigeral,* then a watch must be a watchlet." "For example," I said, " 'Boy' is a youth, therefore a little one is a *boytchik* and a very small one is a *boytchikel.*" Eli becomes very angry and says to me that from our friend Pinney I've learned to be contrary.

Lucky that Pinney was not there. Had Pinney been there they would have wrangled over the word "watch" as they had quarreled and almost come to blows over the word "breakfish," the early morning meal. Eli said the first meal is called "breakfish" because at the first meal you eat fish or herring. Then Pinney said: "If herring, then why isn't it called 'break-herring'?" Eli said to him: "What an ox you are! What is herring if not fish?" Pinney, realizing his defeat, said: "Do you know what? Let's ask an American Jew." No sooner said than done.

They stopped a smooth-shaven Jew in the street (it was on a Saturday) and they asked him, out of curiosity: "Uncle, how long have you been in America?" He answered: "Thirty years. What's the matter?" They answered: "We'd like to ask you something. Tell us why you Americans call the first meal in the morning 'breakfish'?" The Jew looked at them and then said: "Who told you that we call it 'breakfish'?" "Then what do you call it?"

"Breakfast! Breakfast! Breakfast!" the man yelled right into their faces and paid his respects to them by adding: "Green creatures!"

I'm very much afraid that our stay in the shop will not be for long. My brother Eli says the workers are always in trouble with the foreman. Every shop has a foreman, a headman, a supervisor. And not merely one foreman. Every loft has its own foreman. The foreman in the loft where Eli works is a Haman, a tyrant of tyrants. He had been an operator himself at one time. But he worked himself up and became a foreman. The workers say he is worse than the "boss." "Boss" is a Hebrew word and comes from Bel Habeth, my brother Eli says, and Pinney must hold his tongue because he has no knowledge of Hebrew, as compared with Eli. After all, Eli is a cantor's son!

But to get back to the foreman, a rumor spread through the shop that the foreman moves the clock hands, so that no matter when you come you are late. What do you say to the scoundrel! And our friend tells even prettier tales about his shop. Their foreman, he says, won't permit the workers to glance at a newspaper. To read a paper at work— is to risk your life! To say nothing about smoking. And they may not say a word to one another. It is so quiet in the shop that, aside from the pounding and clatter of the machines, he says you can hear a fly.

His shop has another virtue. The irons there are heated by *gozz*. Of course it's not called that here. Here it is called "gas." Nevertheless, it stinks the same as our *gozz*. But you must not call it *gozz*. You must say "gas." The exact opposite. Had it been called "gas" in the old country, it would most likely be called "gozz" here.

In short, the fumes of the gas go to the heads of the workers and they fall in a faint and must stop work. Their pay is deducted, that is, when they are to get their pay for the week's work, they find it has been cut. Late five minutes: half a day's pay; left work too early: half a day's pay. You fainted—lost a day.

No. We can't bear it any longer. We will have to go out on strike!

Point of a Needle

ZALMON LIBIN ⎯⎯⎯⎯⎯⎯⎯⎯⎯⎯⎯⎯⎯⎯⎯⎯⎯⎯⎯⎯⎯⎯

STRANGELY QUIET IN THE SHOP TODAY! Not because of slack time. There's the hum and commotion of the wheels of sewing machines; there's the clacking of shears; there's the whistling and whining of steam. But this is the turmoil of dumb noises—the unchanging speech of cold iron which is without knowledge, without feeling, without understanding, and which remains indifferent no matter what happens.

But the workers themselves are quiet.

Operators, basters, finishers are seated at their work like mutes, sadly quiet . . .

Abe, the jester, utters no quips and there is no laughter; Sam and Hymie, always at odds with one another, are not wrangling today and are no source of joy to anyone; Hanna, the finisher, is not singing; Dave, her accompanist, is not humming and no ear is turned toward them.

Among the men there is no discussion of the news of the day . . . among the women there is no gossip mongering . . . Quiet—all are seated as if transfixed . . . All seem to be mournful . . . On the faces of all there is the sign of secret suffering, giving the impression that all of them are sorrowing over the death of a dear one and that they are engaged in sewing shrouds.

The cause of this breathless silence is a cut in wages—a fresh and still bleeding wound in the hearts of the workers, left there last night by the foreman, the employer's dull and rusted knife.

And no one speaks, no one laughs, no one jests, and no one sings . . . Everyone is preoccupied with this fresh wound. Everyone is embittered, irritated, everyone alone with his pain.

There is quiet in the shop.

Dolbin, one of the operators, is steeped in his work but his thoughts are figuring the extent of his loss and measuring the cost, in blood money, which the decreased pay envelope will reveal . . . It will be quite a sum . . . he is hurt and deeply vexed.

On top of this, Dolbin has another worry: He has drawn a bad lot, a pack of sorrows, and he cannot extricate himself—his bundle of work consists of such cheap, hard cloth. Once he has driven the needle in, he must labor and sweat to draw it out again. The pattern, too, is difficult and from time to time he must rip open what he has sewn with such an outlay of effort and blood.

Dolbin tears his hair, bites his lip till he draws blood . . . his heart grows faint with dismay and pain . . .

Other workers who had drawn their bundles of cloth at the same time Dolbin did are through, and many, in fact, are finishing their second bundles. He, Dolbin, is still laboring over the first lot . . . he feels that his limbs are growing numb.

He is as pale as a corpse . . . his limbs are trembling from suppressed rage and hurt.

Finally he finishes the work, wipes the sweat from his face, and, with a curse, carries the completed work downstairs to the office.

Abe, the jester, suddenly discovers that the point of his needle has broken. He has no other needle; to run out to buy one will be a loss of time. He knows that Dolbin has several needles in the drawer of his machine. But he also knows that today Dolbin is as mad as the devil and he will, under no circumstances, lend or even sell a needle. Abe walks over to Dolbin's machine and tries to find a needle.

The drawer is locked. Abe hits on an idea: He removes the needle from Dolbin's machine and inserts in its place the needle he had taken from his own machine.

The "hands" in the shop smile faintly as Abe resumes his work.

Dolbin returns, bringing back the same bundle of work. His pale face is spotted with red flushes, his eyes flash with terrifying light.

Everyone knows what has happened . . . No one dares to ask a question . . . A sudden shiver runs over Abe's body.

Dolbin hurls the bundle beside his machine, flings himself into his chair, digs his hands into his hair, and sits, bewildered, beaten as by an overpowering blow.

"Do them over?" someone asks.

Dolbin remains silent.

"The whole damned business?" someone else wants to know.

Dolbin says nothing but his eyes are suddenly overrun with tears.

Dolbin picks up a garment . . . his hands are trembling . . . he examines his work and sighs—sighs so strangely that it seems as if the place from which the sigh escaped was a rent in his heart. In silence he puts the garment in place under the needle.

The wheel turns—there is a screech from the broken needle.

"What's this? Who did it?" And Dolbin casts a wild and terrifying glance around him.

Abraham turns pale.

"You, Abe?"

"You have a few others . . . I'll pay you . . ."

A pair of large steel shears flies straight at Abe with terrific force . . .

A shout of terror breaks from all the workers.

The shears pierce Abe's shoulder, pierce deep into the flesh, and remain there . . . blood flows . . . Abe's head falls forward . . . there is an outcry and wild commotion . . .

Dolbin stands up, a terrifying figure . . .

"Serves you right . . . don't grab. . . ," he says and his body shakes as if from cold and he smiles with a frozen, diabolic smile.

Suddenly the boss runs in.

Apparently someone has informed him about what has taken place because he has no sooner come in than he is shrieking: "All because of a needle! Murderers, cutthroats, the whole gang of you should be sent to Sing Sing."

Chaim Thanks God for Deliverance

TASHRAK _____

IF YOU ARE FATED to have troubles, they need not necessarily come through your own wife but may come through a stranger, just as well. I once got into such a mess with a strange young married woman, that I am actually ashamed to tell of it.

But if I don't tell of it you may suspect me of—who knows what? It is, therefore, better for me to tell the whole story before my enemies smear me with their lies.

And I have many enemies, indeed—what customer-peddler doesn't?

I was walking in the street with my bundle and my clock when a young woman stopped me, a very good-looking woman, I think, peaches and cream, although I don't like to stare. Good-looking, not good-looking, what do I care? What am I, a youngster looking for romance? After all, it's business I'm interested in! So when she stopped me I had no hesitation talking to her in the street; the bundle and clock in my hand were evidence enough that I was talking business, not foolishness, compliments, love, nonsense.

The young woman told me a tale about wanting to buy some trifles for the house, on the installment plan, but she added that she did not want her husband to know about it because he disliked dealing with customer-peddlers and buying on the installment plan.

I told her: "We can arrange it without his knowledge; your credit is good." I ought to tell you that the best credit risk is the woman who buys without her husband's knowledge: She must pay, because she doesn't want any kind of to-do lest her husband learn about the matter.

She said to me: "I really intend to buy some things from you with-out his knowing. I'll tell him I obtained them for trading coupons. You can tell a man anything. I'll pay you on my own, on installments. But you will come to collect only in the daytime when he is not at home."

She invited me to come upstairs with her, and I followed her. She conducted me into a pleasant room and asked me to be seated. Then she spoke about a picture album and described the kind she wanted, and we began to talk about the price and the purchasing conditions.

In the midst of our talk we heard heavy steps in the hall. The young woman leaped up, terrified. "Oh, my husband is coming!" she said, wringing her hands. Suddenly she flung her arms about me and said, in a hushed voice: "I'll hide you in the wardrobe." The wardrobe was close by. With both hands she pushed me into it, together with my bun-dle, and shut the door. I remained standing in the dark, among coats, trousers, dresses, and rags. I could not even see my nose.

It is easy to understand that I was quite a bit frightened. What would happen if her husband remained at home the whole day? I would have to spend the night, in the clothes closet. In a little while I heard the husband's voice and that of the young woman, too.

I shall set down, exactly as I heard them, what both voices said:

"Hello, darling."

"Jake! What's the matter? So early?"

"I'm not well, darling. A fearful headache. I have the grippe. Had to quit work. Devil take it! Get me a bit of tea, dear, and then I'll lie down."

"If you have a headache, you shouldn't have any tea. A walk out-doors will do you more good."

"Go on, silly. It's the grippe. I must remain indoors at least a few days, and not leave the house at all."

When I heard that, I thought I would faint on the spot. I began to think of what to do. But what could I do? A thousand times nothing. I could only pledge a quarter to the Foundation of Rabbi Meyer Bel Haness, the master of miracles, if I should get out alive.

In the meantime the thought struck me that perhaps the entire in-cident was a put-up job, a scheme to trick me and to extort some money from me! Things like that occur in America. But I soon realized that, though I was in a mess, the young woman was as innocent as a young calf.

"Whose hat is that on the couch?" I heard the husband ask.

My hard luck! When I came into the room, I had removed my hat and put it on the couch. And when I crept into the wardrobe, I left my hat behind.

"Whose hat is it?" I heard the same voice ask again.

"How do I know whose hat that is?" the young woman said. "Perhaps an old one of yours; it probably just turned up."

"A bum's hat like that! Such a sweaty hat! What are you talking about?"

He burst into laughter and I became enraged. The impertinence of saying that mine was a bum's hat! It was sweaty, all right, because I had bought it secondhand, but to say it was a bum's hat was plain impertinence. But what was I to do? I had to stand silent.

I felt, at the same time, that I was growing hot. I could hardly breathe. I thought, another five minutes and I would leap out of the wardrobe and give myself up, as a soldier does when he sees that all is lost on the field of battle.

"Who was smoking cigarettes here?" the same masculine voice demanded suddenly.

"No one," the young woman answered.

"What are you talking about, Rosie? There's the butt of a cigarette in the ashtray—a pretty bum cigarette, too. The kind you get four for a cent."

"What do I know?" the woman answered. "Nobody was here."

"Say!" the masculine voice insisted. "Don't give me any monkey business. Was anybody here? Here are two chairs close together. Someone was here! Listen, Rosie, I won't stand for any monkey business!"

His voice rose in pitch and in anger.

"Jake, calm down," the young woman said. "Remember you are sick. I just reminded myself the grocer was here. We went over some bills."

"And he forgot his hat? How does any one forget his hat?"

"I'll ask him," the young woman said.

"Rosie, you're lying to me!" the husband shrieked.

"Jake, oh Jake! How can you say that? You know how faithful I am to you, how I love you!" I heard her break into sobs.

I became fearfully hot. I began to fan myself with a pair of trousers that was hanging close to me.

There was a brief silence. Then the wife said: "Go, have your tea."

"Bring the tea to me. I want to take my bathrobe out of the clothes closet," he said.

"What do you need your bathrobe for? Sit in your jacket," she began to stammer. I got a sour taste in the mouth.

"I'm not asking you," he said angrily. "If I say I want the bathrobe, I'll take the bathrobe."

In that moment the light of day struck my eyes. The door of the wardrobe opened and there I stood, trembling like a leaf, soaked in perspiration, with my face aflame.

The first thing I knew, I was hurled to the ground and almost broke my feet. Then the young woman rushed over, stood between us, and pleaded:

"Jake, darling dearest, leave him alone; the peddler is innocent. I asked him to come up. I wanted to buy something without your knowing it. Hit me all you like, but leave him alone. Beat me, darling, slap me, call me what you like, but leave the peddler alone."

She wept like a child. Her husband looked as if bewildered.

"Mister," I said, confronting him, "have pity on your wife. She has suffered enough today, poor thing. If you wish to punish anyone, punish me. I am a man who can take a beating. I get enough from loafers every day, nothing personal intended, Heaven forbid. But you can beat me, you can pull my beard, but have pity on your wife. Leave her alone."

The man broke into a laugh.

"This is a true love scene such as you see on the stage. All right, Mister," he said. "Now take your sweaty hat and get out. Don't you worry about my wife. That's my business. Go on!"

I did not wait for any leave-taking and went. When I got home the first thing I did was to drop a quarter into the box: Foundation of Rabbi Meyer Bel Haness, and in that way fulfilled my vow.

I certainly got into a mess, but it could have been much worse.

Saturday, in shul, I gave thanks for deliverance from peril.

The Quiet Jubilee

ZALMON LIBIN

IT WAS A QUIET JUBILEE. A summer evening, a room furnished in commonplace style in a New York tenement house.

Gittel, the wife of Hirsh, the capmaker, was almost finished with her chores.

Supper had been fully prepared a long time ago. Now it simmered and bubbled in the pot standing over a small flame on the kerosene stove. The supper thumped and knocked against the cover of the pot.

A quiet, justified protest.

The lamp chimney sparkled with cleanliness and the light burned proudly within the lamp; the table was set—the cloth had been removed, until after the meal, to keep it clean; the white oilcloth on the table was gleaming; the dishes were in place, and there were several slices of bread with the hard crust cut away. Neither Hirsh nor Gittel had teeth. In a small tray lay slices of tomatoes; nearby stood an empty pitcher—the water was in a bottle on the ice in a washtub. In a word, this was a table set for a king. The baby's face was washed, and in its freshly combed hair a ribbon stood up in bows.

Gittel herself had washed, combed, and put on a clean wrapper; everything was in readiness and the housewife awaited the arrival of her husband.

And then Hirsh came home from work.

Hirsh entered cheerfully and gaily, not at all as was his wont after work, and his eyes revealed that his mind was bent on some cheerful object. He stepped quickly to the side of the child, looking happily at the baby, and turning a good-natured smile upon his wife.

"There is something holidayish in your manner today," Gittel said and regarded him with satisfaction.

"We should really be celebrating some kind of a holiday today," Hirsh answered and continued to smile.

"Did the boss raise your wages?" Gittel voiced the thought that came suddenly.

"The weather is truly hot," Hirsh said, "but the boss has not gone crazy yet."

"Then what's the holiday?" she asked inquisitively.

"Because I've cast up my accounts today," Hirsh answered.

"What did you say?" Gittel did not understand.

"Because I did a little figuring today."

"What accounts? What figuring?" Gittel looked at her husband, with the blank eyes of a simpleton.

"Wait till you hear," Hirsh answered calmly as if hiding a secret. "In the meantime, tell me, wife, whether we have a decent supper."

"It's a very good supper," Gittel informed him and looked proudly at the pot in which the supper was cooking.

"What, for example?" Hirsh asked, and now it was not the wife who was inquisitive, but the husband.

"Roast meat with potatoes," Gittel told him, speaking the words as if the taste and aroma of the food were actually in her mouth.

"Fine!" Hirsh expressed his delight.

"So you're pleased?"

"Greatly pleased because I was afraid it was soup."

"What if it were soup?" Gittel wondered. "You always like soup."

"But today I want some beer with my supper, and beer doesn't go well with soup but is delicious with roast meat."

"But why beer? There is water on ice." Gittel did not fall in with her husband's preference.

"No matter," Hirsh answered, went to the table, and took the empty pitcher.

"Who will drink a pint of beer?" Gittel asked.

"You and I," Hirsh said calmly.

"But what is the holiday, anyway?"

"Something I figured out today."

"Again figures and accounts?"

"Wait till you hear," Hirsh answered and went out for the beer.

For a while Gittel remained uncertain about what to do, but soon found work to keep her busy.

She set the supper on the table, making sure to cover the warm food with dishes to keep it from cooling before they ate, then placed two glasses in readiness, and looked after a few other details.

The capmaker brought the beer and the family sat down to supper. Hirsh gave the baby a sip of beer, which the baby tasted. At the grimaces on the child's face the parents broke into laughter.

"How long since we were married?" Hirsh asked his wife suddenly and he swallowed another glass of beer.

"I think—about six years," Gittel answered.

"A good six years, I'd say," Hirsh conceded.

"On the contrary; let's figure it out," Gittel proposed thoughtfully and began counting on her fingers.

"Well—is that right?" Hirsh asked impatiently.

"Listen," Gittel went on figuring. "How long did we live on Ludlow Street?"

"Fully six months," Hirsh answered.

"And in Gouverneur Street?"

"Also six months."

"And in Suffolk Street?"

"Just a year."

"There we have two years."

"Two years," Hirsh agreed.

"And in Delancey Street?"

"I don't remember," Hirsh said.

"Neither do I," and Gittel gave up figuring by the places they had lived in.

"I know it's six years," Hirsh announced curtly.

"Certainly it's six years," Gittel said. "You remember when you went to the baths?"

"Two years ago this summer, God preserve us, when I began getting those pains."

"Well, then, don't you remember when you were going to the baths you said: 'Today is just four years since we were married?' "

"Certainly I remember."

"That's six years ago."

"Just what I say."

"And last year, when our son was born," Gittel spoke again, "we figured and calculated that it was five years since our wedding."

"Six years today."

"Yes, six years," Gittel agreed.

"Then it's right," Hirsh said. "Six and four—that makes ten."

"What four?" Gittel asked in wonder.

"The four years I worked at the machine before we were married," Hirsh explained. "Today is just ten years. I remember as if it were today, I came to America just before Shavuot and two days after the holiday I sat down in front of the machine and, thank God, I've been driving that 'donkey' for ten years."

Hirsh became thoughtful for a moment and looked into the glass of beer in which the lamplight was reflected. When he spoke again his voice had changed in tone.

"Ten long, long years," Hirsh said with deep feeling, as he shook his head.

"Then this is your holiday?" Gittel burst suddenly into laughter. It was evident that the glass of beer she had drunk had a share in the sudden outburst.

"Don't laugh, my wife," Hirsh said. "It really is a holiday."

Gittel smiled and shrugged her shoulders.

"It is a holiday," Hirsh spoke on, "if I begin to consider that it is ten years that I have been at the machine and, thank God, I am still all right."

On Gittel's pale cheeks a rosy flush began to spread. She smiled, listened to her husband without speaking. Hirsh went on:

"Many of those who sat down with me at the machine, the very same time I did, have gone—no one knows where. Where is Buchholz now? Came on the same boat with me, sat himself down to work with me—it's almost two years that the grass has been growing on his grave, Heaven spare us."

The smile left Gittel's lips; Hirsh went on more loudly and more spiritedly:

"Where is Drob? Also got down before the donkey at the same time . . . almost. His third year now living in the hospital, taking a slow farewell of his life."

"May you be spared," Gittel interrupted quickly and now there was no trace of a smile on her lips. Her face became serious as Hirsh continued:

"Chaim Zaviesse has lost his legs; Poltiel Kolb suffers from asthma and is struggling for life somewhere in a candy store; Zalmon Shlimel began to spit blood after six years at the machine and now he is a newsboy, selling papers in the streets . . . and I, God be praised, am still all right."

"Thank God, thank God," Gittel murmured quietly and earnestly.

"My legs still serve me," Hirsh went on, "my hands are as skillful as ever, and if I put on steam I can, even to this day, turn out a sizable lot of work a week."

"Please don't push yourself," Gittel scolded him good-naturedly.

"And today is the tenth year. Well, tell me, Gittel, isn't this a holiday?"

"May the Almighty grant us health," Gittel answered as Hirsh emptied the pitcher quietly. Then he spoke again:

"For the fun of it, today I figured up how many caps I made in these ten years."

"It must be a lot." Gittel spoke quickly.

"Guess how many? Try."

She smiled again and shrugged her shoulders.

"I wasn't too finicky about every last cap, or dozen caps, for that matter. Nevertheless, in whatever way I summed it up, it came to nearly three hundred thousand caps."

"Oh, oh," Gittel said without understanding.

"Silly! Why, that's enormous; it's a great number—a world," Hirsh explained. "Why, you can't even conceive how many that is."

"I guess it's a lot," Gittel answered.

"An ocean of human beings, a world of men wear my caps, and I dare say that not one of the dopes knows that I, Hirsh, did all that work."

"How should anyone know?" Gittel said.

"Not that it matters any: It doesn't bother me a bit," Hirsh said and raised his glass of beer.

"L'chaim, Gittel!"

"L'chaim, l'chaim, my mad Hirsh."

"Ten years at the donkey and I'm still OK. May God grant that I get no worse in the next ten years."

Hirsh began to smile to the baby, who was sucking a bone and crooning with delight.

"L'chaim, son! Your dad's been driving the donkey for ten years!

It's his holiday today. May God grant, my child, that you should never know of these shops, of these bosses and donkeys, or of this accursed work."

Hirsh drank to the last drop.

Gittel was growing drowsy: She took up the child, left the table, and began to rock the baby to sleep in the rocking chair as she hummed a melancholy tune.

"Ten years of laboring like an ass, like an ox," Hirsh suddenly took up his refrain, "and what do I have to show for it? A blood—a bloody pauper . . ." He could not go on. His body was weary and exhausted with work; his head was dulled with the cheap beer. He was drowsy.

"No more strength; I'm buckling under the yoke . . . hi, brother Buchholz, we'll be meeting soon," murmured the master of the feast. "I'm half-dead, half-dead . . . soon, soon . . . the grave . . . it won't be long now . . ."

And Hirsh fell asleep seated in his chair, and from the closed eyelids two tears ran down.

Gittel fell asleep rocking the child, and the quiet jubilee came to an end.

Reb Yankele Pickpocket

CHONE GOTTESFELD _____

YANKELE PICKPOCKET, that's my name, and I'm not ashamed of it. What's there to be ashamed of? That's my business, my trade. It calls for skill; it takes guts. It's no cinch to crawl into someone's pocket and withdraw your hand without a touch or stir, put on an innocent look, and vanish quickly so there's no trace of hide or hair of you. It's a difficult trade and it takes talent and experience.

But I'm not like other thieves who are rowdies, bums, and don't fear God. I am a sober citizen and am pious. I fear God greatly. I have myself seen how some of the mightiest men have died of a cold. A little breeze from God laid them flat. I'll not start anything with God. Because of that my friends, thieves all, call me Reb Yankel.

I'm a man who believes in giving to God what is God's and to Caesar what is Caesar's.

I must steal because I have no better profession. But I am one of your finer thieves. No holdups for me. I steal only when no one is looking. If anyone sees me, off I run.

There are those who play the role of respectability and rob and swindle others out of very big sums and are men of great wealth. I am not rich. There's no wealth in lifting pocketbooks. I just make a decent living and have nothing to complain of.

That's why I give to God what is His due. I will not work on the Sabbath even if the best job should come my way.

On the Sabbath I go to the synagogue to pray. On Friday, Sabbath eve, I say 'Sholem Aleichem,' make the benediction, eat gefilte fish, and sing hymns. Saturday morning I read the portion for the week.

True, the Sabbath costs me a goodly sum. On Saturdays the best jobs are to be found. People go traveling, go to the theater, leave the house unattended. On Saturday, people get their wages and carry money in their pockets.

It has happened to me more than once that, after the Sabbath, when I stuck my hand into someone's pocket I found it empty because the wages had been taken by some other thief on the Sabbath. But I will not work on that day for any money in the world. I am a Jew and must pay for it. If God wishes, He can make it up to me on a Sunday for ten Sabbaths running. We have an Almighty in Heaven.

At the end of the Sabbath, I say the havdalah, the prayer of separation between the holy day and the weekdays, greet my wife with: "May we have a good week, a fortunate week," and start out to earn my daily bread.

I am, may no harm come to me, always in need. What I spend on charity alone would provide a fine living for anyone else. I contribute to hospitals, to synagogues, and, especially, to parochial schools. I'm greatly in favor of parochial schools and education. I want Jewish children to study the Bible; let them learn, let them know, and let them not grow up thieves like me.

True, once I robbed the collector for a parochial school. I gave him a five-dollar bill for the school, and stole all that he had collected. But that's making a living for you! If a man comes into the house with some money, am I going to let him out, money and all, so that someone else, a competitor, will swipe it all from him? I'm not that crazy!

I also think very highly of rabbis, holy men. If holy men have taken the trouble to come to us in America, to give us their blessing, they are worth a great deal. What would we do, I ask you, if they did not want to come to America and we had to go to them, all the way to Europe, for their benediction? No matter what we spend on these saints, we are still getting the better part of the bargain.

A little while ago, I went to a rabbi for counsel. The first thing he asked was what I work at. I answered: "I do jobs for different people, on different streets, in different cities. I never work in the same place."

He listened, long life to him, and asked: "Do you work on the Sabbath?"

"Heaven forbid! God forbid! I wouldn't work on the Sabbath for any money."

Then the rabbi, may he live long, raised his shining eyes and said: "I wish you prosperity!"

I was just leaving the rabbi's house when a Chasid went by. I slipped my hand into his pocket and got a wallet full of bills—prosperity!

Recently, I had some trouble with a rabbi. I went to him for a consultation. He, too, wished me prosperity when I caught the glitter of a diamond stickpin in his tie. After all, I am Yankele Pickpocket and I was tempted to take the pin. My livelihood, isn't it? How long would it be before another such opportunity came my way! And it was an easy job, too. The rabbi was apparently thinking about divine things, and I could take the pin from him without his knowing about it for a long time.

But the Reb Yankel in me said: "Nothing doing. Hands off! That belongs to the rabbi. For the money spent on the pin, he gave some Jew many blessings. You may not rob a rabbi!" But the Yankele Pickpocket in me said: "Don't be a dolt! The rabbi does not look for blessings. He will give new blessings and get a new stickpin." Yankele Pickpocket and Reb Yankel in me carried on a debate. Yankele Pickpocket said: "Take it!" Reb Yankel said: "Don't take it." Finally it was too late. The beadle came in with several other people. In thieving there is a law: Don't procrastinate!

In short, I went home without the rabbi's stickpin. The Reb Yankel in me was victorious.

Time passed, I needed a great deal of money. I was to marry off a daughter. The Yankele Pickpocket in me reminded me of the stickpin of the rabbi, long life to him. "Go," he said, "take the pin. You are about to marry off a child!"

I called on the same rabbi to take counsel with him. I poured out my heart to him, told him of my great need in view of the coming marriage. When he gave me his blessing, I already had his stickpin.

I got six hundred dollars for it in the pawnshop. Blessings on him for wearing such a fine stickpin. What would I have done if he were a miser of a rabbi and wore a pin worth only a quarter?

PART THREE

And What of the Children?

Yossele

SHOLEM ASCH ————————————————————————

YOSSELE WAS SITTING in a large room, among many people, waiting
for his mother. He did not cry, he had not detained his mother when
they called her. He was silent.

From the very moment when the misfortune occurred, he understood thoroughly what had befallen him and regarded himself as guilty
of some secret crime. And there arose in this tiny Jew all the humility
and patience with which his people had endured their troubles, and he
found himself prepared for sorrow as if his parents and grandparents—
his forefathers in all generations—had beaten for him a pathway to misery. Silent and withholding himself, he sat beside his mother, like a
full-grown, thoughtful adult, as if he were taking everything philosophically and regretted only that they had torn his mother away from his
brothers and thus marred the joy of seeing his father.

The place in which he found himself was called, in the language of
the common man, the Island of Tears. It actually was an island of tears.
In this room were gathered all those who had been sentenced to be sent
back on the ships that had brought them, or about whom negotiations
were still going on with Washington. For the most part, they were
lonely, desolate souls who had found no relative—no one—to receive
them; or older folk, or some so young that they could not vouch for
themselves, and needed someone who would give assurance that he
would take them to his home. That someone they did not find. They
were strangers in the land. And they looked like fragments, particles, as
if there had been a vast scattering of human beings between Europe and

America, of whom part had fallen among the ships, like granules of barley on the piers when grain is shifted from one vessel to another.

There were those who still hoped they would be admitted to the country; they had relatives here, deep in the interior, to whom they had written. They were more fortunate, better off than the others whom they had already promised to help if, God willing, they were allowed to enter. In that case, they would make every effort to have the rest admitted. Most prominent was an elderly woman, Aunty, who had a nephew living in Chicago. This nephew was, supposedly, a bigwig and a thorough American. "Let him but come," she kept on saying, "and he will take us all out of here." When she was led to the dining hall, she asked everyone she met in the corridor about her nephew and whether he was already on his way, as if everyone must know her nephew in Chicago, the bigwig and thorough American.

The others sat quietly. The old Jews who had not found their children sat repeating the Psalms; the women were weeping, and the children among them hid in whatever nooks they could find. Upon all of them lay the melancholy of the outcast, and over them floated the fear of the sea, which they would have to cross again in their homelessness.

"It makes no difference to me, let them send me even to Goshen; it's all the same to me. To whom shall I go, whom do I have at home?" one woman addressed the others.

"Oh, home," a second woman moaned. "But you, the less said the better, went and sold your bedding, and wandered off into the barren world."

"I told you at once that you should not go—Sarah, do not go. That fellow got lost somewhere. I know he sent photographs, but who believes them? Even the Psalm reader was doubtful and spoke in such a tone as if he doubted America itself or that anything like it could even be."

"And is bedding all that matters?" a third broke in. "Never mind the bedding. Do you have a home waiting for you? And whom are you going to?" She pointed to her husband as if to indicate that for herself alone, she would be provided for.

While the women were speaking thus among themselves, Yossele found a companion. This was a boy of his age who was also wandering about in the room. Several times he had wanted to approach the other, and the other him, and each had circled the other in bashfulness and silence. Finally they became acquainted, took one another by the hand, sat down in a corner, and, in the manner of the grown-ups, began to speak:

"They sending you back, too?"

"Yes. And you?"

"Me also."

"Why?"

"They say I have sore eyes."

"Typhus left its trace on my head," and Yossele took off his cap and lowered his head.

"Is your father here?"

"Yes. And yours?"

"I am an orphan. I was sent to an uncle of mine," came the answer.

Yossele felt deep respect for the boy because he was an orphan, and felt himself inferior to the other. Like true sons of their people, there was not a trace of a smile on their lips, and the last glimpse of childishness had disappeared from their faces. Like wise, aged adults they sat and opened their hearts to one another.

Soon, Yossele's mother came in. Her tears were still on her face and her moist eyes turned compassionate looks upon her son. Yossele realized how desolate, how unfortunate he was—all his fault—and felt guilty as if he had brought all of this about.

ל

In a few days the verdict came from Washington. There was no help for it. Yossele must leave on the next ship.

The family was standing in a group. They were all silent and all knew what was going on, though not a word had been said. The question was, who was to accompany Yossele?

The mother had to remain with the other children, now that they were here. Nevertheless, she wept:

"I will not let him go alone; my child will be lost; I won't let him— I'd sooner lose everything in the sea; I'll go back with the child."

Rachel spoke up like an adult:

"In whose care will you leave the children? Father must go to work. You stay here, stay here. I'll go back." She straightened the kerchief on her head, as if all that was involved was a short walk to her uncle's house.

In silence, Yossele merely looked at Rachel, while the mother continued to cry:

"Where will I leave you all alone? You are yourself only a child; how will I leave you to yourselves across this vast sea?"

"Just look, Mother—I'll manage somehow, I'll surely manage," Rachel answered, and once more patted the kerchief on her head as if in readiness to start on the trip.

"My poor child, my poor child," her mother fell upon her.

In tears, Rachel embraced and kissed her mother as if she had become an old woman herself. Her father said nothing but stood staring and biting his lips.

And when they conducted Yossele to the ship on which he was to embark, he said nothing, as though the heart within this tiny Jew had turned to stone. Silently he accepted his father's kisses, felt his mother's warm tears descend on his head; he did not speak, he felt that he was at fault, to blame for everything. As for himself—well, he was hopelessly lost, but here he was dragging Rachel with him. He knew fully, and understood, what it meant to his sister that she should now leave everything behind her and travel back with him.

He kept quiet, quiet, and his head bowed toward the ground.

Yet, when he stepped on the gangplank, looked about, and beheld his mother and father, the child within him awoke and he suddenly cried: "Mama!"

And that was unseemly in the little eight-year-old Jew.

A Sign of Summer

ZALMON LIBIN _____

IT WAS EARLY MORNING in the lovely month of May. But on Orchard Street where I happened to be, little of its loveliness was to be found; no fresh odors came from the garbage cans; the tall tenement barracks on whose fire escapes were being aired mattresses, quilts, and pillows, had little to suggest the lovely month of May. The same dirt, the same heavy choking air, the same heartbreaking tumult of haggling and trading—of the unending, eternal struggle for a piece of bread. Tumult, confusion—a running and dashing about—killing yourself trying to keep alive . . .

It was here that I came upon the old woman.

Small, thin, stooped, cane in hand, clothed in rags, she stood and looked about her with frightened eyes. Upon her wrinkled face there lay a look of deep, deep worry.

I looked at her closely. She noticed this, glanced at me a few times, then turned to me and said: "Good health to you. Are you a Jew?"

"Yes, Granny," I answered. "I am a Jew."

"Have pity on me and show me where I can see a tree," the old woman went on.

"What? A tree?"

"Yes," the old woman answered. "A tree that grows summers, as in the old country"—and she heaved a heavy sigh.

"Why do you need a tree?" I asked and, looking at the worried old woman, waited curiously for her answer.

"Why? Because God has punished me bitterly," the woman answered, and her eyes overflowed with tears.

Pain constricted my heart. I asked no more questions but hurried to ease the old woman as I said: "Yes, Granny, I'll show you a tree."

"May God bless you," she answered with sincere gratitude.

I began to look about. I knew the section well and began to think of where I could find a tree, nearby, for the old lady. I could not recall ever having seen a growing tree in the immediate neighborhood. That meant I would need to take her to Jackson Street Park.

That made me stop: Perhaps the walk would be too far for her. I asked: "Where do you live, Granny?"

"With my sick son," she answered.

"And where does your sick son live?" I asked again.

"Not far from here, in a back yard, beside a big stable."

Then I asked: "Granny, if we walk a few blocks from here, will you be able to find your way home?"

"I'll ask my way—" the old woman assured me.

"Come, Granny, I'll show you a tree."

We started out toward Jackson Street Park. While walking, the old woman unburdened her troubled heart, and I learned why she was looking for a tree.

The old woman was still a greenhorn on Orchard Street. She had come to her son, in New York, only eight months ago.

He was her only son and she had no relative other than him in all the world. Her son had a wife and three small children. In the old country he had been a teacher and in New York he had become a fur worker. Recently, after her arrival, he had become seriously ill, apparently with tuberculosis. He was bedridden at home and his wife was the breadwinner, bringing trousers from shops to sew at home, and doing the washing for neighbors.

A few weeks ago a doctor who called on the sick man said that if the invalid could hold out until summer, he would be "all right." The old woman, who had already observed that in this country winter was not a real winter, had asked the doctor when summer came, in America. The doctor said that when the trees began to bud and burst into leaf, that was a sign of summer.

Now that Passover had come and gone and, in the old country, summer would have arrived, the old woman wanted to know whether summer had already come in America, and whether her son had survived the winter. Although it was warm this was little proof to the old woman, since there are warm days in winter, too. She wanted to see the doctor's prescribed sign, a green leaf—that was all!

ত

Jackson Street Park . . . a green oasis in a horrible desert. Green trees, green grass.

"Well, here are all the trees you want," I said to the old woman.

"I see them," she answered. "Thanks to His Beloved Name."

And she looked at the trees. Her face lighted up and became free of its cares. In her eyes I caught a gleam of hope and I heard her quiet whisper:

"The lovely summer has come, my darling son. Perhaps Our Father in Heaven will have pity on you and send you a cure."

Then she turned to me and said, pleadingly: "Maybe you will do something else for me?"

"What, Granny?"

"Get me a few leaves, no matter what kind. I'll take them to my son to show him that summer has come."

I found a green leafy twig and gave it to the old woman.

She took it with trembling hands, blessed me with an overflowing heart, and asked me how to go home. I showed her the way and the old woman went to the yard, beside the large stable, to tell her ailing son that summer had come to America.

The American Europeans

WHEN AMELIA WAS STILL in elementary school she would observe
that, at the house of her father, Dr. Wolfson, on certain evenings, people would gather who, in many respects, were "funny." Her father,
however, would welcome them eagerly, grow excited, gesticulate, and,
in general, take these guests of both sexes and varied ages very seriously.
And since her father did not laugh at them, Amelia herself would regard
them more or less respectfully, although she could not free herself entirely of the sense of the comic which several of the visitors aroused in
her. When, finally, the guests began to depart, one after the other, and
because she was not yet ready to go to sleep, she would climb to her
father's lap and, studying his eyes, searchingly, would ask, half in jest,
half in earnest, and in English, naturally:

"Pa, who are they?

"What do you mean 'who'?" Dr. Wolfson would fondle her well-
shaped, charming chin. "Didn't you see, for yourself? People, cultivated people . . ."

"Socialists?" she would ask again, not without timidity.

Dr. Wolfson would smile and answer: "There are all kinds among
them: Socialists, anarchists, Zionists, Paoli Zionis. . ."

"Do they also play baseball?" Amelia cut short the catalogue of
"ists."

Her father would laugh and answer: "No, my baby, they are not real
Americans . . . they have not yet attained to baseball . . . they don't
take to it—"

"They come from Europe?"

"Yes, my child."

"And you, Pa, are you also a European?" Again Amelia asked, although she had known the answer for a long time. How she would like him to deny it once!

However, Dr. Wolfson was proud of Europe and he smiled: "Sure, child, I am a European . . ."

And because Amelia, after receiving this bit of news from her father, would become somewhat distressed, he would be compelled to console her: "It's a long, long time since I came from Europe."

This announcement afforded Amelia great relief and, fully contented, she would ask, regarding the guests: "Did they also leave Europe long ago?"

"No, my child . . . there are those among them who have been here only half a year . . . splendid people!"

"But they are funny. Aren't they, Pa?"

"Funny? Why? You are silly! They are educated. All of them educated; all of them have ideals."

"Pa, what are ideals?" Amelia would ask with some uneasiness.

"Ideals . . . Ideals . . ." Dr. Wolfson began to stammer and, not knowing how to explain this simple word to his twelve-year-old daughter, he was forced to leave the explanation to a later time, when she would graduate from elementary school.

ভ

When she finished elementary school, however, she no longer asked: "What are ideals?" To begin with, she was taking lessons in dancing then; secondly, she was preparing to enter high school and was dreaming about longer dresses and about giving up her elementary school boyfriend for a high school boy. At the same time, she began to observe that among her father's visitors there were also several boys. She became interested in one of them. Even though he was as "funny" as the others, she understood some of the phrases which poured from him so ecstatically, and she would occasionally seat herself nearby and listen to what these people were talking about and wonder why they became so excited.

One time she asked her father about this young man who became most excited of all. Her father introduced him, half-jestingly, half-seriously. She did not hear his name distinctly. It ended in "ski" and when she wanted to have him repeat it, she was ashamed to turn to him without knowing his name.

Several years went by. She finished high school and wore the clothing of a grown-up. What ideals were, she now knew herself, but she herself had no ideal as yet. However, she was drawn to whatever ideal was offered!

"Pa, you have so many ideals," she said to Dr. Wolfson, poutingly, one day. "Give me some kind of ideal. I'm so at a loss . . ."

Dr. Wolfson, whose hair was turning gray and whose temples had become entirely white, smiled bitterly and answered: "I, also, have almost no ideals left . . . after thirty years in this country, it's about time to lose them all."

So Amelia began to listen more attentively to the discussions that took place in her father's house. At times she wanted to take part, but since the discussions were in Yiddish she did not want to cause a dissonance by speaking English. She would not voice her opinions in Yiddish because she feared they would laugh at her pronunciation. She remained silent, giving the visitors the impression that she was an undeveloped American miss.

ק

On one occasion Dr. Wolfson realized that Amelia had not gone anywhere for a long time. She was bored and was complaining about headaches. "Why don't you go somewhere, my daughter?" he asked her with concern.

"I have nowhere to go," she smiled.

"What do you mean, nowhere? Where are all your boyfriends?" the doctor asked in amazement.

"They're not the least bit interesting to me, Pa," she finally confessed, as if ashamed. "After all the conversations I have listened to among your guests, I can hardly speak with my friends; the things they discuss are so foreign to me . . . Pa." After a brief pause, she turned to him with a smile. "You've brought me up badly. From your friends . . . strange as they are to me . . . I have gained something, anyway. However, they are entirely to my liking. But my own are too dull, and not developed. I am really unhappy."

Her father kept quiet and wondered how he might bring Amelia closer to his own circle.

At this time Amelia became acquainted with a young man. Having the freedom of her parents' home, Amelia would occasionally have him come to the house. Her father presented him to his guests of the various "isms."

They put him to the test. It became apparent that, although he was a graduate engineer, he was hopelessly ignorant of all other matters. The European visitors smiled to themselves and wondered about the strange creatures who were beginning to come to Dr. Wolfson's house.

Amelia dropped the engineer and chose a young man from among her father's guests. She went to call on some of her acquaintances with him and suffered great embarrassment there, through him. He would speak nothing but Yiddish, and perhaps only once throughout the entire visit did he say: "Excuse me!"

One girlfriend whispered in her ear: "Wherever did you pick up this kike?"

And in this way Amelia went from pillar to post among her young men. Now she went about with one of the guests; another time she went out with an "American" and experienced embarrassment through both kinds. American friends laughed at the foreigners; the guests at home laughed at the Americans.

Would she have to live alone all her life?

House on Goerick Street

JOSEPH OPATOSHU

THEY LIVE IN TWO SMALL ROOMS on Goerick Street. The small, dim rooms are packed full of rags. Sacks stuffed with oilcloth for tailors reach almost up to the ceiling. Rolls of braid, lace, and ribbons of all colors are scattered all about, and unrolled ribbons are suspended on strings stretched across the rooms. On entering, the first sight is of hairy Reb Mendel, with his black earlocks like long curls, as he walks in thought among the many-colored ribbons, making one think he is a sorcerer.

On the rags is seated Reb Mendel's wife, Leah, a small woman, shriveled, gray, with a threadbare kerchief down to her eyes. She is intoning aloud from a thick Yiddish novel, as if it were a book of prayer for women.

Beside her, to her right, is her only daughter, a pale girl, supple as a sprig which, having sunk root in a damp, dark cellar, now blooms amid decaying vegetation. She is sorting mother-of-pearl buttons from a bag, and is listening dreamily to her mother's reading. At the mother's left side is seated the only son of the house, a twelve-year-old cripple, with bowlegs, who is smiling idiotically as he fixes hooks and eyes on pasteboard cards.

Looking at them, it would seem that all three have grown out of this soil of rags, and that they never emerge from the dim rooms, and it is hard to believe that they live in close proximity to the gigantic Williamsburg Bridge.

Reb Mendel removes a pot of groats from the small gas stove, pours himself a plateful, and eats them with chunks of bread. His long beard and moustache fall into the plate, making it difficult for him to eat, and he swallows the food quickly, without chewing, as if he will not permit himself to take pleasure in eating. In a little while, he says grace, covers his face with his beard, and a muffled, mournful melody spreads through the rooms.

Leah stops reading, listens as her husband says grace, and the thought fills her mind that since she has given birth to the cripple, Mendel has grown completely away from her. He does little business, spends entire days studying, grows more pious day by day, and they live in great want. In other homes, a grown daughter counts for something; raising a daughter is no small matter. Yet here—her daughter is of no account! She is weary of arguing . . .

Nostalgically, Leah watches her husband as he paces from one corner to another and, in bitterness, she asks him for the hundredth time: "Mendel, what's going to come of all this?"

"What do you mean?" Mendel stops suddenly, twists his head and a hand at the same time, as if a fly which he had driven off several times has settled on him again.

"I mean, and let us not deceive ourselves, Feigale is no longer a youngster . . . Already eighteen years old and you are not the least bit concerned . . . You're a father, aren't you? As far as I know, other girls go to parties, to dance halls, meet young men. You won't even let her go out in the daytime, so you must do something for her . . ."

Feigale blushes at her mother's words, plucks at her apron, and almost breaks into tears: "What do you want? I won't have any bridegroom!"

The cripple shoves a finger into his sister's face, opens his mouth, and, baring his teeth, laughs a soundless laugh . . .

Reb Mendel, tall, stooped, his long black beard reaching below his belt, his fiery eyes avoiding everyone, does not reply. He lifts a sack of "trimmings" to his back, stands for a little while with open mouth as if preparing to speak, waves a hand aimlessly, kisses the mezuzah, and walks out.

Reb Mendel is well disposed. He has sold all the merchandise in his sack at the two shops to which he has gone. Now he is walking in the middle of the street, the sack under his arm, and feels that this will be a lucky day.

A short, stocky man, his beard stuck into his vest, with a sack on his back, stops Reb Mendel in midstreet.

"Hello, Reb Mendel, how are you?"

"Hello, Reb Moishe. I haven't seen you in a long time. I hear you're not living in this neighborhood any more, eh?"

"Ever since my wife died, I've been living in Brownsville."

"And how's it going?"

"As far as business goes, if only God allowed other Jews to do as well. But," here Reb Moishe brushes his beard which was stuck in his vest, and sighs, "it's hard, Reb Mendel, doing without a wife; no one to look after the young ones. The oldest, you must know, is twelve and while it is true she is a clever girl, she is still a child and needs someone to look after her. If I could make a decent match, Reb Mendel—I'm not interested in money—I would get married."

"I believe you have four children, isn't that so? May they all be well."

"I have, let no evil befall them, four children—the youngest is three. They can do errands, wash dishes. But . . . no matter . . . I tell you, Reb Mendel, America is full of so many kinds—how would I know it was a proper match? That's why, rather than search in the dark, if I could find a decent girl . . . Who knows . . ."

"You'll surely find someone," Reb Mendel assures him. "Why don't you drop in sometime, when you are downtown?"

"I'll tell you the truth, I was planning to come to see you these last few days. But I just couldn't make it. You are still in the same place?"

"Yes, on Goerick Street. Will you come?"

"I'll come."

"Good-bye!"

"Good-bye!"

Reb Mendel continues his walk in the middle of the street, sunk in thought and admitting to himself that Leah is right—time to think about Feigale. It occurs to him that Moishe would be a good match for her, a trimmings peddler with a good business and, above all, an honest man and not an ignoramus.

ק

Leah and her daughter are seated on the rags. Feigale, on hands spread apart, is holding tape, which her mother is winding into balls.

Not far from them the crippled boy, seated, is catching flies, bringing them close to his ear as he holds them by the wing and listens to the agony of buzzing. In the other room, Reb Mendel by an oil lamp is studying quietly to a sorrowful tune. The quiet melody spreads through the rooms, rings in the ears like a buzzing. It is hard to say whether the buzzing is the tortured flies or Reb Mendel's disquieting song.

Reb Moishe enters in his Sabbath cloak made of flashing alpaca.

"Good evening!"

"Good evening!" Leah and Mendel reply.

Leah puts down the ball of tape and rises. Feigale remains seated, relaxed, retains the strands of tape on her widespread hands, looks at Reb Moishe, and does not speak. She knows this is her bridegroom, come this day to set the wedding. She wants to say that she hates him, that she does not want an old man with whiskers, a father of children, that . . . she is seized with trembling, is filled with loathing for Moishe's beard, with hatred of her parents, and lowers her eyes.

"Take a seat, Reb Moishe!" Leah offers him a chair.

"Be seated—" Reb Mendel reinforces his wife's hospitality, paces about the room with great satisfaction, rubs his hands, turns to Feigale, indicates that she is still only a child, an American girl, to boot, and does not know Yiddish well. She remains silent. He asks Feigale to give him a glass of tea, looks into her eyes, and is happy.

Feigale feels that she is most unfortunate; how will she be able to appear before her friends with such a husband? She sits down in a corner and loses herself in thought.

She frequently meets Sidney on the stairs. He seems to be growing taller and more handsome from day to day. She has even observed that he has begun to shave. Ever since she got out of school, she has stopped talking with him, and if they meet on the stairs, both of them blush and greet each other. She loves him so much, she will tell him today that her parents want her to marry an old man with whiskers . . . He will rescue her from under the canopy . . .

The mother embraces her daughter, kisses her on the head, and says: "Daughter darling, you still have time; if the match is not to your liking, speak! I will not urge it."

"Certainly, certainly," Reb Moishe breaks in, opening his eyes wide as he does so, and trembling in every limb for fear that the girl may be struck by some foolish thought.

Feigale does not speak, but bursts into tears.

"A young girl is bashful—I, too, wept.—Done!"

They sit late into the night, speaking of familiar things and at parting, the date of the wedding is set. Reb Moishe is overjoyed as he takes his leave. The cripple, still catching flies, torments them while they toss about and buzz. The father steeps himself once more in a sacred book, singing more quietly and more plaintively than before. The mother shuffles over to the daughter with a feeling of guilt, embraces her, and without speaking wipes her eyes on Feigale's soft throat.

The plaintive melody, spreading through the rooms, fills the ears like a buzzing and it is hard to say whether it comes from the tortured flies or from Reb Mendel's sorrowful song.

The Father

(A Monologue)

ABRAHAM RAISIN _____

YOU ASK WHERE IS my older boy. Benny is . . . thanks for your interest in him, although your mentioning him makes my heart melt. Imagine it yourself, my Benny is chasing Villa . . .

What Villa? you ask. What? Don't you read the papers? Strange! I mean Villa, the Mexican, the man America must seize, dead or alive.

That's the Villa he is chasing, Benny, long life to him . . .

You're wondering what my Benny is doing in Mexico. Two years ago, as you remember, he was working in New York or going about without work, depending on the way times were. He was fed up with both of them, working or going about idle, because in either case a workingman's life isn't too easy. It was too hard for him to work in a shop; not, God forbid, that he lacked the strength for it—not at all. What then? He couldn't bear being walled in, in the shop—that was his argument.

As for going about idle? That's when I put in my lick: Think of a fellow sitting on his father's neck!

Early one fine morning he made up his mind and enlisted as a soldier in the American army . . .

There's America for you! Would you ever suppose that at home, I mean there in the old country, anyone would enlist voluntarily? Everyone there thanks God if he has a disability—if he has a ringing or a whistling in the ear, or if he is blessed with varicose veins, or if he lacks a dozen and a half teeth, or some other lucky trouble—which the czar

will treat with respect . . . My Benny, thank God, had none of these dis-
abilities, outside of the one trouble, whistling. However, that was not in
the ears, only in the mouth. Whenever Benny whistled, I used to think
that all the ghosts that live in the deserts would come crowding around
him, as we used to believe in the old home.

As I said, he enlisted in the American army. However, it didn't go as
easy as it sounds. As hard as it used to be, in our backward old country,
to escape from service, so difficult was it to get into the service of our
happy land. Not that they wouldn't take him. They took him, all right.
But there was some kind of paper I, as his father, had to sign.

One day my Benny comes to me, shoves a paper, in English, under
my nose, and tells me a story that since he hates to work in a shop and I
hate to have him go about without work, he has made up his mind to
enter the army and, with God's help, when he finishes his term of service he hopes to become a mounted policeman.

Why a mounted policeman? I ask him. Why not a patrolman who
maintains order and keeps his feet on the ground?

My Benny explains that because he has long legs he will go into the
cavalry and because of that, at the end of his service, he can become a
mounted policeman . . . That means he would maintain order from on
high . . .

The affair both pleased and displeased me. What I didn't like about
it was that my Benny who, because he was older by seven years than my
smaller boy, would have had a chance, in Russia, to escape service on the
payment of a hundred rubles, should become a soldier in free America!

True, he was doing this voluntarily, of his own free will. No one
forced him to do it, nevertheless I was unwilling. On the other hand, I
did want my son to be a policeman—especially a mounted policeman.
As a policeman on horseback, he would certainly not be sent to Hester
Street but, instead, would be stationed on Fifth Avenue where the automobiles dash by and where all the millionaires take their walks!

Well, to make a long story short, I consulted friends, discussed the
matter with the lawyer for our society, to find out what others thought
about my son becoming a soldier. The lawyer explained, first of all, that
I would become something of a "citizen" through this enlistment.
Then, suppose I were to make a trip to Europe sometime in the future
and return—I must be readmitted and cannot be sent back. Then if I

wanted to open a saloon, I stood a better chance of getting a license than anyone else. In other words, I have a claim—you get the point?

Well, I hesitated and wavered until, finally, I signed the paper meaning I was willing that my son, Benny, would be of service to the United States of America. What pleased me particularly was that I would become a kind of "citizen" at the same time.

To become a full-fledged citizen was simply beyond me. It is true I have been here for a full fifteen years, long enough to have become a citizen three times over, if not for my troubled mind. Who could learn all the seven points you have to remember? Maybe if I had a day off, on a Saturday or Sunday, depending on the shop where I work, with nothing else to do, I could take up some new tricks, like learn the names of the presidents!

Naturally, how should I know they would assign him to the other end of America—just a hop, skip, and jump from Mexico—and that Villa would explode and tangle with the United States? I certainly never expected that! Who can be a prophet and anticipate such events? As a matter of fact, at that time I didn't even know that Mexico was a country by itself and that it did not belong to us.

Things aren't too cheerful right now. I'm sure that my Benny is there, in Mexico, dashing after Villa, because I haven't had a letter from my boy in a long time. Ordinarily he writes me every week and sends me some of his pay, as well. He's pretty well paid: fifteen dollars a month, with food and lodging. It's a pretty good job, if not for that Villa . . .

Of one thing I am sure—if Villa lets himself be captured, my Benny will take him. Benny is a devil of a fellow. I'd like him to catch Villa alive because I don't see the point in spilling human blood. I'm a great opponent of all fighting and wars. I just want to know—what's the good of them and what's the world coming to if America cannot get out of— I won't say a war, but—this manhunt?

And who must help to capture him—Villa, I mean? Why, it's my Benny who has been in the country only a short ten years! I'm not saying he was ordered to do it, but who knows, if he had had steady work and the work was not so hard, maybe he would not have been drawn to the army and I might know what it means to sleep peacefully again. As it is, I can only see my Benny running after him, Villa, that is, and Villa, not being a fool, keeps running away. And Benny dashes after him! He must capture him, it is clear.

Not long ago I went to the "movies" where they were showing a picture of the way we are carrying on in Mexico . . . People sat, gaped with pleasure, and applauded. I, too, might be as good a patriot as any of them if my Benny were not mixed up in it. I couldn't raise my hands in applause—I had to wipe my eyes . . . it seemed to me that one of the men on horseback looked just like my Benny and he looked at me so sadly, I could tell he regretted the whole business. I wanted to take a second look but this picture ended and soon they showed a ship with a big cannon. Everyone went wild with joy—a ship with a cannon! What jubilation—Uncle Sam has a cannon. Never mind that when their sons have to go to war, they won't be so jubilant over cannons.

Kaddish

AARON MAIZEL _____

I KNOW A JEW who is half-Polish. He comes from a town in the wooded, muddy region between White Russia and Poland. He is a man in the fifties, still powerful, with a wrinkled, pious face, warm eyes, and a gray, thick beard like sprigs of fir on a *succoh* in a rainy day.

He is now living in a city in New England. Till now, he lived there with his son, who was seventeen or eighteen. Now the father is in mourning; his son died and the old man says Kaddish for him:

"Ysgadal Veyiskaddash Shmay Rabbo."

But the old man is not through with the mere saying of Kaddish. He is a scholar, well informed, and knows various ways to pacify the soul, to gladden it with holy joys of the Torah.

At night, in his rented front room where his iron bed waits in readiness for him, he lights the fainthearted, yellow gas jet (there is no other lighting in the room), opens an old, damp-smelling volume of the Mishnah (which he had brought in his bag from the old country, as nourishment for his journey), rocks to and fro, and, in a tremulous voice intones the chapters in Rashi whose initial letters spell out the name of his dead one: the youth, Yehiel, may his soul be bound in the bundle of life. After that, he lies down in his bed, cannot fall asleep for a long time, groans wearily, urges his soul to leave his suffering body for the night and to float off into the everlasting heavens.

In the morning (after his first prayers) he unbends his rounded, age-stiffened back, fastens all the buttons of his short coat, and, with heavy feet, sets out for the shop where he worked with his son Yehiel, peace to his memory.

How depressing the morning is for a lonely man! What can he do about it? A misfortune befell his son. What's to be done about it? Who is to blame for it? All decreed from above . . .

It was probably decreed that Yehiel, may his soul be bound in the bundle of life, was to lose his life at that hour, in that place, and in just that way.

On that morning, as on all other days, they walked to the shop together. They walked in silence—a morning silence. Nevertheless, the father carried a grievance in his heart against his son. It seemed to the older man that the youth was drifting away from him, was seeking to go off on a separate path.

After that they arrived, after that whistles blew, and they set to work.

Father and son stood side by side because their machines, too, were set close to one another.

The factory, as was usual in New England, produced articles made of iron, steel, brass, copper, and tin. Skates were the chief output—all sorts of skates. Roller skates for youngsters, sharp-pointed ice skates, and sporting skates for men and women, all of many kinds and designs.

It was a huge plant and employed several hundred workers. Wide belts slid up and down like waves of black water, and the machines, oil-stained and immovable, bit into the sheets of iron and pressed them into different shapes.

The windows of the dirty, red brick building were tall—from close to the floor almost up to the ceiling. The windowpanes were overgrown with a dull skin of dust and were enclosed, on the outside, by a heavy steel frame, which was divided into squares. There were thirty panes in all, in each window.

At nightfall, when an electric bulb was lit beside each machine, it seemed to the eyes of the passersby that a restless black stream of water, inside the building, was flecked with sparkling diamonds. They would stop, look, and wait in expectation of something within.

But that which happened took place in daytime, in the flaming light of the sun which stubbornly persisted in piercing the dull layer of dust and spreading its rays over the hard, manufactured goods of this New England factory.

This is how it was:

The father drilled holes in ironware, and the son stuck iron nails into the holes, hammered, and riveted them down.

The father was dressed in a short jacket which did not go well with the passive, small-townish look of his face with its sparse beard; the son—in a red, roomy sweater with long sleeves that were too wide and in which, looking like rods, were the thin, elongated arms of this growing boy of seventeen or eighteen.

The father urged the son to speed up:

"Yehiel, well? Get things out of the way; look, here's a mountain of skates."

At that moment, the boy's mind was on altogether different things. He might have noticed, close by, a girl whose white neck showed through the unbuttoned collar of her blouse. Or, perhaps he was wondering at the rays of the sun, which had pierced through the dirt of a window.

He turned a disgruntled face to his father, his forehead pale and thoughtful, and asked: "Wha-a-at?"

"Get through with these skates!"

On occasion, even New England machines for the making of hardware go wrong. The old man saw his son stoop to repair his machine.

"What's the matter?"

A leather belt had come off a block. Yehiel seized it, drew it, and prepared to leap over the shield. In the meantime, the steel axle, uncovered, with a flashing metal gash—a sliver wound—was spinning. The youth crouched, measured the distance, and suddenly leaped, belt in hand, on the dizzily spinning axle. In his haste, a small edge of the sleeve of his red sweater, a tiny edge of it, caught somewhere. The billowing black water drew him in, lifted him up, and carried off the boy in his red sweater.

The whole thing took a second, a fraction of a second. The old man saw it and at the same time heard a cry:

"Mo-ther!"

In the midst of belts, mounting like ladders, with the flash of the dark red sweater, Yehiel was carried to the ceiling. Relentless, dizzying axles, floating belts, a red flash, two shoes like twisted rods, up-down, up-down, and screams:

"Mo-ther! Mo-ther!"

After that he broke out of that whirling circle, tumbled awkwardly in the air, among oil-smeared spikes-shoes, like twisted rods, shooting in different directions from time to time, swung out, and—crash—right into a window.

He struck a large window, from close to the floor and up to the ceiling, smashed all the panes, thirty in all. The splinters of glass, some smeared with clinging dust, scattered and caught the rainbow gleam of the rays that thrust through the barred iron frame and now, freely, poured in streaming gaiety into all the dark corners of the dark factory.

And the single sound of the body, as it struck the iron frame, was like that of ground meat under flailing chopping knives, and then it fell to the floor with a dull, heavy thud, a blue-masked, soiled piece of meat.

"Je-sus!"

That, uttered as from one mouth, by a couple of hundred workers gathered to turn out hardware in a New England factory.

"Praised be the True Judge!"

A father stooped down, looked at the blue bundle of flesh, no longer a seventeen—or eighteen-year-old being, not a trace of his son Yehiel.

Who can feel a father's heart? Was he counting the warm drops of blood on that ruddy flesh? But what does it matter? Who is to blame for it? All decreed from above.

Probably decreed that the youth, Yehiel, may his soul be bound in the bundle of life, was to lose his life here, at that hour, in that way.

So the old man is a mourner, has rent his garment—torn a gash in the lapel of his jacket—and says Kaddish for his son:

"Ysgadal Veyiskaddash Shmay Rabbo . . ."

Madame Marquis

JOSEPH OPATOSHU

TALL, BLONDE, with two thick flaxen braids resting carelessly on the back of her neck and seeming, momentarily, about to uncoil down her shoulders; a pair of large, myopic eyes which, at the same time, are deep blue; loose garments falling from the shoulders in soft folds; and a body in every movement of which there lies an exciting lassitude—that is Madame Marquis.

She is lying on a soft divan, ostensibly reading a book, but with half-closed eyes she is watching her mother-in-law, a tall, gray-haired Italian, playing with her five-year-old son.

Suddenly the old woman breaks into laughter, draws her daughter-in-law's attention to the child, says something, and kisses the boy on the head and on the eyelids. The daughter-in-law shakes her head without knowing what the old woman has said, drops the book, and falls into contemplation.

She cannot communicate with her mother-in-law, who, in her old age, has recently come to this country from Florence to live with her children. The two resort to sign language, use their fingers, and never know precisely what they are saying to each other. The daughter-in-law wonders at her Irving, who sits, open-mouthed, listening to his grandmother's recital in Italian. The old woman talks with her hands, face, and all her limbs, and the little boy listens with rapt attention as if he understood every word. And who knows? Perhaps they are conversing in baby talk?

The daughter-in-law turns around, drops a comb from her head, picks it up, and shoves it into her disheveled hair as one drives a pitchfork into a bundle of hay. She burrows into the soft cushions and feels that she is unhappy.

From the time her mother-in-law came into the house, Madame Marquis has felt that everything around her is strange, as if the old woman were her conscience, and she has begun to yearn for her old home.

She was born, raised, and had grown up in a courtyard by the Black Sea. From early childhood she had avoided people, preoccupied with herself alone. As she grew up, the brokers who came to see her father began to speak of matches for her, but she would not hear of them. She was always dreaming that "Petshorin," bronzed by sun and wind, with black locks in disarray, would appear in his vessel under her window on some stormy night. He would seize her, as she slept, and carry her off into Crimea or the Caucasus where, among mountain peaks far from human settlement, they would dwell.

The brokers and indigent folk who called on her father would often come to her with letters from their children in America. She read the letters to them and felt that there, on the other side of the ocean, life must be more expansive. She determined that she would travel there. After endless quarrels with her parents, she, Mary Stein, a sixteen-year-old girl, landed in New York. She went to work in a shop. Her first day there disillusioned her and, if she had not been ashamed, she would have returned to her home.

In a little while she became acquainted, by means of gestures and sign language, with Philip Marquis, a bronzed Italian with hair black enough to serve as a mirror. This Italian with black, dreamy eyes, with agile movements, took her fancy. But what pleased her more than anything else was the name—Marquis! How well it sounded! After the day's hard work, in which Mary sewed buttons all day, bent double in a narrow, filthy shop, Marquis, neatly dressed and scented, came to call on her. Every evening he took her to a different place and entertained her until she came to love him, discovered in him her old hero "Petshorin," and married him.

Marquis owned several barbershops and was well-to-do, so he furnished their home to satisfy her every desire. However, she spent her days visiting in their circle, mostly Americans and Americanized Italians. She had no time to think about herself, had forgotten that she was Jewish and that she had parents in Russia. When Irving was born the thought came to her vaguely that the boy ought to be circumcised, but she was ashamed of her husband and realized that he did not know she was Jewish. For a time she thought of naming the child Abraham, after her grandfather. However, calling him Abe would be too Jewish; Gentiles do not use such names. She compromised on the name, and decided on Irving. After the confinement she forgot all about the matter, simply had no time to think about it. She wondered why people had a poor opinion of Italians, why it was thought Italians mistreated their wives. Her experience contradicted that general impression. She had never heard Philip raise his voice.

But since the arrival from Italy of the old woman, her own mind had undergone a complete change. She resented the old woman's talking Italian to Irving and, for the first time in years, she found herself thinking in Yiddish. She did not know why, but when she remained at home with her mother-in-law she found herself trembling and had the feeling that the old woman was a witch who might leap at her, at any moment, with her bony hands. At such times she had a sense of guilt.

Of late, her parents had begun to appear in her dreams. They wept and pleaded that she should have the boy circumcised, and that she should divorce her husband. Time and again, she would awaken exhausted and stare about her. She found her husband beside her and moved away to the edge of the bed as if she were in terror of him. And always when she had these visitations in her dreams, she would find on her hands and feet bluish bruises—as if she had been pinched by the dead.

She felt that all were conspiring against her, that they were lying hidden in various nooks, under the bed, and that at the first opportunity they would leap at her in chastisement. Now she began to observe things that she had not noticed before. When she went visiting with Philip, she could no longer listen to his stories. It seemed to her that everything he said was crude, that he was himself an ignoramus, and that any day now he would begin to mistreat her, become jealous, like all Italians, and slash her face with a razor.

For entire days she went about thinking how she could have the child circumcised. At first she wanted to tell Philip about it. Then she decided that in summer, when she went to the mountains, she would have it done without her husband's knowledge. She had heard that many Italians became converts when they married Jewish girls and for a brief time the hope brightened her thoughts—who knows? Perhaps, if she pleaded with Philip, if she fell to his feet, wept—she had her way in everything—he might do it, too? In that case she would invite her parents to her home . . . how mean she was! She had not written them in more than three years. Her mother was surely old now, aged for sorrow; has probably been weeping . . . and her father? She began to feel a growing warmth at the heart, a swelling in the throat. Her eyes became wet.

On a soft divan the old grandmother was holding Irving on her lap and singing to him.

Mary shuddered, wanted to seize her little boy and to tell the old woman not to come into this room again but to remain in the kitchen, and in her mind she mimicked the old lady's song:

" 'Capusheto, Sti-letto, Man-zetto'—old witch!"

She sat bolt upright and shouted: "Irving, come here."

Irving tore himself free from his grandmother and leaped into his mother's arms: "Ma . . . Ma . . ."

The mother kissed and caressed him and for the first time in years spoke to him in Yiddish:

"My little son, Abraham darling, do you want to go to your grandfather? You have such a fine grandfather with a long, gray beard, my little Abraham!"

Irving seemed to be frightened, repelled her with his hands, and, not understanding what she had said, looked at her with fear.

"What are you saying, Ma? I don't understand . . ."

"Do you love Mother?" she asked.

Irving embraced her with his hands and clung to her with his little legs as he kissed her face. The mother, almost in tears, rocked on the divan with her little son and, half in English, half in Yiddish, told him about herself, about her parents, and, as she was talking, began to feel a great relief.

Simcha and Sammy

CHONE GOTTESFELD _____

MY BABY IS CALLED SIMCHA and my boss's baby is called Sammy. My baby's nurse is—a bottle of sugar water. Sammy's nurse is—a Polish maid.

My Simcha's mother is weak and lean; she can hardly stand on her feet. Sammy's nurse is strong and healthy. When she walks across the kitchen floor all the dishes rattle in the cupboard.

If I could take the Polish maid from Sammy and give her to Simcha for even one day! How greatly he needs her!

My boss's brother was married one day. Well, I am a kind of relative, so all of us workers in the shop went to the wedding and brought a present for the groom.

I went to the wedding with my wife, my Simcha, the baby carriage, and Simcha's nurse—the bottle of sugar water.

We went to the hall. The boss was there already, with little Sammy in his arms. The boss was smacking his lips to him: "Putchie, Kutchie, Lutchie," but Sammy would not smile. He was as sweet as his father. The workers were all gathered about Sammy's baby carriage and beamed on Sammy. "How clever he is," they said, and took Sammy and, in a little while, were carrying him about in the hall.

That hurt me. My little Simcha has more sense in his socks than Sammy has in his head. My little Simcha is able to say: "Pa." True, Simcha is very pale, poor thing, but he is not to blame, poor fellow. How can he look well on his bottle of sugar water?

I took Simcha in my arms and began doing a few dance steps with him on the dance floor. When I became tired, I asked one of the work-

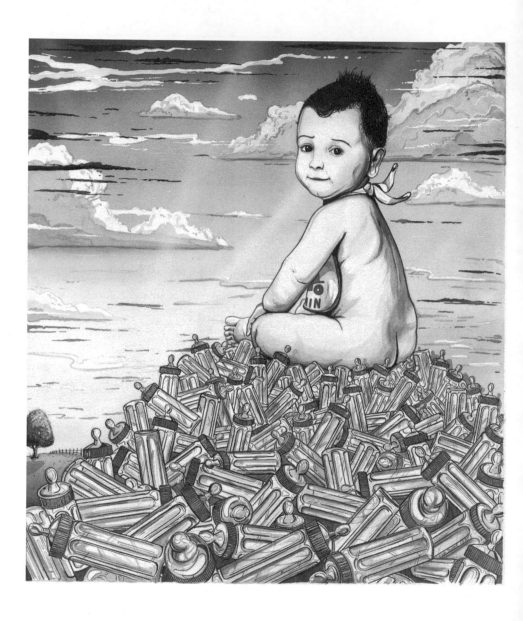

ers to take Simcha, for a minute. He refused. Then I said to him: "This is the boss's baby!"

"The boss's baby?" he said. "Why didn't you say so at once?" He grabbed my Simcha as if the child were a piece of the wedding cake.

Now they were trundling two babies about, in the hall, Simcha and Sammy.

One of the workers handed me the boss's baby. I put him into my Simcha's baby carriage. Later I got hold of my Simcha and put him into Sammy's carriage and wrapped him in a warm blanket. The Polish maid, seated near the carriage, was drowsing to the music.

After the wedding we went home with the boss's baby. The baby cried at night. My wife gave him a bottle of sugar water. Sammy did not want it. He was used to better fare.

"What's wrong with the child?" my wife asked me. "He's crying dreadfully. That's not his way."

"Devil take him," I said. "Crying is good for the lungs. Let him cry a bit."

It was early morning. My wife took one glance at the baby and shrieked: "Help! They've changed our baby!"

I said to her: "Don't worry. Our child is in better hands. He is with the Polish maid." Then I told her the whole story.

"Go to the boss at once," she commanded, "and get our baby back."

"Don't rush so," I told her. "Let little Simcha have a good meal first."

But my wife insisted that I should bring our baby back at once.

I went. When I came to my boss's home, they were all still asleep after the wedding. I told the Polish maid that Sammy was at my house.

"How's that possible?" she said. "I was suckling Sammy all night long."

"That was little Simcha," I explained to her. "Did he, at least, seem to enjoy his meal?"

"What a gourmand he is!" she said. "He almost ate me up alive. He's sleeping now as if after a wedding feast."

We exchanged our babies.

Since then, Simcha will not touch his bottle of sugar water. He longs for the Polish maid.

PART FOUR

There's Laughter, Too

Why the Taracans Are My Enemies

ZALMON LIBIN _____

WHEREVER LIVES A MAN from Taracan in New York, he is a confirmed enemy of mine. All natives of Taracan, without exception, are my sworn enemies.

I assure you I haven't the faintest idea where Taracan is. I have never in my life spoken ill of Taracan itself, or of a native of Taracan, and yet all the natives of Taracan are my foes, and here is the reason:

On a certain beautiful morning two young men knocked at my door.

"Is this the home of Mr. So-and-So?" they asked and mentioned my name.

"Yes, I'm the very man. Come in!"

"We are a committee," the young men informed me.

"What kind of committee?"

"Of the Independent Taracan Society."

"A pleasure. What can I do for you?"

"As we are running a concert and ball for our annual festival, we are issuing a journal and would like you to write something for us—something comical befitting a journal for a festive occasion."

"I am very busy and really have no time." I began to reject the honor which they proffered me.

One of the young men interrupted me: "You'd better not oppose the Independent Taracans."

"They're no trifle, the Independent Taracans!" The second member of the committee supported the first. "Trifling with our society! Don't forget we count our membership in the thousands—thousands in good standing; we have influence!"

"And the natives of Taracan are people who never forget a favor—besides, they play an important role in New York!"

Well, you know how bitter is the writer's loaf—how he is always dependent on the views of others . . . even a cat can interfere with a writer's livelihood. Also, I didn't want to offend anyone. I promised to write something for the Independent Taracan Society. I kept this promise, wrote something comical, and sent it to the designated address.

"Good riddance to them," I thought to myself. "Now I know that I've won the goodwill of all the natives of Taracan."

A week later another committee of two came to see me.

"Are you Mr. So-and-So?"

"Yes, my friends."

"We have come to you as a committee of Taracans."

I knew that I had just done them a favor, and I also knew that they were to have a ball about this time; it occurred to me that these genial young men had come, therefore, to express the gratitude of the Taracans and invite me to their celebration. The mere thought warmed my heart and I answered: "Oh, from the Taracans! What a pleasure!"

"We have come to ask for a trifle," one of the members of the committee began. "Since, at about this time we have our annual affair . . ."

"We are asking that you come to our festivities"—my heart prompted the words I expected him to speak. However, I did not hear these words.

"We would like you," the speaker continued, "to do something for us."

"What is it?" It seemed to me the whole business was bringing me new difficulties.

"In connection with our celebration we are going to publish a journal."

"I know. I know that."

"How do you know?"

"I have already written for your journal . . ."

"When? What? For whom?" Both members of the committee interrupted me and stared.

"A committee came to see me."

"From whom?"

"From the Taracans."

"What Taracans?" shouted the committee. "What Taracans?"

"The Taracan Taracans . . ."

"There are various Taracans," a committee man assured me. "Which ones came to you?"

"Members of the 'Independent' Taracans."

"What a shame! You've been fooled!"

"What do you mean?"

"They're not Taracans at all."

"What then are they?"

"Oh, just a few charlatans who broke off from our society and set up for themselves. That's what they are!"

Gloomily, I asked them: "Who are you?"

"We? We are true Taracans, the United Brotherhood of Taracan, the most powerful organization in New York."

I began to offer excuses, but they were of little help. The committee declared, brusquely and pointedly, that since I had written for the "Independent Taracans" who were obviously the open enemies of the true Taracans, represented only by the "United Brotherhood of Taracan," it would be taken to mean that I exposed myself as an enemy of the Taracans, something they would advise me against. I must bear in mind that the "United Brotherhood of Taracan" are people who remember a favor, but never forget an injury. And I, as something of a public figure, must not under any circumstance offend such a powerful organization.

The committee actually terrified me. I promised to write for their journal and I kept my second promise, too.

A few days later a third committee called on me.

"Taracans?" I asked, frightened.

"Yes," the committee answered. "We are Taracans."

"What would you like?"

"Since we are about to celebrate our fifth anniversary, we want to print a journal and would like your name to appear among our contributors."

"Who are you?" I began to shout.

"What do you mean who we are?" The committee looked at me as at a savage. "We are Taracans."

"Which ones?"

"The true, the genuine, the well-known, famous, historical Taracans known as the Federated Taracans of New York."

When I told the committee about the other two organizations, these representatives of the "Federated Taracans of New York" laughed me to scorn and assured me I had been imposed upon. They were the only genuine organization of Taracans, and if I really wished to seal the bond of friendship with the natives of Taracan I had better write for their journal alone and see to it that I wrote something worthwhile . . .

Well, as the saying goes, if you are in a hole you must get out of it as well as you can. I became a contributor also to the anniversary journal of the "Federated Taracans of New York."

In a few days a fourth committee came on the scene—again Taracans! The "Taracan Young Men."

All right. An article for them.

Obviously, you cannot satisfy everyone in the world. The natives of Taracan, all Taracans, without exception, are now enemies of mine.

Chaim Does His Duty as a Citizen

TASHRAK _____

WHEN ELECTION DAY CAME, the day for voting, I began to feel festive. Benele, my youngest, a boy of seven, hung out the American flag from our window and told me that this was an important holiday for all citizens. For on this day you could witness American equality, namely: Today I am the equal of the president of the United States because he has no more than one vote and so do I. Thus we are really equally privileged.

I thought to myself: Granted, but after all there is still a slight difference between us, a great difference one might say; however, I dislike to contradict a child. Since Benele said so, so be it. Why should I cause him unnecessary irritation?

We had had enough annoyance in the house for several weeks before Election Day. The household was turned topsy-turvy, our domestic peace disturbed, and neither I nor my old woman could have a moment's rest.

It was always this: My son, Shloimke, a boy of fifteen, supported the Republican candidate. My second son, Jakey, ready for bar mitzvah, was immovably in favor of the Democratic candidate, and the youngest, my Benele, who was a great prankster, was a devoted Socialist. So much for the boys of the family.

There are, however, three girls, all older than the boys, and all of them also deep in politics. My eldest daughter, Betsy, who is a schoolteacher, told me that I must vote for a Mr. Rendel. I asked: "Who is this Mr. Rendel? It seems to me nobody even mentions him." She explained that Mr. Rendel was the candidate of the Prohibition Party, which wanted to close all the beer saloons. So I reflected: "Rather a good idea.

135

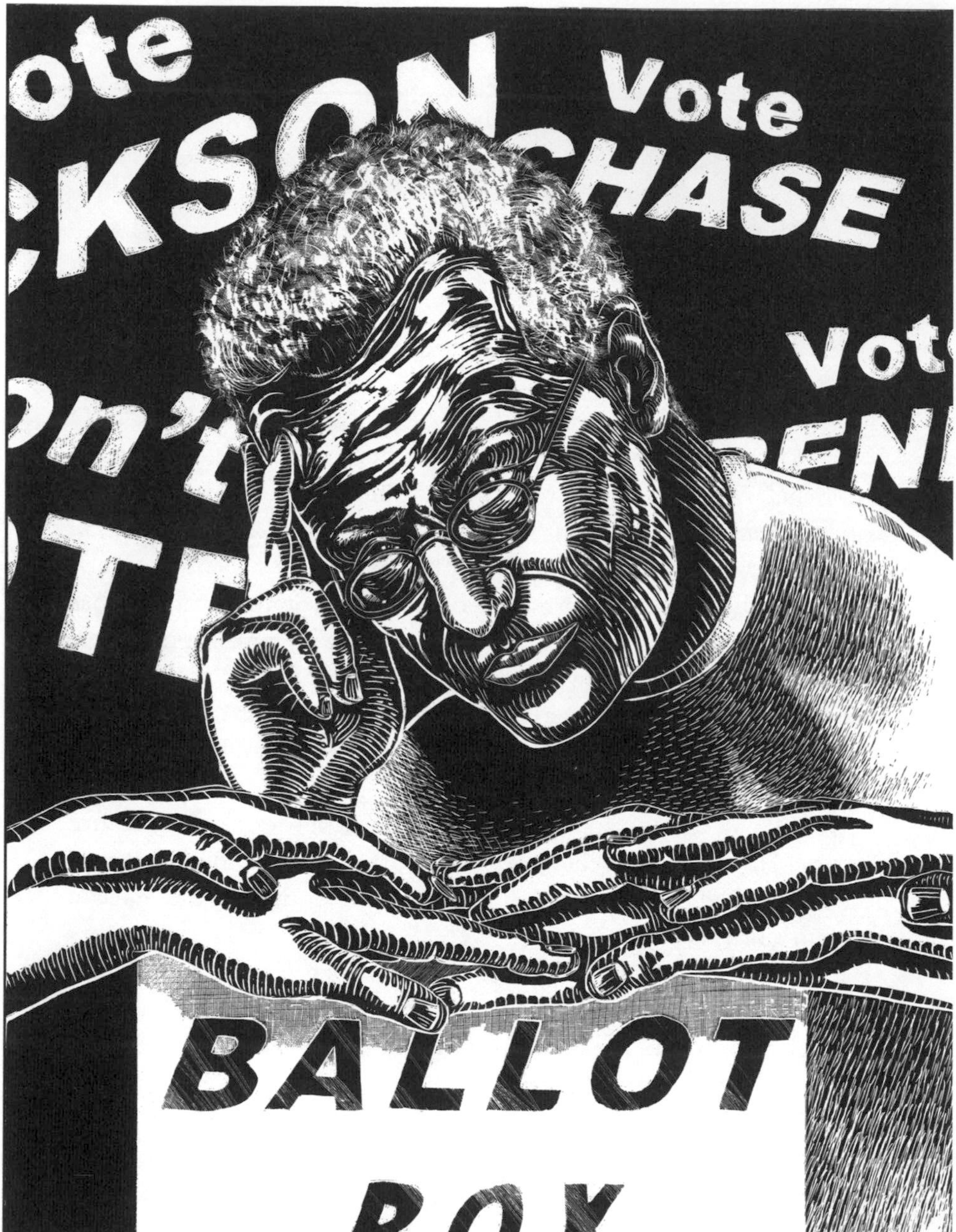

ote
CKSON
Vote
CHASE
Vote
On't
OTE
BALLOT
BOX

If all my customers who drink stopped getting drunk, they'd be able to pay regularly for the merchandise they buy from me. But how do you vote for a man nobody has heard of and nobody knows anything about?"

My second daughter, Flossie, is a milliner, and she wanted me to vote for a Mr. Jackson. "Who is he?" I asked. She explained that he is a Socialist, but a genuine Socialist, not like Mr. Chase for whom Benele is ready to split a gut with his outcries. And my third daughter, Jenny, slightly foolish and something of an anarchist, insisted that I should not vote at all. She tried to make me see that elections are a capitalistic fraud to trap the poor—to lead the poor into thinking that they determine the government, but that in reality the government pays as much attention to them as to a cat. Well, as you can see for yourself, there is no sense in arguing with such a fool.

As I have told you, the election war went on in my house for weeks before Election Day. But when the day drew near, my children were at dagger points with one another. I said to them: "What are you quarreling for? Let my enemies possess all that the candidates will gain from your talk. And you, foolish fellows, are too young to worry about it. Stop arguing!" But my words were of no use, and they continued quarreling.

It was always thus: Flossie and Benele quarreled about their Socialist candidates. Benny said that Flossie's Socialist wasn't even a Socialist. Benny said: "Your man is a faker!" Flossie said: "Your man is a demagogue!" Then Shloimke and Jakey shouted at the top of their lungs. Jakey: "Oh, so you are for the lousy trusts and corporations." Shloimke: "You favor those who are ruining the credit of the country." Jakey became enraged and shrieked: "What about the coal trust, the milk trust, the meat trust, and the Panama Canal?"

Shloimke waved a hand and said: "That's easy talk." I saw that Jakey, who is soon to be bar mitzvahed, was ready to explode and that they would come to blows. But my oldest daughter, the teacher, intervened, took each of them by an ear, and told them to behave, that is, to cool off. Then she herself began to argue with Jenny and they quarreled, shrieked until they began to weep and sob and gasp, may the Merciful One save us!

On the eve of Election Day, I came home tired, exhausted. I had had a hard day. Women buy my merchandise on the installment plan and as soon as they get some ready cash they carry it off to the dressmaker's or the department store. As soon as I entered the house, my wife met me in the kitchen and said, somewhat bashfully: "Chaim, I want to tell you something, but I am ashamed."

"What are you ashamed about?" I asked. "What are you—a little girl? You're the mother of six children, may they live long."

She answered: "Well, Chaim, he persuaded me."

I looked her in the face, amazed by her talk, and shouted angrily: "Woman! What's the babbling about? Who is he, this he?"

She said: "Our Benele, the dear child, attached himself to me and insisted that I should support the Socialists, and our Betsy begged, in the name of mercy, that I should support those who want to close the beer saloons. I just didn't know what to do. My heart, I felt, was being torn to pieces. I wanted to satisfy both of them. So I said to Betsy: 'After all, you're a grown-up; don't let Benele suffer so, he's only a child. Let me be on his side. It is easy to understand that if people have enough to eat they will cease being drunkards.' Then Betsy said: 'I don't care. I'll see to it Papa votes as I wish.' "

At supper, I begged the children that they should not speak a word of politics at table. But Jenny would not refrain. She grabbed a button with the picture of the candidate from Shloimke's lapel, and flung it into the soup tureen. Benele and Jakey burst into laughter. Angrily, Shloimke tore off their campaign buttons and—into the soup with them! At this point I was in a rage and told them that I would vote for Mr. Rendel who means to close the saloons.

Then I saw my Flossie become angry and she said she didn't want any supper: "Why," she wanted to know, "should I yield to Betsy?" Was it because she, Flossie, had labored in the shop so Betsy might go to college? And she burst into a loud weeping. Now I was beside myself and cried out: "I will not vote at all. I will do as Jenny says."

"Hurrah for the Social Revolution!" Jenny shouted, standing up on a chair. "Down with the ballot box and the corrupt capitalist gang with their camp followers, the betrayers of the people!"

"In Heaven's name!" my wife cried out. "Sit down, maniac! What are you standing up to shout for? People will come running at your carryings-on, you silly dolt!"

I must be stronger than iron to have survived that night. Those children of mine did not let me sleep a wink. They quarreled and shrieked and did their best to win their mother to their way of thinking.

Early in the morning I saw, from the window, that the street was lively, with neighbors on the street on their way to the polling place. My Benele enlarged on my joy at being a free citizen and on how lucky I must consider myself for being in America.

Whereupon I said: "I would be lucky indeed if you, my children, did not make my life miserable with your goings-on."

Betsy came in, all dressed for the holiday and as pretty as you please. She whispered in my ear the secret that Mother now favored her candidate and that I should be a good father, support her party, and vote against schnapps and drunkenness.

I thought to myself: "You, my daughter, are happy? You have a good job; you have a holiday today. But Flossie and Jenny are working, poor things, and they are working—for you. Should I vote for Mr. Rendel and embitter hearts?"

Shloimke, Jakey, and Benele wouldn't leave me alone and announced that they would accompany me to the ballot box and each of them pestered me with his arguments. I pushed them away and put off voting—I wanted to give the matter more thought, and something inside me prompted the idea: Perhaps it would be a solution to take Jenny's advice and not cast my ballot? It is sometimes wise to take a fool's advice.

Finally, I made up my mind and went to vote. How I should vote, I still did not know. I thought to myself that perhaps, at the last minute, the Almighty would put something into my mind which would help me to overcome all the difficulties.

When I walked in (the polling place was in a real estate office), and I told them my name, they all looked at me as if I were a greenhorn and told me that their books showed that I had already voted.

I asked them: "How can you say that? I have not left my house until now!" But they smiled, those clerks seated there, and the burly policeman also smiled, and a man with a badge called me aside and said to me, in Yiddish:

"Too bad, Mister. There's been a fraud here. Someone came in, earlier, and voted in your name."

"Long life to him," I said. "A blessing on his head. He spared me a very unwelcome job, and my children will have no more grievances."

As I went away, I heard the man with the badge break into a laugh. When I told the story to my children they also laughed. May they always have something to laugh at!

First Row Balcony

ABRAHAM RAISIN _____

EVERY BUSINESS at which Zalmon had tried his hand in the few years since he had arrived in New York, he ran into the ground.

"Can't make a go of it, do what I will." That's what Zalmon himself said with a smile.

Bystanders would smile back at him. To tell the truth, what did such people care what Zalmon felt after all his failures? Naturally, not all people are as heartless as these. Others gave Zalmon advice. One told him to learn the language and become an insurance agent because he made a good impression and if he tried to "insure" anyone, he would certainly not be turned away. Another gave better advice—there were too many insurance agents, but a "paper stand" would be just right. Not too much money was needed for that, and people were reading a great deal today. To a third, it occurred that it would be good for Zalmon to move to a small country town. A fourth told him to remain in New York despite everything, but if he really wanted to seek his fortune it would be best for him to go on to San Francisco. There, it was said, money was as cheap as dirt; you never even saw a penny, but only nickels and nickels . . .

But despite all this advice Zalmon was without a "business" for almost a year, and though he still retained his pride, it was obvious that he was completely crushed. He had reached the stage when a fellow countryman of his, better off than Zalmon, offered him a few dollars as a loan.

However, Zalmon was not the sort of person to borrow money lightly. That is to say, the lender might be a decent person, but the bor-

140

rower was lost. "A man," Zalmon would tell those close to him, "must make his own way. He should not turn to others for help."

Zalmon might indeed have gone hungry without anyone knowing it, but his wife, Ethel, was a different kind of person. She meant to have a living, as God had decreed, and she had grievances against the world.

"What's the meaning of it?" she demanded once, when she descended on some relatives and *landsleit*. "Why should my Zalmon be allowed to sink? When he had money he would always give generously." But never mind; she hoped that he would be on his feet again and that he would again help others.

In the meantime she wanted to help him, though in such a manner that he would not know. He might, God forbid, do himself some mischief—and she burst into tears. He was really mad on this point. If others were caught in such a tight spot, friends and relatives helped to open some kind of store. But that was the misfortune in his case—he simply would not turn to anyone.

For that reason he must be helped, but only in the most delicate way and secretly.

Ethel was a clever woman and devised a plan, which was that a theater benefit be arranged for Zalmon, and the profit given to her. She would say that she had received it from her parents.

Two young men volunteered to carry out the project.

A week later, Zalmon was seated in the home of one of his countrymen. It was a Sunday afternoon. Zalmon was feeling elated—that morning he had collected an old debt—five dollars—of which he had left three for his household. The remaining two, in his possession, were to be paid, next morning, to the grocer. Meanwhile, however, he felt the money in his pocket, and this gave him a sense of security and strength. When his friend's wife said that she needed two singles for a two-dollar bill, he was the first to answer that he could make the exchange.

"Zalmon is still the richest among us," the woman said and smiled.

"Who else?" the husband conceded readily, and knowing of the benefit performance that was to be given for Zalmon, he added: "Zalmon will be the first to become wealthy!"

Zalmon felt even more exhilarated because of this remark and was about to answer, but at this moment the door opened and the two young men who were to arrange the benefit came in.

There was a marriageable girl in the house who was on the lookout for a young man. The two boys were cordially received. The man of the house invited them to be seated. His wife asked them to help themselves to oranges in a bowl.

The young men, however, appeared to be very busy about something and they looked at Zalmon as if he were a source of disturbance. They rapidly exchanged some secrets between them and one spoke up: "We have no time now. We have come on business."

At the word "business," Zalmon was the first to speak out: "If it is business, I certainly want to hear about it."

The young men exchanged looks and smiled lightly, but swiftly turned serious as one began:

"This is not the kind of business for you, Reb Zalmon—a theater benefit is being given on behalf of a poor fellow countryman of ours. We are selling tickets."

"Tickets . . . that's very fine." Zalmon encouraged them. "Helping a countryman is always worthy and just. Sure, sure . . . Who is the man . . . do I know him, too?"

"That's a secret," one of the young men said.

"Well, if it's secret, I will certainly not force you to tell me; I'm not one of those who is curious to know."

"One really should not be curious," Zalmon's friend spoke. "That means, then, you want me to take tickets . . ."

"Certainly!" The two spoke together and one drew out a batch of tickets and suggested various kinds: box, orchestra, first balcony.

Zalmon's friend deliberated which to take: orchestra or balcony; the man's wife suggested balcony seats.

"Why balcony?" Zalmon broke in. "Balcony is too far away. I will take orchestra tickets."

The two young men looked at each other, then one decided it might be better if Zalmon bought a ticket.

"Orchestra tickets, Reb Zalmon?"

"Yes, orchestra—a dollar each . . . a poor countryman . . . Sure, why not? I don't even know who it is, but that makes it an even better deed . . ."

The seller of the ticket could not help laughing.

"What's so funny?" Zalmon asked, somewhat injured. "Isn't it a better deed?"

"Of course," the young man blushed. "I, too, regard it as a worthy deed, that's why I am going around with the tickets." Becoming serious, he handed Zalmon two tickets in the first row, saying: "Reb Zalmon, you are getting tickets in the first row."

Zalmon felt very proud. He took the tickets, examined them on all sides, and with a contented smile took out his last two dollars.

"Here you are—two dollars . . . now, when is it?"

One of the two gave him the date of the performance.

"Very good! That's very good!" Zalmon was delighted. "I will go with my Ethel."

After the young men left, Zalmon turned proudly to his friend: "So you, it appears, bought balcony tickets at seventy-five cents."

His friend was silent, but his friend's wife spoke with a sigh: "In these days, even this comes hard, but what are you to do with a poor fellow countryman?"

Her saddened tone roused Zalmon from his dream; he remembered that he had parted with his last two dollars for tickets in the first row.

He could sit still no longer; he left the house.

Depressed, without a nickel for carfare, he set out for home on foot, with the two tickets, first row, for his own benefit performance.

I—as Echo

MOISHE NADIR _____

TIMES WERE BAD. The times were bitter, much bitterer than you think. There was nothing to eat, and what little there was did not belong to me but to others.

People whom I did not know and whose names I had never even heard walked freely about the streets and ate juicy pears and apples and red cherries from cone-shaped paper bags, and they peeled bananas and flung the skins under my feet. And I alone, who am no stranger to myself and know myself so well, went about idle and my teeth went about idle, too. And in each of my two eyes there hung a dream of a fine breakfast. And in each of my nostrils there trembled the longing for a kosher restaurant, for a warm meal.

I walked about the streets, twirled my cane in the air, and wished for a quick death or a happy future.

Death did not come and if he had come he would not have found me at home anyway, because I had moved from my old room; and the happy future was far away, as far away as she always is, somewhere in the future.

There was nothing left but—to look for work.

Look for work! Look for work! Let's look around for some work, I pleaded with myself because the word "work" frightened me. I had long become unaccustomed to it. Besides that, I was afraid I would have to soil my hands and my nails would lose their polish.

I had very beautiful nails!

I was in a tight spot, very tight. My cheeks became more sunken day by day, my chest became as flat as a matzoh, my eyes withdrew from the outer world, hid in their sockets, and were too listless to observe the sated world. My hands became weak, as did my hope. She no longer waved like a silken flag in the wind, but lay on my soul like a quilt that hangs from the window and would like to slide off, but cannot . . .

Oh, what groans and sighs escaped from my breast at that time! From my eyes there flowed—not bloody tears, but hot bloody tears! I let these tears flow freely down on my vest. Then I would take my vest, wring it, and hang it out to dry.

For a long time I looked for work and, may it not happen to you, may you be spared such agony, did not find any. Wherever I went in search of work I got the same reply—as if they had conspired together—"Nothing doing."

When things were at their worst—so bad, in fact, that the waters of despair had risen so high (pointing to my tie)—I received a letter from a friend, a farmer, in which he invited me to become an echo for $2.40 a day with laundry thrown in.

I—an echo? No longer the handsome, charming young man of commanding stature in society, with the bright smile and eyes, I became but an echo, an answering voice, a reverberation . . . thus I soliloquized as I tore the hairs from my head and let them fly out of the train which was carrying me to my career as an echo.

When I arrived at the farm and greeted my farmer friend, the following conversation took place between us:

I: What will constitute my duty as an echo, please?

He: You will be stationed all day near the small bridge by my lake and will make echoes.

I: To what purpose?

He: As you know, there are people, great nature lovers, who are especially fond of echoes. And since my competitor hired a man last year and set him beside a bridge to produce echoes, I advertised this year that we have even stronger echoes in our woods. I want you to be the echo because you have a strong voice.

Eight minutes later I was stuck away in a swampy little woods and waited for the opportunity to test my gifts as an echo.

In a little while a man went by and from the way he waved his hands, as if to catch flies, I understood that he was a worshipper of Mother Nature, and a seeker of—echoes.

Soon I heard a call: "Hello! Who's there?"

I promptly responded: "Hello! Who's there?"

"A fine day!" the approaching voice said.

"That's right!" I answered—"A fine day!"

The "that's right" was superfluous, but natural.

"So we are in the country," the voice called out.

I answered tone for tone: "So we are in the country."

"Ha-ha," the voice laughed.

"Ha-ha," I laughed back.

"Where are you?" asked the voice.

"Where are you?" I asked in return.

"Ha-ha-ha!" the voice split its sides for laughter.

"Ha-ha-ha!" I laughed back, with a few more "ha-ha's" than were necessary.

There was silence for a while. Meantime I lighted a cigarette and soon the voice asked: "How are tricks?"

"Thank you!" I answered. "I am all right. How are tricks with you?"

Half an hour later I held the $2.40 in the palm of my hand, my wages for the killing work as an echo, and my friend, the farmer, pointed toward the railroad station with the warning that I should be careful in crossing the tracks or I might be run over . . .

Moishe "Liar"

JOSEPH OPATOSHU ⸻

BY TWELVE MIDNIGHT the Romanian wine cellar was packed. Romanian Jews with their wives and young men with their girls were seated around the tables, cracking roasted almonds, smoking, and enjoying glasses of "native" wine. The owner, tall, lean, with his few hairs seemingly pasted to the naked skull, sat gracefully beside his musical instrument, shoved a wooden hammer and his fingers over the metal strings, and played sorrowful Romanian folk tunes. The audience accompanied him with quiet singing and beat time with their feet.

From time to time a couple emerged from behind a table. The audience made room and the two, moving in a dance so lazy that they seemed almost fastened to one spot, excited the onlookers with every provocative turn and step. A street singer moved from table to table. He stopped before one, occupied by stout women with double chins. The women, feet slightly spread, had almonds in their laps. They threw the nuts into their mouths, cracked the shells, and spat them out on the floor. They held their sides for laughter at the singer's spicy couplets, winked to an elderly, bald man with greasy eyes who was seated among them, and joined in singing, suggestively:

"Oh, what a bomb; oh, what a bomb!"

At the cash register, the owner's wife, a stout woman with cat's eyes, sat over a platter of sweetbreads and chewed lazily and drowsily.

From the singing women and the stringed instrument there rose a tumult that filled the cellar. In the deafening turmoil, the glaring lights, and the smell of roasting meats, throats grew dry and brought more and more orders for "native" wine.

147

Moishe "Liar" was sitting in a corner. His hat was cocked jauntily on his right ear and he wore his shiny, almost threadbare, Prince Albert—buttoned—and his striped trousers—newly pressed. He twirled his cane between two fingers and whistled. Every now and then he touched his inflamed nose, which was blue at the tip like a flame of alcohol.

Moishe was a fixture in the Romanian wine cellar. He spent whole days here, on the lookout for a "sucker" who would treat him to wine or invite him to a meal. These victims he would find among new visitors, greenhorns, and writers. If he caught a writer, he had a new lease on life. He knew that a talk with a writer would put no money in his pocket, would not even yield him a glass of wine; on the other hand, it was a source of satisfaction to him that he was understood, that he had been able to unburden himself to a colleague.

He told tales made of whole cloth and shed tears. Very rapidly, he affected stupidity, slipped into the role, forgot himself, and began to believe the stories he was telling. And if the writer sat with mouth agape, Moishe triumphantly laid one hand on his auditor while he beat himself on the chest with the fingers of the other hand and chortled:

"And you are probably thinking of writing a story with Moishe for your hero, ha-ha-ha."

If he victimized a greenhorn, he would begin by talking him deaf and dumb about the ease with which one could become rich in America. In proof, he would demonstrate that all his fellow countrymen, cobblers and drivers at home, had become wealthy here. And when he observed that the listener was lost in a dream of fancied fortunes, he would really let himself go. The man, breathless now, would learn about the wealth that Moishe had had at one time, and about the prosperous life he had led, and how Moishe's partner, a Litvak, may his memory be blotted out, had robbed him, taken his wife, and ruined his twenty-one-year-old daughter. He talked with such a tearful voice and watery eyes that the man was moved to pity. At such times Moishe easily gained a few pennies.

Moishe looked about him on all sides, wondering where to turn. Almost all the tables were occupied and at tables that were filled no one would listen to him and there probably would always be someone who knew him. On top of that, the singer was running about from table to table, shrieking at the top of his lungs, and Moishe felt that moving in his direction was not propitious.

At a small table near the door sat Benny, a six-footer, who was pouring himself a glass of wine from a pitcher. Moishe hesitated about approaching him. For the last few days, since Benny had appeared in the wine cellar, Moishe had cast an eye in his direction. However, he was frightened because he knew that the fellow was in some "shady" business and that breaking a person's ribs was as simple a matter to Benny as emptying a pitcher of wine. Moreover, Benny always had his companions around him. Yet the more Moishe was afraid, the more strongly he was tempted to go over to him, certain that, with any kind of luck, he would come away with a good haul. After all, what was money to a tough guy like Benny?

Moishe arose, straightened his Prince Albert, touched his inflamed nose, and sat down near Benny. The gangster made room for him. Moishe went through the motions of calling the waiter, blustered, cursed, and swore he would never put foot in this swinish place again—more than an hour since he had asked for a pitcher of wine and he'd not been served yet.

Benny shoved an empty glass toward him and pointed to his pitcher: "Help yourself to a glass of wine in the meantime."

"Thank you, sir." Moishe bowed, poured himself a glass, drank it, and felt emboldened. "In Europe, a thing like this could never happen! If the scoundrel didn't serve my wine, I'd break his head! But he's a big shot here, belongs to a union. Try to tangle with him!"

Moishe took out his cigar case, offered it to Benny: "If you please!"

They lighted up, sat quietly, while Moishe's mind, spurred by the glass of wine, raced with ideas for snaring and holding Benny captive.

"A fellow countryman, I see. By your pronunciation I would say from Yassy—eh?"

"Are you from Yassy, too?" Benny smiled.

"And from where in Yassy? Right from the heart of it!" Moishe almost shrieked and then sighed. "But I had to flee. And would you believe it! My picture was stuck up in every railway station along the borders and, as I live, the government offered a cash reward to anyone who would take me alive!"

Benny who, up to this moment, had seemed not to pay any attention to what was being said, suddenly planted both hands on the table, looked at Moishe with such piercing eyes that he was chilled, and asked with intense interest: "What do you mean the government offered a cash reward?"

Moishe felt that Benny was already snared. He was sure Benny would not disentangle himself very easily now.

"That, Mister, is an interesting story," Moishe drew out the words—"But this is hardly the time, a chance meeting . . . when we meet again, I'll tell you all about it. But, would you believe it? Even here, in America, I was not safe at first! Romanian spies were after me, at every step, and I was in terror that they would turn me over to the Romanian Consul. As I live, I've gone through quite a bit in my life!"

The waiter came over.

"Another pitcher of wine," Benny said and turned to Moishe. "Have something."

Good-naturedly, Moishe pressed the waiter's hand, slapped him on the back as if they were old friends, and almost yelled in his ear:

"Let me have a steak with french fries. Fresh broiled, do you hear, Rudolph?"

The wine cellar became more lively. The wine was having its effect on the crowd, making the aged youthful and the young old. Elderly men embraced young girls, threw back their bald heads, and hoarsely accompanied the musical instrument. In a little while Moishe was crouching over a steak, taking pleasure in every stroke of the knife which released a flow of blood. He sipped wine and felt that the screws of his mind were loosening as was his tongue. He moved closer to Benny and pathetically confided in his ear:

"And do you suppose things are better now? It may be that right now as I am talking with you, a pair of eyes are watching me. I am followed at every step!"

Instinctively, Benny looked about. He shuddered. In a corner, a man with a checkered cap was seated before a glass of wine. The man did not take his eyes off Benny, who was sure this was a detective. Benny did not look in his direction again. He shuddered, felt the eyes burn into his flesh, and waited momentarily for the stranger to rise, lay a hand on him, and arrest him. Benny no longer listened to Moishe's talk, but thought only about escaping from the cellar until it occurred to him, suddenly, that perhaps the stranger with whom he was talking was also a detective!

"Let me ask you." Moishe seized Benny's hand. "Can anything be more dreadful than to think, all your life, that someone is after you? Why are you trembling? Are you cold?"

"Where do you get that stuff?" Benny muttered as he thought to himself: He probably takes me for a dope! We'll see!

"Wherever you set a foot," Moishe said, holding Benny more securely. "Whenever you yawn—it is known! Not to spend two nights in the same place! You know what that means? A man endures all this, suffers a living death from day to day, and no one cares about it!"

Look at this guy, playing dumb, the son of a gun, trying to talk me deaf, dumb, and blind! If he doesn't let go of me, I'll break every bone in his body, Benny thought to himself, but he said: "Why wouldn't I know what that means?"

"Here are hundreds, seated right here," Moishe continued, "drinking wine, having a gay time with the ladies. At home there are warm beds waiting for them and not one of them even stops to think that I, in my shabby Prince Albert, will have to sleep in a park with . . ."

Benny saw that the man in the checkered cap arose and started to walk toward his table. He tore himself free from Moishe's hand and almost threw Moishe off his chair. Forgetting the change, which the waiter had left on the table, the six-foot gangster dashed out of the wine cellar.

A Eulogist

CHONE GOTTESFELD

I AM ONE OF THE BEST SPEAKERS at a funeral. I speak in a touching voice with a sorrowful tone and use words that pluck at the heart and cause tears and mournful sobs.

For that reason, I am called to many funerals to deliver eulogies. I speak at several burials a day. I am always a hit. If applause were permitted at a funeral, I would receive the greatest applause. But instead, my talks are interrupted by wailing. At funerals I am the second greatest attraction, after the corpse.

One time an acquaintance of mine called me on the telephone and told me in a sad voice that he had just read in a newspaper that our friend Moishe Lipkin had died. The funeral was taking place at that very time. He himself had to go away and, therefore, could not attend. He begged me to go. He said: "One of your eulogies will be an honor to the deceased and to the family." He gave me the address of the cemetery and assured me that if I hurried I would still be there in time to deliver a bit of a talk.

I asked no more questions, started out at once, arrived, and delivered a eulogy. The number of mourners was small. My friend deserved a larger funeral. I made use of this fact in my oration. I thundered against those who had failed to pay their respects to the deceased, a person who had been of warm heart and generous hand. He had given to all, had helped everyone. He had been the pride of his fellow men, of his Galician fellow countrymen, of his friends and family.

I spoke with the greatest warmth about him, but I felt about me only the cold wind of the burial place. I compared him with Tolstoy,

152

LaSalle, and Socrates, and said, with pathos: "To take such a good man, a man with such a countenance, and to bury him in the earth!" Such words always brought an outburst of tears. But here I was the only one who wept. None of my talks had ever had such a cold reception at a cemetery.

I traveled home dissatisfied and began to think about the causes of my failure. Had the mourners been people whom no tragedy can move? Had my talk been at fault? Had I aged and grown unable to speak as formerly?

Suddenly, not far from me in the streetcar, I saw a man who was returning from the same funeral and decided to find out from him whether my conclusions were correct: that my talk had not been any good.

"How did you like my talk?" I asked him.

"I didn't like it at all," he answered.

"Why not?"

"Because there wasn't a word of truth in what you said," he announced. "You said that the deceased had been charitable. I never knew a bigger hog in my life. You said he was a Galician; it happens that he was born in Bialistok. He . . ."

I didn't want to talk with this man any longer. I thought he had taken leave of his mind. I had known the deceased well, his warmheartedness, and this man called him a hog. I knew the very city in Galicia from which the deceased had come, and this man was making a Bialistoker of him. The man was crazy, I was sure.

When I returned to my office, I found waiting for me my friend Mr. Zaikin. I told him that our friend Mr. Lipkin had died, that I had spoken at the funeral, and that my eulogy had been a total failure.

Mr. Zaikin had been a close friend of the deceased and was also a friend of the family's.

He was deeply shocked by the sad news. He wanted more details. Had he been ailing? I could not give him any more information.

He thought for a while and then said: "I must go to the widow at once and express my sympathy. Since I have my car, I can also take you along."

I explained that, as I did not know the widow personally, it was not proper for me to go. However, he said that did not matter. "First of all, she knows you, even if you don't know her. Secondly, she has just listened to your eulogy at the cemetery and is certainly grateful for the kind words you have spoken about her husband. She will regard it as an honor that you have come."

He convinced me and we went.

We arrived at the home of the deceased. We rang. A young, pretty, charming woman opened the door, extended her hand to my friend, and said, smilingly: "What a welcome guest! Come in!"

We went.

He introduced me. "This is Mr. Zhipitz."

She gave me her hand as she said: "I have heard a good deal about you. Be seated!"

We sat down and the widow excused herself, saying she was going to get us some drinks.

I was amazed at her demeanor—not a trace of mourning. Not a word about my speaking at the cemetery. Ordinarily, widows thanked me for my eulogy at the funeral.

I said to my friend: "She is a queer kind of widow."

"You don't know Mrs. Lipkin," he said. "Her heart is bleeding and she puts on a cheerful face. She is a remarkable woman. Her love for her husband was extraordinary, and she is hiding her grief."

"One meets women like that very infrequently," I declared. "I should like to know what she thinks of my eulogy. You ask her."

"She will probably tell you herself," he said. "She will surely thank you. She never leaves a debt of thanks unpaid."

"Nevertheless, you ask her," I said. "It isn't right for me to ask."

The widow returned and brought wine and cookies, and said: "Eat and drink, my welcome guests. The living must drink the toast!"

All of us, the widow included, drank two or three small glasses apiece.

"Mrs. Lipkin, you are to be admired," my friend spoke up, "for your spirit, your bearing. Bravo!"

"Mrs. Lipkin," I chimed in, "you are a great being. Your late husband was a great man and you are a great being."

"What did you say—my—husband?" she asked, not knowing what I meant.

"In my eulogy at your husband's funeral, I compared him with Tolstoy," I said.

She cut me off with a hysterical shriek.

"Pardon me," I said. "As I understand, you do not wish any mention of your late husband."

"Help! Woe is me! When did he die?" She began to scream and wail. "When? How? Why didn't I know?"

I and my friend looked at one another, not knowing what this meant. Was it possible she was just learning of her husband's death?

"Why don't you speak? Why don't you explain?" she kept on screaming.

My friend threw all the blame on me. "He told me about it," he said.

"I received the news from a friend, over the telephone," I said. But before I could give her any more information, the door opened and the "dead" Moishe Lipkin came in.

Chaim Buys a Piano for His Daughter

TASHRAK ────────────────────────────────

LONG AGO I HAD PROMISED my daughter, Betsy, the teacher, that I would buy her a piano. And, as I live, she deserves it. First of all, she is a fine child, good, and gifted. Secondly, she earns a good salary and gives me all her earnings except the few dollars she keeps for pocket money and her clothes. And, in addition, it is sheer pleasure to have a piano at home and to hear a bit of music, occasionally.

I went to Gudilsky, the storekeeper from whom I buy my merchandise, and asked him to give me the fine points of purchasing a piano. Mr. Gudilsky told me it is best to buy a piano through a friend. You asked the friend to act, ostensibly as the agent, the commission broker. An agent receives a twenty-five-dollar commission and these twenty-five dollars you get back from your friend and put into your pocket. You have already saved twenty-five dollars in cash.

On the day when the piano was brought to the house, the entire block turned into a fair. All day long, around the house where we live, there was a crowd of people, old and young, who looked with enmity up at the floor from which long thick ropes were suspended. The tenants in the house regarded me as a millionaire, and all my children became so stuck up that day, that it was beneath them to talk to one another. Even my wife began to put on airs and on that day told the butcher that he should be good enough to deliver the order instead of her dragging herself to his store with her basket. She had suddenly become a lady!

Even before this, my Betsy had been able to play the piano fairly well. She had taken piano lessons, and at night, after supper, we all gath-

156

ered in the parlor, and Betsy said she would play us something from an opera. She opened a sheet of music and began to work her fingers. But work—till doomsday! The piano squealed like a wagon on which someone has forgotten to grease the axles. And although I cannot read a note, I realized instantly that the piano had diphtheria and needed a doctor.

"Papa," my Betsy said, "you have been fooled. This must be an old piano varnished over to look like new."

All of us crowded around the piano. Each of us caressed it, tickled the ivories with gentle persuasiveness, and then gave way to anger and banged, banged. It was no go! The piano did not work. Even my wife took a bang at the ivories. She, too, wanted to try.

"Woman!" I shouted at her. "Two is company: Three is a crowd. Do you think you know what a piano is? A piano is a delicate machine. It is a machine with a soul. Every key has a separate tone. One strikes 'do,' the next 're,' the third 'le,' and after that come 'mi,' 'fa,' and 'sol.' And then they go down the scale 'sol, fa, mi, le, re, do.' Isn't that so, Betsy? And you, Woman, want to teach us how to play the piano!"

"Oh, what a genius you are!" my wife yelled. "A sage, a know-it-all, and everyone puts it over on you. Prove what a genius you are and try to get your money back or get another piano."

"I'll show you what a genius I am!" I said. I got my coat and ran to the piano store on the avenue.

I ran more than I walked, and I was boiling because of the shame of it. Imagine, to take me in so stupidly and to give me a piano that is dumb! But when I got to the place, I saw that the store was already closed. By now it was about ten o'clock at night but it seemed to me the store had purposely closed early because of me.

In the door of the store I saw a card on which was written the address of the storekeeper's home. I started off immediately; it was not far away. I rang the bell. A sleepy servant girl came out and asked whom I was looking for.

"I want to see Mr. Toplitsky," I answered.

"He is sleeping already," the girl said.

"Wake him up. It is very important," I told her.

In ten minutes, Mr. Toplitsky came out in his nightclothes, and as soon as he saw me called out, "What is the matter?"

"The piano I bought from you doesn't play," I said.

Mr. Toplitsky looked at me for a few minutes, and then he asked: "Mister, are you in your right mind?"

"Yes," I answered him, "I am in my right mind now. I have just discovered that you have put one over on me—a fine piece of secondhand junk."

"Say, Mister," Mr. Toplitsky said in anger, "I want you to know that I am a reputable man. Probably nobody among you knows how to play, or there is some other reason. Whatever the story is, tomorrow I'll send a man over to see what is the matter. At any rate, what are you making such a fuss about? Altogether, you've paid only six dollars down and, anyway, what are you so hot under the collar for? Go on home, and we'll fix the whole matter tomorrow. Good night!"

When I got home I was simply amazed. Betsy was playing "Rozshinkes mit Mondlen," playing so well, so beautifully, it filled me with delight. While I was away, the piano suddenly recovered.

"The piano is all better?" I asked in astonishment.

They all burst into laughter at my question. Only my wife failed to laugh.

"What happened?" I asked.

"If you won't shout at Mother, I'll tell you," Betsy answered.

I had to promise that I wouldn't shout. Then Betsy explained:

"It was nothing, Pa. It was just a trifle. Mother had opened the top of the piano and hid a bag of apples and a bag of fancy cakes inside, so that the children should not get at them."

"Woman!" I began to shout because I could not contain myself. But Betsy gave me a look and I became silent.

A few days later something happened which must make you laugh, and again the piano was to blame.

After we took the piano into the house everyone began to look askance at the sewing machine, which had been in the house a good number of years. Before the piano came, the sewing machine used to stand in the parlor. Because of the piano, the machine was put into one of the bedrooms, until, finally, my wife bethought herself and said: "Chaim, why don't you sell the machine?"

At Betsy's suggestion, I began to look through newspaper advertisements for someone who wanted to buy a sewing machine.

I found an advertisement in which a man indicated that he was looking for a sewing machine, somewhat used. He asked that anyone having such a machine should write to Box Number 23, care of the paper.

I sat down and wrote him a card in the following words:

"Mister, dear sir, Box Number 23: Call on me in the evening. I have an article for you which will surely please you. You will be thankful to me. Chaim, the Customer-Peddler."

Naturally, I included my address.

By curious mischance, when the postcard arrived at the newspaper office, the bookkeeper put it into another box.

The box into which he put my card happened to belong to a young man who had advertised that he was looking for a bride, a girl of respectable parents.

Just imagine the situation: When that young man received my card, it never occurred to him that a mistake had taken place. I had written that "I have an article for you which will surely please." I was writing about a sewing machine, but the young man was thinking about a bride.

That evening there came to the house a young man of about twenty-eight, dressed like a fop, with a silk hat and a flower in his lapel. He said he wished to speak with me, in private.

"With the greatest pleasure," I answered. "What can I do for you?"

"I have received your card," he said, "and I have come to see the article." At this, he began to throw glances toward the front room where my daughters were sitting.

"With pleasure," I said. "She is still almost new."

"What do you mean new?" he asked.

"I mean she is in good condition. She sews very well."

"At what kind of work?" he asked.

"At everything. She is capable of everything. She can sew anything in the world," I said.

"Very well," he said with a smile. "But thank God, I will not need to have her work."

"Well," I said, "she is still really new. In my house only four years.

"She would be an ornament in any home. She is a 'beaut.' "

"I don't understand," he said, questioningly. "You keep on hammering away that she is new. What do you mean new?"

"I am saying that she is not old," I explained.

"Oh," he said and smiled. "And where was she before? You say she had been with you only four years."

"How do I know where she was before? In the factory."

"In what factory?" he asked.

"A factory where they make sewing machines."

"And what is she doing now?"

"She is idle. And that's why I want to sell her."

"What do you mean sell?" he asked in surprise.

"I say," I said, "that you may have her for ten dollars. But you will have to hire an express yourself to take her away."

"What's going on here?" the young man called out and rubbed his brow. "We can't seem to understand one another."

"I understand you perfectly," I said. "You want to buy a sewing machine and I want to sell one. Come and take a look. And if you like the machine, pay me ten dollars and she is yours."

"Oh!" The young man put his hand to his heart. He looked at me so strangely I did not know whether he wanted to cry or laugh.

And then, when he told me what he had come for, we both realized that there had been a mistake in the newspaper office.

In the meantime, the machine is still at home.

PART FIVE

Not Lost in the Crowd

Story about a Greenhorn

SHOLEM ALEICHEM _____

YOU SAY: America is a land of business—never mind. That's as it should be. But, after all, to get married and sell yourself for business— that, you must excuse me, is piggish. I'm not preaching morals, but I tell you, and it's a fact, 99 percent of the greenhorns among us marry for business. That distresses me and if I lay my hands on a greenhorn, he's not the same when I get through with him. Leave it to me, and I will tell you a good one.

One time I am seated in my office, going through my mail, when a greenhorn, hardly more than a boy, comes in, accompanied by a sweet young thing—how shall I describe her to you? Blood and milk, lovely as the day and fresh as an apple just off the tree. Once inside, he calls to me: "How do you do? Are you Mr. Baraban, the business broker?"

"Sit down! What's the good news?"

He opens his heart to me and tells me a long story, so-and-so, how he is a boy who has been here only ten years, that he is a knee-pants maker by trade, and that the little lady had fallen in love with him, she a working girl with a thousand dollars in cash, that he has married her and is looking for a business where they can make a living and give up working in the shop because he has, may you be spared, a touch of rheumatism—may he hold onto it—and so forth.

I look at the little lady and say to him: "Into what kind of business would you like to go?"

He answers: "I want to open a stationery store."

And he explains to me that in a stationery store, "she" would be able to help him.

Do you get the greenhorn's drift? It's not sufficient that he has nabbed himself a wife, a little peach, and not enough that she has brought him a thousand in cash—oh, no! What's more—he would like her to work for him while he sits with his crowd, plays pinochle, and so forth—I know my customers!

So I think to myself: A plague of a stationery store you'll get from me! It suits me more to have you tied, like a dog, to a laundry. That's what I'll make of you—a laundryman.

Why do I happen to think of a laundry? It happens that I just have a laundry at hand to sell. And I say to my greenhorn:

"Why do you need to bother with a stationery store with its eighteen hours a day, and worry about a schoolboy who may steal a candy worth a penny, and so forth? Instead of that, leave it to me—I'll give you a better business, a laundry in the Bronx, and you'll work regular hours and live like a lord!"

I take a pencil and figure things out for him so that, after all expenses: rent and shirt ironer and family ironer and delivery boy and laundry bill, he has left thirty-odd dollars a week, clear—what more does he want?

"What will it cost?"

"It's a bargain at a thousand," I say, "but leave it to me—I'll let you have it for eight hundred. All you'll need to do," I tell him, "will be to make a small down payment, blindfold your eyes, take possession, and you're all set. In the meantime," I say, "go in good health and come back in three days' time, because I have no time now, and good-bye."

ත

And I myself go off to my laundryman and congratulate him. "God has sent me just the right fish," I tell him, a greenhorn, and he, the laundryman, now has a chance, if he is sensible, to get rid of the laundry for even money; let him do the right thing, and so forth.

The knave understands what I mean and says to me: "Just bring that fish here and everything will be all right."

In three days, the greenhorn appears, leaves a deposit, takes his place, with his wife, in the laundry for a week's trial, as is customary, and my laundryman has probably seen to it that the week's trial is all right and even better than all right—and the business is settled. The greenhorn pays the agreed sum; the laundryman turns over the books and the key; I take my commission from both parties, and so forth—Mr. Baraban, the business broker, knows his business and—what do you say: *Finita la Comedia?* Isn't that so? That's what you say!

For me the comedy is just beginning. For now that everything is completely and finally finished, my wrath first blazes up in me at that greenhorn. Why does he, the rascal, deserve pigeon's milk brought right to his lips—his little wife—a thousand dollars cash, and a going business without a headache?

That laundry must be bought back from him at half the price and go back to the original laundryman. How? That's exactly why I am Mr. Baraban, the business broker. In my experience there is no objective I cannot carry out! I go to the corner on the next street, exactly opposite the laundry, rent a small place from the agent, slip him a ten-dollar deposit, and hang a sign in the window:

"LAUNDRY WILL OPEN HERE."

Not a full day has gone by and my greenhorn appears, with a head that's all in the air. How come! He is simply ruined!

"What is the trouble?"

He tells me of his misfortune: Some plague of a fellow has rented a store directly opposite his and is opening a laundry!

"Well, what do you want, greenhorn?"

He wants me to find him a customer for his laundry; he will show his thankfulness in the nicest way and he will always pray for me and so forth.

I calm him and tell him it is not so easy to find a customer. But he is to rely on me and I'll try my best. In the meantime he is to go home and return in three days because I'm just flooded with business, and so forth—and good-bye!

තු

And I send for my old laundryman and tell him so-and-so: "You now have a chance to buy back your laundry for half the money."

He says to me: "How will you work it?"

I say: "How does that concern you? Leave it to me—that's why I am Mr. Baraban, the business broker."

He says: "All right."

I say: "Will I get my commission?"

He says: "All right."

I say: "I must have a hundred for the job."

He says: "All right."

Meanwhile the three days pass—my greenhorn arrives with his little wife. She has become a little bit pale, but is still as beautiful as the sun.

"What's the news?"

"What news do you expect?" I say. "You ought to thank God," I say, "that I have just barely succeeded in finding someone for your laundry. However, you will have to," I say, "lose money."

"How much?"

"Don't ask," I say, "how much you are losing. Ask how much you are gaining. Because, however little you get, it is found money . . . Are you going to start up," I say, "with American competitors? They can drive you," I say, "into such outlays that you will have to," I say, "get up in the middle of the night and flee in your last shirt."

No point in going on. I throw them into such a fright that they take half of what they had paid, and even give me a commission. After all, I'm in no condition to bother for nothing and—no more laundry!

But take it easy, we're not through. If your mind is working you must remember that I gave an agent a ten-dollar tip for a store, and hung up a sign announcing a laundry. Then here's a question: Why should I let ten dollars go to waste, willy-nilly? Is Mr. Baraban's, the business broker's, money stolen money? That's item number one. Secondly, the thought of that greenhorn burns me up and keeps on prodding me: That scoundrel still has a few hundreds in pocket and a sweet little wife—purest gold—besides. Why does he deserve it?

Mr. Baraban, the biggest business broker on the East Side, must have a wife who is, excuse me, a sight to behold and a Xantippe to boot. And God sends the greenhorn such a doll, you know, a little mezuzah—a charm to kiss. Let him atone for it!

So I don't put it off but write him a postal card that he should come at a certain time: I have a business for him.

He needs no persuasion and comes at the appointed time and, sure enough, with her, his pretty wife. I seat them, my cherished guests, and tell them so-and-so: "You don't know American fakers! If you knew the trick that that thief, the laundryman, has put over on you, your hair would stand upside down!"

"What's the point?"

"What's the point?" I say. "It was he," I say, "who rented the store opposite you and hung up the sign," I say, "in order to cause you to take fright and return him his laundry for half the sum."

Hearing this story, the couple begin to look at one another and turn red—especially the young wife. Her eyes burn like coals afire.

"It is only just," I say, "you should settle accounts with him, that thief, so he will have something to remember you by!"

"How can we settle accounts with him?"

"Leave it to me," I say. "I will fix him so well, the gay bird, that through me," I say, "he will not rise again even on Resurrection Day, and you," I say, "will derive much good; you will," I say, "have an even better business than before!"

They look at me like doves, as one saying: "From your mouth to God's ear, and long life to you," and such like.

And I lay out a plan for them: Why should you buy a strange business and pay the owner to the crack of doom? Let me go to the landlord and rent the small store that knave had wanted to rent, and I will fit up for them, for three or four hundred, a laundry directly opposite his and begin my competition: Whatever he charges, I will charge less, and in three or four weeks I will make him move—or my name isn't Baraban!

Why labor the point? I unscrew them so that the greenhorn almost embraces me and that pretty little wife of his blushes and grows even prettier.

On that same day I rent for them the little store and in a short time we have a finished laundry with a sign and counters and all the trimmings, and my young couple takes to the job and a fiery competition begins between them and the old laundryman. They beat one another's rates down as far as they can. If he charges twenty-four cents for a dozen flat, they charge eighteen and do a spread free of charge. If he lowers shirts to eight cents, they reduce collars to a cent and a half and force him down to a penny, and so forth.

The point is, they fight so long that the greenhorn shakes himself free of every dollar and remains without a cent; he has nothing for his rent, closes the laundry, and is left as on the day he was born, as the Good Book says.

And now I have him resting where I want him, in Ludlow Street jail, and I have found his wife a lawyer who, on her behalf, is asking three things: 1) her money—the dowry of a thousand dollars; 2) a divorce; and 3) until she obtains the divorce, alimony for her support, according to the law of the land.

Accursed be all his generations, that greenhorn!

She Reads the *World*

ABRAHAM RAISIN ⎯⎯⎯⎯⎯⎯⎯⎯⎯⎯⎯⎯⎯⎯⎯⎯⎯⎯⎯⎯⎯⎯⎯⎯

AFTER THE "SEASON," Lena is left with a few ten-dollar bills to carry her through the several months of "slack" time. This sum she takes to the post office. The attendant behind the window, a tall, thin young man, knows her and when she deposits the last pay of the season he gives her a friendly smile and says: "You'll accumulate a fortune!"

Lena explains that in a little while she will begin making withdrawals because the season is over.

And she really begins to withdraw small sums every week until, in the course of two months, she has just one dollar left in the post office.

This dollar she does not withdraw.

Why she leaves it there she hardly knows herself.

Perhaps, by leaving it there, she wishes not to break the ties with the man at the window who greets her in such a friendly way and, then again, perhaps she does not want to risk finding herself without even one dollar. After all, it is cheering, when you wake in the morning, to remember that the situation is not really desperate: There is that dollar, safe in the post office, and if it comes to the worst, she can lay her hands on her money.

Lena has had the experience of being left without a cent, with the season a long way off and nothing left of her postal savings book except the covers.

For the most part, however, she is careful with her savings. She budgets her expenses so she will not need to suffer too great deprivation while waiting for the new season, and for that reason she is able to leave the dollar in her savings until the coming of the next season.

The post office attendant greets her with his friendly smile and, examining her old savings book, tells her the joyous news: "You still have a dollar left!"

Lena does not wait for the last minute but as soon as she has reached her last dollar she begins to look for work.

Early Sunday morning she buys a *World* for five cents. In the *World* she always finds a shop for the new season.

But she does not turn to the want ads immediately. First she looks at all of the pictures in the magazine section and through the feature stories about actresses, singers, and dancers.

One actress, with large black eyes, earns two hundred thousand dollars a year. The *World* stresses the fact that she is paid this sum wholly for her beautiful eyes.

In Lena's heart there is a sudden flow of enmity.

She stops before the mirror fixed to the wall in her room, opens her eyes wide, and studies them. She is certain her eyes are not a whit uglier than those of the actress in the *World*.

And why has she overlooked such a job at two hundred thousand a year? Especially since that other one cannot act either, and is paid solely for her eyes . . .

Lena feels insulted and hurt. She continues reading once more.

Here is a dancer with whom a millionaire fell in love and now she is demanding two hundred thousand for her broken heart.

And Lena remembers that someone has broken her heart, too—really broken it. But she has never told anyone about it, never complained to anyone, never demanded anything from anyone. She had merely been sick for an entire month and had not been able to go to work. She is still paying for her love . . .

She gulps a tear, set flowing by her recollections, and now reads about a wealthy girl to whom an aunt has left an inheritance of three million dollars. The girl has just married a poor student.

Lena quickly figures out that for three million dollars all the girls in the shop where she had last worked could be married. Again, she tells herself that if she had the three million, she would certainly not get married because it is simply impossible to fall in love with a girl who has so much money.

And having read all the sensations in the world of love, she reminds herself that she had not bought the *World* for this purpose.

What she wanted was the want ads. She was looking for a shop.

However, after reading about all the strange strokes of fortune in the magazine section, it is difficult for Lena to take to the densely printed sheets, their print dismal and cold like a cemetery, with every want ad like a tiny grave.

What is there to do? She has only one dollar in her savings, and there are just a few nickels in her pocketbook.

She turns from the gay pages to the cemetery of want ads . . . She selects some of the ads, cuts them out of the paper, and hides them in her pocketbook.

Tomorrow, she must rise early, hurry to the waiting lines, and wait until some total stranger will admit her to a job.

Her mind made up, she again poses before the mirror, studies her eyes once more, and is again convinced that they are in no way uglier than the eyes of the actress who gets two hundred thousand dollars a year . . .

However, Lena knows that no one will give a cent for her eyes. All they need is her hands.

Now she examines her thin, delicate fingers, one of them still not entirely healed of the stab made by the needle in the shop . . .

And early the next morning there is Lena already at work at a small table, beside a new acquaintance.

She looks at the eyes of her new friend and it seems to her that her friend's eyes are just as beautiful as the eyes of that actress.

When they go out for lunch to the nearby workers' restaurant, Lena cannot contain herself and turns to her friend with a question: "Do you read the *World*?"

"From time to time," the other answers. "What's up?"

"I read in yesterday's *World* that there is an actress who gets two hundred thousand dollars a year for her beautiful eyes . . ."

"Why, yes . . . I know her. . . ," her friend answers with pleasure. "I saw her in the movies . . . She is beautiful . . . very beautiful!"

Lena looks at her almost in anger: What a fool! She does not understand that her eyes are also as beautiful and it is only by accident that she is working in a shop.

But Lena does not dare to utter her thoughts. Her friend will not understand.

Moishe the Poet

CHAVER PAVER ⎯⎯⎯⎯⎯⎯⎯⎯⎯⎯⎯⎯⎯⎯⎯⎯⎯⎯⎯⎯⎯⎯⎯⎯⎯⎯⎯

EARLY IN THE MORNING, he had his coffee and roll and was off to the library. Toward evening, he had some soup and bread in a cafeteria and again was off to the library.

It was warm in the library, and quiet. This place did not close until nine. There was a full eternity until nine o'clock. He would have nothing to worry about in those hours. He would be at rest and at peace. He was certainly not hungry. His belly was full of vegetable soup and the three slices of bread. Now there was a rumbling in his belly. There were some stabbing pains. But he would pay no attention to them.

The great lamps lit up all over the spacious room with its tall bookcases! How he loved this beautiful brightness! And what did it recall to him, this lovely brilliance? It reminded him that outdoors it was cold and dark, that the stinging wind lashed the shoulders—that to venture outdoors would be to perish . . .

Tall cases with books. So many books. Perhaps, sometime, a book of his would find a place in one of these bookcases. His name began with the letter *B*. That meant one would have to look on the shelves for books of writers whose names begin with *B*.

A young man would come in, or a young woman, who would go straightaway to the bookcase marked *B*, would look among the books and would find him immediately, would take a seat at this brightly

From *Die Tzen Landsleit*.

lighted brown table, would open his book, bend over it, and read one wonderful song after another.

"Daydreaming, Moishe? How you are daydreaming!" he laughed at himself. "You are rich in dreams but a pauper in every pocket. Early this morning you still had your coffee and roll and in the evening some vegetable soup and three slices of bread. But tomorrow you will have—nothing. Empty pockets. And what excuse will you give the landlady today? What do you want of the poor woman? Why have you thrust yourself upon her?"

Thoughts like these would certainly not yield him any rest or peace.

"Quiet, quiet, my child," now he said to himself half-mockingly, half-sorrowfully. "Be quiet. Better look around at the hundreds of volumes set out in the bookcases. The people who wrote these richly inspiring books must also have suffered enough. Better take a book in hand and dip into it because the attendants are looking at you too closely."

Perhaps it would be even better to write a poem! In this very library he had written most of his songs. He needed only to shut his eyes, focus his thoughts, and soon he would experience that stimulating pensiveness which brought to his mind completed verses, warm, vivid, melodious verses.

Indeed, he would write about the Yiddish poet who, half-starved, sat in the library and studied the rows of books in the bookcases. And what was he thinking about the books on the shelves, while it was so cold outdoors? For more than two months, he had not paid his rent. His overcoat was worn threadbare. His limbs and body were lean to emaciation. And he had griping pains in his stomach.

And that sad, creative pensiveness actually brought him warm, living lines. His pencil ran rapidly, rapidly across the paper. A poem was being born here. There was plenty of time till the closing of the library at nine o'clock—an entire eternity. In the meantime, it was warm in this lovely brightness, in this solemn stillness.

Moishe Bookbinder, the Yiddish poet, who had eaten almost nothing all day, was writing a song in praise of all the creative beings whose books were set, row upon row, in the bookcases. He addressed them as "my brothers," these wonderful brothers of his who had lived in all the generations of man, in all times, and had given the world wisdom and beauty created in direst misery and in deepest pain . . .

Moishe smiled. He was joyous. His new poem pleased him. He read it again and again. Improved a verse here, found a more fitting word there. It was melodious. He closed his eyes and found he had already memorized the poem.

Now the lights in the library were being put out. He must leave.

He buttoned his overcoat—thin and threadbare. He put up his collar. He walked out and the blood in his veins was chilled instantly, as if he had been immersed in freezing water.

Where to? Home. But what would he tell the landlady? What excuse would he proffer her? . . .

But he did not need to proffer any excuse at all. He found his valise beside the stairs in the hall. A few pieces of his soiled laundry had been scattered about from an unwrapped newspaper bundle. Close by were his few books and manuscripts, scattered here and there. It was clear that the children of the house had busied themselves with his things. There were pages missing from the manuscripts.

There was a candy store on the corner. The storekeeper knew who Moishe was. He always read Moishe's poems and praised Moishe with warm admiration.

"Good evening to you, Chaver Moishe Bookbinder," the storekeeper greeted him respectfully. "It's a long time since a poem of yours has appeared. I've begun to yearn for one of your poems."

Moishe was pleased that this man, running a candy store on Twelfth Street and First Avenue, yearned for one of his poems. He assured him that soon one of his poems would appear in print. In fact, he had written one this very day. In the meantime he would like to leave his valise and things for just a few days. He had to move to new lodgings.

"Certainly—with the greatest pleasure." The storekeeper took the valise and other parcels and carried them into a small room in the rear. "No one will disturb them." He was happy that he could oblige this wonderful poet whose songs delighted his heart and touched him to the quick. "And so, it seems, we will soon read one of your new poems," he said with relish. "Good night, good night. As to your things, have no fears whatever. Safe as in your own home."

The dimly lighted streets, with their blocks of tenements, stretched for mile upon mile. The wind was merciless. It pounded his shoulders, whipped his feet, and pushed and pushed. His hat froze on his head.

His shoes shriveled from the cold. He had written a new poem today. He recited it to himself. He still liked it. He recited it once more, aloud.

The streets were empty, anyway. Everyone who had a roof over his head had taken shelter from the murderous cold. He might just as well repeat the poem in a loud, loud voice for no one would hear it against the malicious wind . . .

He reached the gloomy Bowery. He entered a narrow corridor. Behind a barred window there sat a pale-faced man, looking angry and sleepy. Moishe paid him a quarter, his last coin. The man gave him a key. Moishe mounted the stairs, key in hand. He entered a large room filled with boxlike cells. Row on row of cells. He had previously spent several nights in this "hotel."

"What now, Moishe, you great Yiddish poet?" He spoke to himself, mockingly. "Keep it quiet, don't say a word to anyone."

Moishe began to cough from the sharp odor of antiseptics. This stinging odor was meant to kill off all creeping and biting things, but it could just as well kill a human being.

Moishe stretched out on the iron cot with its thin mattress. He closed his eyes. He was almost stupefied by the odor. His mind became dull and his thoughts confused.

"Sleep, Yiddish poet." He spoke to himself once more, half in jest and half in sorrow. "Sleep, sleep. Greater poets than you have not even had a cot. Sleep, young fellow, and may you dream the sweetest dreams."

And he did dream the sweetest dreams. He dreamt of the Dniester—of a boat with snow-white sails moving swiftly in the wind. It sailed past the hill in Tcheremaiyev. On the hill stood Vera in her white shoes, in a light brown dress, and with her colored scarf around her neck. She beckoned to him with her hands and called: "Moishe, habibi, Moishe, yakiri—Moishe, my beloved, Moishe, my dearest one." He stopped the boat with its snow-white sails, reached out to her, and took her into the boat.

"Where are we sailing, Moishe, my dearest?" Vera asked.

"We're sailing to a new life, *rahyosi mchmad nafshi*, my friend, the desire of my soul. Our former life, Vera, was like the mud of Tcheremaiyev, like the rains of autumn, like the falseness of a dark, wet, winter night. Do you still remember, Vera, those unreal, dark torrential nights in the month of Kislev? It pours and pours, there's chaos outdoors, the sky has disappeared, the Earth has disappeared, and life just mourns and weeps.

"Oh, God, what pains!" And with that he awoke suddenly. He did not know the exact seat of the pains but they cut like knives. His stomach was torn by horrible cramps. He gritted his teeth. He stretched out, stomach to the mattress. What could this be?

"Oh, Mama!"

How very many years since he had called for his mother! Now he called to her. Oh, let her come quickly to save him for he could not bear the pain any longer.

The sharp pain eased somewhat. But a feeling of dull hurt remained. He turned over, his face to the ceiling, and lay that way part of the dismal, suffocating night. When morning came, the pain was gone. However, there was left a feeling of nausea that coursed in his blood. It was like a poison that infected his every limb and bone—a poisonous nausea that made him turn on the world and on all mankind. Now he hated everyone, he hated Vera, he hated his mother, his father, he hated his fellows, he hated everyone with a venomous hatred . . .

ᘐ

Tramps were sitting on the stone steps of Cooper Hall and smiling in the warmth of the sun.

On Third Avenue, El trains rushed back and forth. Machines and trucks, loaded with merchandise, whirled by from Fourth Avenue, from the Bowery, and from nearby side streets. Hundreds of pedestrians poured from side streets, cut across Cooper Square, hurried by swiftly and noisily.

All the passersby had a destination. All the rushing trucks and machines had a goal. The tramps who were sitting on the steps of Cooper Hall had no destination, had no goal.

Moishe was seated among them. He, too, had neither destination nor goal. He was just like them. His shirt—filthy, the collar—dirty; he had lost his tie in a municipal lodging house. The boxing of his shoes was split. His coat was crumpled and stained. His hair—disheveled, dusty. His face—a dirty red, windblown, soiled, frostbitten.

Now, nothing mattered to him. Now it was delightfully warm. Such a lovely early spring sun. If only he might stretch out full length, close his eyes, and doze off. But you could not stretch out here in the open street.

The tramps sat and looked at the bustling streets all around them. Their look was aimless. They looked and saw nothing. Moishe, too, looked at the bustling streets around him—also looked aimlessly—looked and saw nothing.

He had learned from his fellow tramps how to sustain life on nothing—on miracles. For six weeks now he had kept himself going on nothing. Like them he had gone to the free city and charity soup kitchens where they were fed a bowl of soup and a cup of coffee. And since he did not smoke, he did not need to panhandle cigarettes from passersby or pick up butts from the streets. As for sleeping, he slept wherever occasion offered or wherever it was possible. On very cold nights he begged for a handout from pedestrians. On milder nights he would sit on the steps in some hallway—sit and doze.

Moishe hated everybody and everything. He hated his poems. He hated Vera and his fellow writers. He was through with everyone—needed no one anymore. He would lose himself in the world so no trace of him would be left anywhere. He would roam across the country like many of the tramps who roam the highways and byways of America when spring comes. He would die behind a fence, somewhere, and good riddance to his stupid, fruitless life . . .

But the sun was warming him so tenderly, warming every vein and fiber . . . the sun was bringing him comfort—was bringing him hope . . . that pensive sadness was coming on which winged his thoughts. He would like to work out a poem—such a poem as would sing to those who were as he was now—a poem that would comfort and give hope to him, Moishe, and to thousands of Moishes like him. And suddenly a beautiful line leaped into his eager mind; this line called forth a second line, and a third, and a fourth—and slowly, bit by bit, a new poem was being born—it was not human beings he should dislike, he was saying in his new poem, and not life that he should hate. What he should hate were the unjust practices in life—the injustices all about him. Now, in his poem, he was addressing the young chap who wanted to lose himself and sink into the unreality of tramp life. He was calling him back. Let him rise up on his young strong feet. Let him stride back into this hard, merciless life and set it astir . . .

His Brother's Check

ABRAHAM RAISIN _____

MR. GOLDBERG, a man in his thirties, with a long, lean face wearing a careworn expression, was looking through the morning mail in his office. There was little to read in the letters. A few words, clearly set down as only a typewriter can do it (handwritten letters hardly ever came to him), informed him of the business at hand. The letters were not only written on a machine, but seemed machinelike in content, and Goldberg, who was romantically inclined, felt, as he read them, that he was walking along a smooth pavement without a tree on either side, without a flower or a blade of grass.

It was even more difficult for him to answer the letters, that is, to dictate the answers to his stenographer. The words dropped from his mouth mechanically while the girl set them down in shorthand, then began hammering them out on the machine. Only for his signature did Goldberg need to use a pen. But even the signature seemed to come out from a machine. One signature did not differ from another. His name, Harry Goldberg, was always of the same length, width and height, somewhat angular and written brusquely. The last stroke ended in a small hook . . .

Often he himself would wonder that his signature was so unchanging. When he was a boy, he recalled, he would always sign his name differently. The memory of those varying signatures sometimes filled him with longing. But some important business matter would tear him from the sentimental mood and he became again the businessman governed by duties, laws, and rules . . .

A man entered the office.

Goldberg answered his greeting, pointed to a chair, and was soon engaged in going over some accounts with the caller. Then he wrote a check, gave it to the man, and waited for him to leave.

However, after putting the check into his pocket, the man remained seated and with a friendlier expression he said: "You know, Mr. Goldberg, I bring you regards."

"From whom?" Goldberg asked with slight interest.

"From a brother of yours—"

"A brother!" Goldberg now spoke with more feeling. "I have only one brother here—"

"That's your brother, then. We happen to live in the same house . . . He's a very fine person . . . not very rich . . . A child of his is sick . . ."

Goldberg flushed with a sudden embarrassment, but quickly his gray eyes brightened and he murmured:

"So, from my brother . . . Yes, thanks very much . . . a child of his is sick? Oh, that's bad, too bad."

His scattered words sounded so strange in the office that Goldberg, the stenographer, and the visitor looked surprised.

Goldberg was almost shamed by this unforeseen occurrence, and when the man left he felt greatly relieved.

His brother's face kept floating before Goldberg's—this brother whom he had not seen for a long time because he was always busy. It seemed to fill the office . . . wherever Goldberg turned, there was his brother whom he had always loved . . .

Now he wanted to go to him at once, to find out about the ailing child. But—there were such important business matters today. Tomorrow? No, tomorrow would be impossible, too . . . or the entire week.

I'll write him a letter, meanwhile, send him a check. . . , Goldberg decided, and in his agitation he said aloud: "I must write him a letter!"

The stenographer, hearing the words "a letter," took her place at Goldberg's desk with her pad.

"No, no," Goldberg began to stammer bashfully. "This is a different kind of letter . . . I must write this one myself." He added with a smile: "This is a letter to a brother."

At first the girl looked at Goldberg as if she did not understand, then she said: "Oh, to a brother . . . That's nice!"

There was a wave of brotherly feeling in the air.

In his own hand Goldberg wrote to his brother, the letters full and carefully formed, as he had written them in his boyhood; they poured themselves out onto the white sheet, and at every sentence Goldberg stopped to admire his script. A new kind of letter for him.

Even on the check which he drew for his brother, Goldberg wrote each letter with fond care. The word "fifty" looked as if it had been etched, and his brother's name was spread across the entire line. He took particular pains over his own signature. It had been a long time since he took such pleasure in signing a check. If only he might add to his signature the word "brother"! Let them know in the bank that this was not just an ordinary check, but a check for his brother . . .

A few days later, going through the morning's mail, Goldberg opened a letter and found in it a familiar check—the check he had sent to his brother.

His brother thanked him for his kindness and regretted that the check had been returned by the bank because it seemed improperly drawn. He hoped that it would be corrected.

Goldberg examined the check and looked for the flaw.

He smiled bitterly: The signature was not like his accustomed one. This was a different Goldberg: full, round, and firm. No! The bank knew another Goldberg! This one was unknown!

And Goldberg was deeply ashamed.

The Dog

SHEEN MILLER _____

TWILIGHT.

The evening star had already pierced the sky, evening stillness was swaying in the air, the evening shadows were already spreading on the ground. The man—between Heaven and Earth—himself a shadow, a silhouette—scarcely moving, muffled steps on woolly ground, felt, rather than heard, that someone, something, was following him. He turned his head, sharply stopped. Man and dog looked at one another.

The dog was not to his liking. Nothing evil about him that he saw. Muzzle pointed, sharp, but not wicked. With such a muzzle a dog nudges sheep, helps the shepherd guard and guide his flock; however, peaceful, friendly though he was, the dog was not to his liking. How hairy he was! Really like a bear, and reddish-brown, as if somewhat rusty not only in individual hairs, but in strands and tufts. Must be frightfully filthy. He made a motion with his hand—Go away!

The dog made a move sideways, stood still, looked the man in the eye: "It won't help you to chase me" . . . and the man felt that he was helpless. He turned around and began walking slowly, so slowly that the dog could hardly hold that pace. He followed nevertheless.

What do you care if the dog is following? Barking dogs don't bite. But this dog doesn't bark, a stealthy dog—without warning he'll snap at your calf . . . What a fool you are! You saw for yourself—a collie—he won't bite. It's the Jew in you that's frightened by the dog. A goy would have patted his head, spoken to him, played with him. Touch that filthy dog? He is filthy, much too filthy to . . . Is he still following? I'll stop walking—see what he'll do.

He stopped, and the dog also stopped. A standstill. A contest as to who would stir first . . . Motionless as during the Eighteen Benedictions. He did not look at the dog. It was the sky he looked at, where he could see three stars already. What about turning back, going home? No good: The dog would follow. But just standing here was no good either. Just then the dog saw a tree and was drawn to it. And now he has raised a hind leg—good, very good! Quickly the man turned and as quickly started on the way back to his home. A few steps and he realized the dog was running after him. Defeated. Let him follow. But at home . . .

Getting home, he sneaked into the house, stood stock still, listened. He heard a scratching at the door: Let me in!

He wouldn't think of letting him in. But how about opening the door to drive him away? No. He'll go away himself. No more scratching. Gone? He shoved aside a curtain, looked to one side and then another. Not there. Must have gone. Obviously a lost dog, strayed from his owner. Perhaps he should have taken him in, after all: A dog can serve as a watchman, can even prove a good companion. But he hated dogs. Good riddance.

He switched on a light. Radiance leaped into being, the dog leaped off into nonexistence, into nonbeing, in fact, had never been. But when he had seated himself, looked at his watch, seen that it was twelve after, and bethought himself: Autumn, days are short, nights are long, long nights . . . He suddenly shuddered and feared to look down at the side of his chair: He actually felt that the dog was lying there . . . Nerves. He passed his hand over his hair. His hair, still thick all his fifty-seven years, was brushed smooth . . . those nerves . . . He saw a book on the table and picked it up. The down-turned corner of the page said: "Here's your place; go on from here." He started to read. The letters—the eyes of a dog, words—the pointed muzzle, lines—tufts of hair. He put the book down, walked into the next room, turned a knob of the radio in the dark by the light of the radio bulb, turned another to Station MPS. They played records, but it was good music.

The dog did not intrude into the music. Later, in the man's sleep, the dog did come in and, in the man's dream, was even angry enough to bite . . . so that he woke with a scream. Devil take it all! He vented his spleen at the dog, tried to fall asleep again, could not, was filled with rage at the animal. However, when the housekeeper came to clean up and prepare his meal in the morning and asked him: "Whose is the dog?" he pretended to wonder and asked: "What dog?"

"Right by the house. Some kind of filthy dog. Must be lost. Doesn't have a tag. I don't like him."

"And what did you do?"

"Drove him away."

"Very well." As the words left his mouth, a hint of a smile shone in his eyes: "Are you sure? I am not so sure."

As was her habit, the woman set to work, prepared meals, and tidied up.

The meat scraps and other leavings she carried out and put into the garbage can.

When, later, she went into the yard to hang up a blanket for airing, he heard her talking and screaming at someone. He went out.

"See what he has done, dirty dog!"

He saw. The can was overturned and the contents were spilled.

"Are you sure that he did it?"

"Who else? I suppose I did it? Just look at the way he stands there, the dirty brute. Away from here, you dirty dog!"

The dog was not at all disturbed by her screams or her gestures to drive him away.

"He must be hungry."

"Hungry! Let him go to his owner, not overturn garbage cans and dirty the yard."

"You said yourself he's a lost dog—he has no owner."

"I'll find an owner for him. I'll call the police, the dogcatchers. They'll give him what he deserves."

And she did just that.

He sat and heard as she spoke, no, screamed into the telephone that the dogcatchers should come at once, and he thought of lost dogs and a civilized society that cannot tolerate such things. Human beings may not beg in the streets unless they are among the privileged . . . cripples, ex-soldiers, and even they must be salesmen . . . pencils, shoelaces, merchants, so to say, on however small a scale . . . only no frank misery. And here is a dog without a license, comes and takes upon himself the privilege of begging of the garbage can . . . What do you mean begging! Actually robbing it! Would the law enforcers, the dogcatchers, really come for him?

They did come. The woman went out to them, he followed, like a child following grown-ups, eager to see, to hear. He heard: "He was right here in the yard while I was calling you."

"Is it a collie with rust-colored hair?"

"Rusty is right. He is one piece of rust. What a dog."

"That's true. He is filthy, but he's also clever."

"Clever?"

"Madame! You are the sixth woman who has called us to catch this dog, but he is so damned clever that as soon as he sees us, smells the wagon, he runs off like a hare, like a deer."

"Can't you catch him?" The woman's tone said: "Dogcatchers!"

"I tell you he runs like a hare . . ."

"Can't you shoot him?"

"Hm . . . yes, we could do that but the law doesn't allow it. You might shoot at the dog and hit a person, a passerby. No, we can't do that, but we'll get him. Just don't worry. We'll surely get him and you can help us. Yes, you can help. The next time he comes, don't chase him away. Feed him instead, and fool him into going there, into that toolhouse; lock him in, then call us."

The dogcatcher was so pleased with his scheme that he looked smilingly at the woman: How do you like my idea?

Her look: How clever of you! If I lock him in, you'll catch him. Nevertheless, she promised to do it.

The dogcatcher said: "That's it. The next time we come we'll not leave empty-handed." He smiled, said good-bye, and drove off.

"Great dogcatchers," the woman remarked. The man smiled. Had the dog appeared just then, the man would have patted him: pretty shrewd fellow!

The dog did not come. Days passed, a week, two weeks—no sign of the dog. The first few days, on going out for his evening stroll, the man would look about. Perhaps the dog was following him. After that, he did not even do this; he had already forgotten the dog. Until one evening.

All that day he had not felt too well; nevertheless, he had started out on his stroll which, in the course of years, had become a kind of ritual. Walking thus, slowly to be sure, he felt in the dusk and stillness that he was part of the world, that he was in close union with it. Therefore the slightest rustle could break this unity with the world, and he had become so sensitive that he could hear, no—even feel—when a leaf fell from a nearby twig.

He felt that something was following him and shuddered as the thought crossed his mind: the dog! In spite of that, when he turned around and saw him he was surprised: Here again? He recalled the dog's cleverness in outwitting the dogcatchers, but instead of calling to pat him—clever fellow that you are—he looked at him and thought: Is he really so clever? Did he recognize me? Maybe his nose did, maybe his nose knew the man by scent, but did his brain do so? Did the dog, recognizing him as the person who had called the dogcatchers (although it was not he), now want to have it out, to square accounts?

He could make nothing out of the dog's posture, out of the movement of his muzzle, but he was altogether in the dark when he saw that his tail was motionless. Was this a sign of enmity?

Whatever the dog felt, friendship or animosity, he himself certainly felt friendly toward the animal. "Next time the dog comes, fool him and call us." No, he had no intention of driving him off, nor would he deceive him, and he would certainly not call the dogcatchers. The dog would follow him? Let him. All the better . . .

When he got to the house he did not enter by the front door. He admitted the dog into the yard, and then went into the house by the rear door, and into the kitchen. The white door of the refrigerator was dazzling. He opened the door and, by the light of the bulb inside, found a piece of meat, a potato. What else? Bread. He closed the refrigerator and opened the bread box. When he had assembled the meal, he carried it out. He did not throw it but, instead, set it down on the ground and pointed to it: "This is for you, or rather, be seated at table."

A grinding of teeth and the table was cleared. The upturned muzzle asked: Is there any more? He had no more food for the dog so he pointed to the grass—you now go to sleep. The dog sniffed the grass, poked it with a paw, scrutinized it: Nothing there, that's clear. The man smiled: You certainly understand, but, at that, it is not easy to communicate with you. That's the way it is. He waved his hand—good night to you—went into the house, and fastened the chain catch on the door.

In the darkness, he sat and thought: Clearly, a dog can reason. He recognizes things, people, so he must remember. Well, yes, he scents, but he no longer recognizes his owner in spite of his sense of smell. He had read about the loyalty of dogs to their owners, to children, and had even read of a dog's suicide after his owner died. Well, all of that is "literature."

But that a dog should be aware of the owner's absence is altogether reasonable—the owner means food. Does the dog see the connection? Pavlov's dog did. Pavlov's dog. Can this dog make the connection, connect this yard with the dogcatchers? Apparently not. But Pavlov? Oh, well, after hard work he succeeded in fashioning a . . . reflex. Whereupon wise ones came and transposed this very reflex to human beings, but these wise ones are, if you will forgive me, great fools. We can remember "via stomach" when it is time to eat, but why and how did it happen that, at this very moment, he remembered Shaya Michael, the son of Chassie? Oh yes, he had read about this sort of thing in so-called scientific works, but in actuality this, too, was "literature." "We recall the pleasurable, forget the painful." Untrue, Rabbi Freud. We forget the good, but if anyone says an evil word to us, we remember it down to our dying day. "A blow will pass, but a word endures." But we remember the blow, too.

To this very day he remembers how, on the first of Pesach, he went out for a game of Nuts and how, after the game, they came to blows and Shmitzie, the Bull (that was what he was called), tore the pocket off his new suit. Not only that, but precisely because of that torn pocket, he remembers the Pesach of fifty years ago. This he remembers, but what he ate the night before he cannot recall. How does one remember? That is, what is the process? How does it work? In old age one remembers his childhood—as the saying goes: "What has been learned in childhood is never forgotten." Then how is it he has forgotten to say the prayer Ashry, he who knew the prayers by heart at the age of six?

Proverbs are not to be taken literally, and theories are not the Laws of Moses. Speculations. What does the laboratory say?

The laboratory?

The electroencephalograph. Although he had never seen one, he imagined it was somewhat like a cardiograph. He had seen a cardiogram of his very own heart. The doctor had been friendly enough to show it to him. He looked at it: lines, flat, pointed. As far as he could see, it might have been a diagram of hills or, for that matter, the skyline of New York. He told that to the doctor. The latter smiled: "It is of your heart, and it shows your heart is normal, the circulation is normal. However, let there be a disturbance—a coronary thrombosis, let us say

. . . What is that? A blood clot forms in the coronary vessels, but the blood must circulate past the clot. In that case the cardiogram would be altogether different. You see, one must be able to read a cardiogram."

That was the specialist talking to the layman.

He had asked nothing more. After all, he had not come for a course in medicine. He supposed that the psychiatrist, in the same way, explained the cephalogram or the psychogram or the psychometer—if there are any such "gadgets." "Such and such a line shows the flow of thought is normal." But—what is the flow of thought? And what is normal?

"Thought waves, brainstorms."

Einstein sits and thinks about the theory of the unified electromagnetic field and a stamp dealer sits and sells stamps. Both are doing their normal work and thoughts are flowing on a normal course. But Einstein comes up with the energy-matter formula—E=mc2—and a gambler comes up with a new scheme for some deal. In both cases, so to say, a "brainstorm" has occurred. Laughable. And here's something else: Did the thought bring the "brainstorm" or did the "brainstorm" occasion the thought? The old story—the chicken and the egg . . .

So little is known about the brain, the all-knowing, but that same brain has come to know a great many things. And not merely to know but to achieve things—to make a machine, for instance, which not only computes complicated figures more rapidly than the human brain, but also remembers them. A machine with a memory! Oh, yes, man himself built the memory into the machine. He knows what button to push to evoke the memory. But where is the button in man, and who or what pushes it? This "machine" is a little too complicated, which may explain why there are so many "machinists"—psychologists, biologists, physicists, chemists. To what effect? Oh, a great deal has been done—all the vaccines and antibiotics—many plagues have been averted, and much more will be uncovered. But when they will have found the remedy for every ill, will they get rid of the plague of death? And if, in the laboratory, they do create life, will they put an end to death?

Abolish death? No, not that. It should not be abolished. To live forever? Dreadful, even to think of it. Billions, trillions of human beings . . . One *must* die. Yes, that one there! As for me . . .

I really don't want to live forever, either, not even the traditional Jewish one hundred and twenty. I'd agree to something less . . . Only not a lingering death, a drawn-out illness. If it is not to be by going to the outskirts of town and sitting down somewhere on a stone and not getting up again, then let it be by getting into bed and falling asleep . . .

And when shall it happen?

Not today, of course, not today and not tomorrow, and not . . . Hypocrite!

The miser, large as his hoard of gold may be . . . still fears that he is dying poor.

The sick man, old and ill as he may be, is afraid of dying before "his hour."

No, he was not afraid.

What then?

Just thinking.

Fool! You want to get to the bottom of all things in one shot, to figure things out to the very end. It's not for you to complete the task.* Should you follow things to the very end, you will arrive only at your own end. However, by the world's reckoning your end may the beginning of . . . worms or the devil knows. So what have you figured out?

He took out his handkerchief and wiped his face and neck. He was drenched in sweat—how man thinks, how he remembers, is far from being clear. But it is clear that thinking is a difficult matter, he thought, not without a smile. And all because of a dog . . . and perhaps it had nothing to do with the dog or thinking: Maybe it was just fatigue, although he had really done nothing but think. Maybe he ought to read something so as not to think? Or it might be better to lie down, get into bed. Call it a night. If he didn't sleep? There was his little drugstore: first of all—the nitroglycerin pills—a sleeping tablet, a glass of water. What else? Perhaps a piece of chocolate? If he did not sleep and felt hungry, he'd have a bite. Or, perhaps, take the Carbitol right now, fall asleep. No, still too early.

He might drowse off himself. Tired. Very tired.

How long he had been sleeping he did not know. He was awakened by the howling of a dog. At first he thought he had dreamt it. But wait, what had he dreamed? As he tried to disentangle the threads of his dream, he definitely heard the baying of a dog, a long, long blowing of a horn. The quavering howl poured down upon his body. He shud-

From "Sayings of the Fathers."

dered. "Baying dogs announce the Angel of Death." Quiet, it has stopped. There it is again! The dog in the yard. May he drop dead! Didn't like him at first sight. Shouldn't have fed him, should have driven him off. Maybe now he . . . There, again!

He turned on a light, slipped into a robe, opened the door, and, speaking quietly but firmly, said: "Go away!" He waved his hand. "Off with you! Off!" The dog did not stir. The man seized the broom in the entrance hall, went out, and made a fanning motion. The dog moved from a sitting to a standing position, but did not leave his place. He remained still without howling.

Nasty dog. I ought to kill him, or at least give him a good beating, chase him away. Nevertheless, he looked about him; somebody might be watching his battle with the dog, with broom-gun in hand . . . The darkness of the neighboring houses, the thick silence, told him he was not being observed, that it must be extremely late. But he appeared comical to himself—in bathrobe and with the broom. He spoke quietly: "Go away!" But now this was no longer a threat, or an order, but a plea. And, leaning on the broom, he went back to the hall, to his room, to bed. He turned out the light, lay, waited.

Five minutes, ten? The dog began to howl again. What to do? Go out again? It would be no use. He'd better take the sleeping pill.

He was already holding the pill between two fingers and was raising the glass of water with the other hand, when the telephone began to ring. The telephone now? He got out of bed, turned on a light, lifted the receiver. "Why, in the devil's name, don't you drive that damned dog away?"

He recognized the voice—that of a neighbor.

"I tried to drive him away, but he won't go."

"Then why the devil don't you call the police?"

"Police?"

"Yes! Po-leece! They'll come, shoot him, seize him, and not let him . . ."

"The dog does not belong to me. You can call the police, too."

"In whose yard is he? Well, then it's y-o-u-r funeral!"

"What! What did you say? My fu . . ."

So sharp was the pain that his hand leaped to his chest. The telephone receiver, telephone, telephone stand, the chair on which he sat, and he himself—all fell as all fall at the broken sounds of the ram's horn.

And—when, after those broken sounds, there ensued the great silence—a silence which filled the vacuum following on the sounds—it chanced that the telephone receiver, a deaf stethoscope, lay against the stilled heart and silently certified . . . dead. And in the yard the dog began anew his loud baying, bay-ay-ing: dead . . . dead . . .

PART SIX

Not All Greenhorns Are Jewish!

Quiet Words

BORECH GLASSMAN _____

IN FRONT OF HER, little flames, tiny electric fires, lit up all the time. It was a cold stormy day in the Catskills. All around the village, where the local telephone exchange was installed, farms and houses were scattered on peaks and on naked, bald hills and white, snow-filled valleys. On such days the farmers could not come to town. They would call up the shops, would find out how an acquaintance on the farther slope of the mountain, in a distant fold of the valley, near a rock fault by the road, was making out. Snow flurries were swinging and tearing through the air. The telephone wires carried warm, close intimacies through the frost, through the white, isolated air of the frozen hills and valleys.

Bundled and wrapped in furs and all sorts of rags, isolated farmers kept carrying armloads of wood from the woodpile in the yard to the kitchen. Again a return to the woodpile and further splitting, with a sharp axe, of the logs of sawn, young trees. Sounds of the axe echoed in the frosty air. After this, the farmers entered the nearby stables to let their frozen limbs thaw out in the warmth of cattle breath and manure. From the heaving flanks of the cattle and from their sweating bodies there issued a steamy vapor like that from warm wrapping when exposed to the icy outdoors.

The girl worked on the second floor of a house near the railroad station. Before her was the low, wide switchboard, which resembled the reading stand of a poor, small, provincial synagogue. Over her head the girl wore a semihoop of steel which ended, on either side, in a small circular cup over the ear.

From minute to minute on the black board in front of her, a little flame lit up, a tiny electric bulb.

"Hello! Hello! Hello! Yes, thank you. Hello? I am ringing your party . . ." And again a tiny flame, and again a voice that always sounded hoarse, cold, excited, discontented, angry, and as distant and moldy as the other side of the Earth.

Like the movements of a dead, metal creature, controlled by invisible springs, were the movements of the girl. She spoke to pieces of iron, to various dead, unknown, metal objects, in all directions of the surrounding region. There was not one movement of thought in her mind while she made telephone connections for callers, answering calls, listening mechanically to see that the conversations were in progress.

The room was cold. From time to time the girl would go to the small stove and throw in a piece of wood. And now for a while the telephone board became quiet. This happened occasionally, somewhat suddenly. Perhaps everywhere, in all places, in the widely scattered houses folks had gone to bed, or were sitting down to meals, or were snowed in by the flurries. The storm had grown more furious; the wires must have been torn.

The girl went to the window. This was a Jewish village. Before her lay one street, wet and trodden. No matter how much it snowed in a winter, in this street the whiteness was always trodden and turned into a yellow porridge. There were a couple of clumsy sleighs, filled with milk cans, which some poor farmers, having no cream separators, had barely driven to the cooperative creamery. A few people, risking life and limb, dashed rapidly from one store to another. They were carrying loaves of bread in sacks. On the small station platform, several tall, lean Jews wandered around with a couple of short, squat, roly-poly women and just could not come to agreement about something that concerned them. They kept looking back, behind them, to see whether they were not being asked to return. These were some New Yorkers who had come betimes to rent boarding places for the summer. The girl listened to the wind whining and hurling dry snow in the biting air.

Across the way, through the window, the girl suddenly saw the face of the young druggist, who was frowning with boredom, describing circles on the glass door with his finger, thus thawing little windows in the frost of the glass through which he looked out on the world outside. Sharply, abruptly, instantaneously, the girl turned her eyes away.

His round, broad face, like a gourd, with hairs bristling all over it, looked to her in that moment like a spider in the midst of its web.

She crossed to the opposite side of the room, and looked out of the windows on that side. These windows opened on the snow-covered land. This land, white and wintry in appearance, brought rest and tranquillity to the girl in the house. There, on the empty slopes of the hills, stretched fields of snow cut up, here and there, by black fences with an occasional upthrust of dark, isolated brush. The girl was tempted to leave her solitary room and go walking along the fences across the dark. To walk, walk, walk ceaselessly, up to one of those distant fields, then to crawl to the last still, greenish field—a dark, a restless, and an unfortunate stain—to lie down there, in the snow, to merge with and pour herself into that dead, tranquil whiteness. That would put an end to her sorrows, uncertainties, and sufferings.

But such white fields on the hillsides were infrequent. Besides, in the whistling hurly-burly of the stinging whirlwind, they would hide from her sight. In the unusually long and marvelously woven net of snow dust, the greater portion of the mountains was covered with nude, plucked, and empty woods, black woods. They looked like mere skeletons of trees. Thin, naked, such dead growth as pointed up the total whiteness around her and in deadly silence spread a menace in the air— like tree-high crows. That, too, was the way the girl felt at heart— naked, dark, emptied, frozen.

As she allowed her eyes to run along the tracks to the distant curve around the hill, her heart was seized with pain and longing. What was she doing here, in this place, where she had met with such misfortune? Perhaps, if she were to leave this place, she would feel easier, she would forget everything. To the east, where the trains ran, there were certainly many cities and towns with new, unknown beings. For example, New York. There lived the girl, the druggist's betrothed, whom he would soon make his wife. With her, the village girl, he had merely trifled. She tried to imagine what kind of girl the other was. In what way was the other better? Most likely she was fat and Jewish. All Jewesses were fat. Unlike her—delicate, slender. With youthful cynicism, born in her recently, after the first disillusionment in her life, she added, her lips grimacing thereby: "They all like them fat."

Suddenly she realized that her thoughts were ugly. To think how low she had fallen!

She felt so depressed. Perhaps she ought to go off to her father, to the small, remote, forsaken farmhouse in the village with the old Indian name, a place the Jews had not yet infected with their turmoil. A few moments of silent thought went by. Then she tossed her head, bit her lip, and dismissed further thought of her father. To what end? Had she even consulted him before this? She had obeyed only this one, and for his sake immured herself in this house, bound to the switchboard all summer and now through the winter, so it would be more comfortable and convenient for him to meet her as he should desire. She had no strength to withstand his demands because she loved him.

Her eyes roamed farther along the tracks, shining, cold, frozen. Above them a frosty vapor fluttered, like heat waves above a radiator. The tracks run past little villages and towns throughout the mountains. Human beings everywhere. What did her pain matter to them? Possibly there were young girls there who were concealing sorrows within themselves. But that could not be. The like of what had happened to her had never happened to anyone.

A railroad worker in blue overalls went by and began climbing a signal post. He lit a deep blue light. Was he happy? She ought to go to this unknown man, throw herself at his feet, tell him of her hurt, of how she had been wronged. He was human, would he not help her? Suddenly she laughed so loudly that she was almost frightened, and looked about in the room to see that there was no one who had overheard her. It came to her that in that moment her former childhood had returned to her, with her faith in people, in all people. She was much brighter now. Although only eighteen, she now knew better after what had happened to her. She knew that every single one is alone in the world, alone with all his sorrows, and no one can look for help to anyone. You must help yourself. And if that be the case, she would surely help herself. She already knew how. She had given it enough thought in the last several weeks. She would help herself, help herself. How? Yes, in this very manner.

The girl's thoughts seemed track-bound. They were cut off only where the rails disappeared behind a hill. Miles and miles away—New York. She would not go to New York. There she would surely be trampled underfoot. She was certain that every woman there was hounded by men who would quickly detect that she had been victimized already, and would hound her the more. That New York! Why, this druggist with the round face framed in tiny yellow bristles, as in a spider's web, was from New York himself.

There was no one to whom she might go, no place to go. She would remain here. It was the same everywhere. The girl was filled with deep doubt and distrust of people. She was afraid to tell anyone about her misfortune or to ask for advice. Should anyone know about what had happened to her, for appearance's sake he would sympathize deeply with her but, at the same time, would certainly be laying plans to snare her for himself. No, there was no place to go. She did not want to and she could not leave this place before she had freed herself of the feeling of degradation by which she was overwhelmed. She would never again know of a day freed from this feeling of depression, of having been trampled upon, a feeling that hung onto her and bent her to the earth. She saw no other way out, if she were to free herself of this feeling, breathe freely, straighten up, and look people in the eyes, save to rid the world, cleanse the world of him.

She had made up her mind what to do. In the papers she had frequently read of similar instances. She had no fears on that score—the court would free her. She was sure of that, as she was sure of her justification. Indeed, she would do it this very evening, when the druggist closed his shop and went home. The house in which he lived was off to a side, almost completely isolated in a field. She would wait for the moment when the last train to New York went clanging by. In the turmoil, surely no one would hear the shot.

Quietly she went to a front window which opened on the street. From a corner, hidden by a curtain, she looked out. The druggist was still standing by the door. She looked at his face, always so dear to her. That childishly full, smiling face. With pain she felt that she still loved him, loved him to the point of hatred. At the same time she touched, in her bosom, the small, cold automatic revolver which she had obtained on the plea of self-protection because she went home late at night. As if in anticipation, that sweet listlessness of total calm and assuagement descended upon the girl.

In the afternoon a telephone operator in New York called her and said she had a long-distance call for someone in her area. The call was to some forlorn farmhouse having a party line.

The girl called the farmhouse and made the connection, with New York. As usual, she listened in to make sure the connection was clear and the conversation was in progress. She heard a man's voice from New York:

"Hello! Hello! Hello! Does Mr. Carlen live here?"

From the farmhouse, noisily and angrily, the coarse voice of a woman shrieked in broken English:

"Who is? Hello! What you want? Who is? Who? Hello! Hello!"

The man's voice tried to explain at first quietly, then more loudly, who he was. But it was futile. In the middle of the talk, the woman in the farmhouse hung up the receiver. For a while, the telephone operator kept ringing but no longer got any response from the woman.

Then the girl explained to the man that she could not make the connection. Thereupon, a man's voice, refined, gentle, and strong, answered. He pleaded urgently that she put the call through. He was going to arrive from New York that very evening, without being expected. He was coming to see his sister on a matter of great importance, and the woman in the farmhouse was his sister. Since the mountain roads were surely covered with snow and the nights were dark, and the farmhouse to which he was going was several miles from the station, and he was not being expected, he wanted to inform his folks that they should have some vehicle await him at the station.

The voice, speaking to her, was refined, hearty, and persuasive. The girl again tried to make the connection. From the farmhouse the shrieking issued once more: now in Yiddish, now in English:

"Hello! Hello! Hello! What you want? Eh? What? Who you want?"

The voice from New York could not achieve any kind of communication with the farm woman. The latter finally took offense, was certain that she was being disturbed for no good reason, that no one in New York could be calling her, that this was all a mistake, that it was surely a call for some other farmer since this was a party line, and besides she had an infant which she was neglecting and which now was crying without letup. With a bang, she hung up the receiver.

The man's well-bred voice was filled with deep concern. The man in distant New York was so deeply troubled that he had obviously forgotten that you do not let yourself slip into private talk with a telephone operator. What should he do now? He could not send a telegram because in such weather they would surely not send a special messenger off to the farmhouse. Besides, it was almost evening and the Western Union in the village closed at five. And he had to get there today—because of a very, very important matter. It was a matter involving—uh, uh—involving—a betrothal. It had to be settled by the very next day.

At this moment he seemed to realize that he had gone too far in these private concerns. He offered a thousand apologies. His voice was soft and awkward.

He was so puzzled about what to do that he must have chewed off her ear.

The girl at the telephone reassured him—she did not mind. She had been so moved that a total stranger would confide in her, that she promised:

"I will try again several times. I will surely get your number. Surely, surely."

The girl was not accustomed to having anyone talk to her so gently and quietly. Usually the voices were coarse, demanding; the callers would quickly flare up in anger if they did not get their numbers at once, or if she made any kind of mistake. Even village folk she knew, when they spoke to her by telephone, would speak in tones that were cold, rude, matter-of-fact, quick to take offense. And here was a total stranger, more than a hundred miles away, a person she had never seen and whom she would never in her life meet, speaking with such softness, gentleness, and refinement in his voice. The stranger's concern suddenly came close to her, became her own, as though a brother were speaking to her.

She tried several times more to call the farm. In vain. The woman there did not understand her. She thereupon rang up the unknown New Yorker to explain, with a smile in her voice, that "the woman must be a greenhorn, a foreigner—it could not be otherwise. I am very sorry, awfully sorry."

The man must have sensed the friendliness in her voice for he also laughed amiably, and thanked her many times for being so kind to him. There was no help for it, he would have to take a chance. Whatever would be, would be. And since he could not cut short the conversation in midcourse, he put some questions to her about the weather.

"It must be very cold up your way, in the country, very cold. Is it?"

"Certainly," she answered him. "It certainly is. The cold burns like fire."

Because they had nothing more to talk about, both of them felt uncomfortable about hanging up.

"Do you know what?" A thought struck her and filled her, suddenly, with a warm glow. "It's possible that because of the distance—more than a hundred miles—and especially in this stormy weather—you and that woman can't get together. However, come up here as you have decided, and call your folks from the railroad station. Over this two—or three-mile distance you'll surely get through to them, and they'll send someone for you."

For the rest of the afternoon the girl felt unusually well disposed, warm, and at ease. She recalled that she had not had a bite to eat all day long. She now went to prepare something at the coal stove in the room. She felt somehow more peaceful and calm. Looking into the glowing red coal, she tried to imagine what that man must look like. That he was a young man—she was sure. And he would always wear a gentle, almost childish smile on his face. And what kind of lips did he have?

It was evening. The cold and wind increased. The train from New York was not due for another three hours. She laughed quietly to herself. It meant that she, too, was waiting for the arrival of the train, much as if a kinsman of hers were about to arrive. Suddenly her heart began to beat more rapidly at the intrusion of a happy thought: She would call the farmhouse immediately, tell the woman that her brother was coming, and that she should dispatch someone to meet him. The girl was now aglow as she pictured the pleasurable surprise that the stranger would have on his arrival.

A moment later she called the farm. There was no answer. She soon realized that the phone was out of order.

For some time she sat as if congealed, and was not able to move from her place. Tiny fires flared up on the switchboard, but she did not lift a hand. The stranger was coming and would not be able to reach his folks by phone. There would be no car at his disposal. It was already late and in winter nights there were no cars or other vehicles at the station. He would have to walk miles in this cold, in pitch darkness, over a twisting road between waste and pitted fields. And she was to blame—she had herself advised him to come.

Pale, uncertain, and her only thought was that when the train arrived she would have to go to the station to offer the stranger a thousand apologies. How would she recognize him? She would observe who lingered and walked about alone in the station. And what would she do after that?

Minute sped after minute in strange, unusual swiftness, more rapidly than ever before in her life. Train time was drawing closer. The girl became nervous and uneasy. She felt a sense of release when the night operator came to relieve her. Swiftly, she left the house.

It was now late evening. One after another, the stores in the village began to close and the streets became empty and dead. It was so dark that only close to the snow was it still possible to distinguish anything. The girl did not want to go for her dinner to the boardinghouse where she was staying. She walked back and forth on the sidewalk, past the stores, as if, in thus walking about, she wished to keep the lighted shops from turning out their lights and the area around the station from turning dead and silent, as it usually was late at night. Hardly anyone ever got off at the station from the eleven o'clock train.

A half hour passed. All the stores were now dark. The druggist had also turned off the large electric light above the door. The street had become gloomy. Only in several houses were lights still showing in the bedrooms, which were being warmed for bedtime. With nights as cold as this, all went to sleep early. All alone, the girl continued to walk the platform of the small railroad station which projected into the very center of the business block. She saw the druggist, vigorous, rotund, and prematurely obese, go home. At that moment she had no feelings about him, no stirring of any kind. She remained strangely unmoved.

On the other side, in a barn deep in a courtyard, a door was opened. There was a burst of light in the darkness. Someone, heavily coated, emerged in the light. That was the bakery, and work was beginning there. This was the only sign of life in the night-engulfed village. The girl crossed to that side.

In the yard, under a shed, there stood a horse and sleigh and a Gentile farmer was attending to the horse and removing a blanket from the animal. He was ready to set off. She knew the farmer. She approached and greeted him. In a moment he began to complain to her about something.

At first the girl did not hear anything. She felt happy in the mere knowledge that there was another living being outdoors with her, who was speaking and warming with his breath the cold and the night. In a little while she began to follow his talk. He had come to town in midday and had brought a few sacks of potatoes. Ordinarily, by midday there was a large number of Jewish farmers from nearby and he had no difficulty finding a buyer for his wares. But today, because of the severe storm and the cold, no one came. He waited and waited. All for nothing. He had left the sacks of potatoes with the Jewish baker. He was going home now—after losing half a day for nothing.

The girl became aware that her heart was beating more rapidly and she made a conscious effort to calm it. She almost screamed in the anxiety that beset her. It seemed to her that she spoke too loudly and excitedly, and that she aroused suspicion. Actually, she was speaking quietly and calmly.

"Why," she said to him, "since you are here now, why shouldn't you wait till the train from New York arrives? You may get a passenger, earn a few dollars, and your trip will be worthwhile."

Indifferently, the farmer waved his hand. "As late as this? No one would be coming to such a desolate place at this hour."

But she herself had seen such an arrival. A few nights ago she went by here—she had stayed late at the home of a friend—and had seen several passengers who went about looking for a conveyance—in vain. And they were willing to pay, and pay well.

The farmer would not believe it. The girl began to persuade, to convince him that she was telling the truth. He regarded her with suspicion. He noticed that her eyes were flashing and that she was aflame. Probably this was all a trick of some kind, hidden from him, he thought, and started to busy himself with the harness and halter, and to fasten the iron fittings of his sleigh.

Now she no longer spoke in this vein. She questioned him about his family and how things were going on the farm. Had his sow given him a good litter? And what about the bull, did they still have to set the dog on him to drive him away from the barn? And did he expect to tap a lot of maple syrup the coming spring? Had he provided himself with new buckets? Three hundred?

She spoke and spoke incessantly, and he could not drive away. Now there remained only a quarter of an hour before the arrival of the train. The farmer began to bethink himself. He got down from his seat, withdrew the blanket from the wagon, and once more covered the horse.

"I forgot something," he said. "I've still to buy a loaf in the bakery."

She bade him good night and went away.

In the still, cold night of the other side of the mountain there sounded the hooting of a train. From a corner of the yard, the girl saw the farmer drive to the station, where, in a little while, through the narrow, last valley before the village, there came flashing the great, panting night train. The train was between her and the small station and concealed what was going on on the other side. The girl's heart beat strongly and evenly. A moment later the train went off, again hurrying away on its important errands.

The girl saw: Over the squeaking, snowy ground, three villagers were returning from nearby places. Rapidly, they disappeared into neighboring houses. There was no one else at the station. Now, however, out of a corner, came a man, tall, somewhat stooped, a stranger. For a while he looked about him as if he were not sure that he had come to the right village. The farmer went up to him and they engaged in talk for a while, as if for a long time both of them had looked forward to this meeting. And soon the sleigh turned to the left, toward the distant, scattered farmhouses in the valleys.

Now the girl felt strangely weak, as weak as if she had worked a full, long, summer day in the field, as if she had done a great deal of work and done it well. She was pleased, although she could hardly stand on her feet. She wanted rest. She began to walk home. Her heart was as peaceful as the tranquil, self-contained night around her. When she passed the large, one-story house where the druggist lived, she drew out the cold, shining, and curiously heavy weapon and flung it far from her into the snow. It was buried in an instant. She walked on. When she got into bed, she could not fall asleep. She wondered to whom she was smiling in the darkness of her room.

Race

JOSEPH OPATOSHU ————————————————————————

IN THE HOT AFTERNOON everything was ripening—the spreading vegetation, the fruit on the trees—and, from a distance, even the bungalows—scattered, brown, red-roofed—looked like ripened fruit.

Behind the bungalows—tiny gardens. In one of the gardens, in a wooden swing which seemed to sway and yet not to sway—sat Helen Rossi. Hair—eyes—shining, golden. Face, neck, hands—suntanned. Helen looked at the roof where creeping vines had spread. She looked at the trimmed bushes that enclosed three sides of the garden and at the fourth side where a white sandy path led to Cedar Lake.

In the stillness there was the sound of the water, lapping the pebbles on the shore, rolling and running on as time was running, as Helen's life was running.

For the first time in the six weeks that Helen and her ten-year-old son, Edgar, had been in Daleville, she sat in the swing. They had no sooner come out to their summer home when Edgar had become ill. At first—the grippe—then tonsillitis. Thus she had spent almost six weeks with her boy in the bungalow. And this was the second day that Edgar had gone to the lake by himself and she had remained alone.

The August sky was blue and deep. The lake was even bluer. The air was constantly changing. Now it carried the odor of ripe fruit and again the moisture and coolness of moving water.

With pleasure and a sense of fullness, Helen's eyes closed of themselves. How happy she was that, somewhere far behind her, she had cast off ten years of living, had cast off every care. And now, seated on the

swing, this was another Helen, a younger Helen, freed from all obligations, indebted to no one, neither to husband nor to ten-year-old son.

A translucence enveloped Helen, translucence coming from the trees and plants in full growth, from the blue transparent air. The many-branched trees were transformed into beings whose supple limbs, stretching over Helen, caressed and warmed her face, neck, and hands. She lowered herself to the grass that was deep and cool. She stretched full length, her feet first, then her hands, and remained lying so. From the lake there was a momentary sound of voices, and then the silence returned. Soon there came the sound of running feet, feet that were beating on the path that came from the lake. The footsteps ran on, into the grass, on to Helen, where, like a sudden downpour, childish fingers fell upon her body.

"Who's that?"

Helen shuddered and sat bolt upright. Beside her stood Edgar, weeping.

"What happened, my child?" Helen was on her feet, studying his bruised eye. "Who struck you? Who punched you in the eye?"

"Our neighbor's boys," Edgar gasped. "They began first."

"Why did they pick a quarrel with you?"

"They called me 'Sheeny' and 'Mocky.' They called me 'Jew bastard.' "

"Why did they call you names?"

"Don't know," and now the boy rubbed his eyes with his little fists and left stains on his cheeks.

"Why don't they call me any nicknames?" Helen drew Edgar close to her.

"Don't know." He extricated himself from her hands. "They belong to the K.K.K."

"How do you know they do? There is no K.K.K. any more."

"They told me themselves." He began to stuff his pockets with pebbles.

"They told me themselves that as soon as they grow up, they'll kill all the Jews and Catholics and blacks. So I said, 'We'll kill all the K.K.K. first.' There they are now."

His pockets bulging with pebbles, Edgar took up his position under a tree. Pete and Ted, the neighbor's boys, were in front; two other boys followed.

"Don't you throw any stones, do you hear?" Helen turned on Edgar. "They're four to one."

"I'll beat them all up, all of them." Edgar threw a stone and struck Pete's foot.

Four stones flew toward Edgar, but none of them struck him. The blood rushed to Helen's temples. She did not know where to run first—to Edgar or to the four boys. She turned to the latter and pleaded:

"Boys, let him alone and he'll stop throwing stones. He's just been sick. Edgar is a nervous boy and if you have any complaints make them to me. I'll punish him myself. Besides, you are four to one and how do four fellows jump on one?"

"Sure we're four," Pete, who had been struck in the foot, said, and stepped forward. "Edgar knows we are four and yet he starts up with us."

"That's a lie, Mother. Don't believe them, the K.K.K.," Edgar shouted, and stamped his feet in rage. "They picked a fight with me. They called me names."

"We started it," Pete went on, "and he calls us the Klan."

"Pete is right." Helen took Pete's part.

"No, he isn't right, Mother." Edgar shook convulsively. "Before I said anything about the Klan, they called me 'Sheeny' and 'Mocky' and they called me 'Jew bastard.' "

The boys burst into laughter, which they suppressed quickly. They avoided one another's eyes. They stood with lowered heads and glanced sideways at Edgar, to see that he did not throw a stone again. Helen stood, confused. She knew that Daleville had no love for Jews. She knew that where the Jews went bathing, the youngsters of Daleville—these "little Klansmen"—strewed broken glass. But she was sure that this was aimed at "greenhorns," who spoke Yiddish, who spoke English with an accent. She wanted to change the subject, to soften the conflict, but in a mild, strange voice the words escaped from her lips: "Boys, is what Edgar says true?"

They did not answer. Edgar shouted at his mother:

"It's true, I tell you. And you go on talking to them, pleading with them."

While Edgar was shouting, Helen's neighbor arrived from her little garden. Tall and gaunt, with her lips pressed thin, she called to her two boys as one calls trained dogs. She looked them up and down as they withdrew. Then she walked toward Helen, close up to Helen, and spat angrily.

"We hate the looks of a Jew and you keep pushing in among us!"

These words came so unexpectedly that Helen lost all speech. By the time she recovered and words began pouring into her mouth, her neighbor was gone. Her unspoken words choked her. Edgar drew close to her.

"Why do they hate us so? Because we are Jews?"

"Because they are Klansmen." Helen led Edgar to the swing where both sat down. "Because they are mean people."

Edgar could not stay seated. He saw a colorful butterfly and dashed after it.

The spacious surroundings shrank suddenly. Helen no longer saw the translucence which came from the trees and the plants in the fullness of their growth and from the blue transparency of the air. The space about had become much too constricted for her. She was grieved and did not understand whence so much malice could come to human beings as to make loathsome Heaven, Earth, and growing things.

Everything under Control

JACOB GORDIN _____

THE TRAIN—Hudson River Railroad Company—was twenty minutes late. Messages sped from one station to another. Passengers on the platform leaned over impatiently and looked for the first sign of the roaring locomotive; anxious passengers asked one another—"What happened?"

A trifle. The rails were torn up at one place. Repairs could be made quickly and everything would be under control.

It was still very early. The train was flying through woods, past green fields, past pretty villages, past wealthy villas . . . Some passengers were dozing in a sweet early morning slumber; others were looking out of the open windows and a fresh breeze brushed their faces. The sun was still a reserved guest and still too bashful to burn and broil. The sun looked down on Earth, modestly and charmingly. Suddenly the locomotive blew an angry blast, shuddered, and the train came to a stop in the middle of a meadow. The frightened passengers leaped up from their seats, several stuck their heads out of the windows, others began to run to the doors . . . many sprang from the steps to the green grass which was covered with dust and dew. For a few minutes there was panic—no one knew what had happened; the train crew ran about, excited; the firemen and engineer were shouting and banging with hammers. What had happened?

Nothing much. The rails were torn up on a bridge. Repairs would be made soon and everything would be under control.

The officials of the Hudson River Railroad Company put a very high value on time—that is to say, on the money it gets for transporting

human flesh from one place to another. The rails were really fixed very rapidly, the passengers were invited to return to the cars, the locomotive blew a gay, lively blast and slowly, quietly began to roll . . . everything was under control.

All of this took place a few miles from Hyde Park, New York, where the beloved F. W. Vanderbilt is building a magnificent palace. Hundreds of laborers sweat every day, lifting and carrying and working hard from early morning to nightfall. The palace is to be built quickly, the surrounding estate cleared, the roadways asphalted, and everything will be under control.

Mr. Vanderbilt will have a beautiful dwelling soon, but in the meanwhile the workers have no place here to sleep or eat. Every night they scatter among the neighboring farms; early in the morning they arrive on foot, some walking two miles, some three miles, some five miles, from their lodgings. They set to work promptly and everything is under control.

Among the men there is a Pole named Krosovski, just an ordinary workingman. Every day he walks five miles to and from Hyde Park. He walks the tracks, observes the woods around him and gardens . . . recalls the fields and the woods of his homeland, sings a melancholy song, and hears the accompaniment of wings in the trees. Suddenly, on a small bridge, he sees that the rails are torn up . . . Soon a train, packed with passengers, will come dashing along . . . All will be hurled into the bog below . . . hundreds will be killed. Cold sweat covers his face as he looks around, not knowing what to do. Where do you go, on whom do you call for help? . . . He decides to save his unknown brothers . . . runs a short distance from the danger spot . . . removes his shabby, old jacket so that his white shirt may more readily be seen by the locomotive engineer. It may be that the engineer will not see him, even so, and run him down and grind him to nothing. But the train will suddenly stop, the passengers will be saved, and everything will be under control . . .

He stands and waits, while time goes by. He knows that he is already late for his work and how malicious the contractor is, but he does not desert his post . . . Now he listens intently . . . the earth shudders under his feet . . . from the distance comes the noise of . . . the train is coming. He raises his hands, he shouts . . . shouts from the middle of the tracks . . . the engineer has seen him, blows an angry blast, stops the roaring locomotive, and everything is under control.

Krosovski loses no time. He expects no gratitude, has no time for talk, and runs off to his job . . . But he is late. The contractor listens to no excuses, he has no use for lazy workers. He orders Krosovski to take the pay that is due him and to leave. Krosovski pleads, explains . . . he knows that now he may remain idle a week, two weeks, or that he may lose out for the entire summer . . . The contractor listens to no arguments . . . He pays out the wages and tells him to be off! Wrapped in this thoughts, Krosovski makes his way back along the same tracks . . . The train has been gone a long time and the passengers have forgotten their terror . . . In Hyde Park they are building the palace without Krosovski and everything is under control.

In a Drugstore

B. APPLEBAUM_____

IN THE STREET, noontime smelled of fresh baking and a sense of free-dom in the world. Spring sang above the roofs of tall buildings. Beyond the city, roadways lay dry, smiling under the sun; fields were turning green and the wind made waves in the grass. In the city, people walked coatless in the streets, with brightened eyes and slightly ruddied faces. They were already abloom with the ease of summer and the joy of vaca-tion time.

But in the drugstore where I sat at the counter, slowly sipping my soda through a straw, it was half-dark.

It was pleasant and quiet. The faded mirrors looked down from the bemused walls; the nickel soda fountains smiled with gentle reflections on those seated at the counter—a couple of young girls, one light, the other dark blonde, with little, smooth faces. They relished their sundaes and carefully guarded their red lips.

A tall young black man, with soft, bronzed features and dreamy eyes, came in. He breathed with the kind of thoughtful reserve you will find in places of higher learning. With careful steps he approached the counter, stopped, and waited.

Patiently he waited. But the attendants in white jackets did not see him. They were standing quietly. One had his right hand on the faucet of the soda fountain and looked into space, but not toward where the young black was standing. This attendant's face was now congealed, his blond hair pressed down on his head, and the part lay like a string that had been pasted on.

The well-dressed young man was silent. His face was steeped in pain—like Jewish pain. Under his arm were several books and note-books. A student? Surely a student . . . He stood, waiting up to his neck in unspoken suffering. His jaws had become taut, set, and his eyes—deep, big, and black—were moist with flashing redness.

Finally his full, finely cut lips parted and, in a well-controlled voice, he said: "Excuse me."

Only then did he in the white jacket turn his head, take an indifferent look, and furrow his brow, lightly. His silence bellowed: "Nonentity!"

Passionate obstinacy flowed suddenly under the dark skin of the black student. He lifted his head proudly.

"A Coca-Cola, please."

For a while they looked at one another. The serf in the white jacket still had his hand on the faucet. On the bronze face of the student there was a look of disgust. The dark skin blanched. The blood ran out of the lips and they trembled on his mouth. At last, the serf in the white jacket removed his hand from the faucet and silently picked up a glass.

"A large one!" The words issued from between the young man's teeth—hidden spitefulness of the deeply offended in his voice.

White jacket took a larger glass. Silently, without looking at the student, he filled the glass, set it down on the marble counter, and stood waiting. In his stance there was the watchfulness, the alertness, of the pointer, which does not shift an eye while, ostensibly, it is not looking.

The young man did not seat himself and drank while standing, and I saw that he was struggling as though it were a bitter draft. Neverthe-less, he did not hurry. His face was tearful, with the silent tearfulness of one, innocent, who is harried and mocked, and who knows there is none to whom he may protest . . .

Finally, he finished his drink and put down the glass. The fellow in white quickly seized the glass in one hand. With the other, he grabbed a cloth and wiped the spot where the glass had stood, made a quick turn, and—crash!

The shattering of glass echoed in the stillness of the richly appointed drugstore. As if accidentally, the glass had slid out of his hand and splin-tered on the stone floor beside the counter.

At first, I did not understand. The young girls, too, it appeared, did not hit on what had occurred. They had merely smiled at the clerk's lack of skill. At that moment I had looked at the young student: He writhed as if a fiery whip had cut into his body; his eyes froze and the eyelids closed halfway.

Another black man—a porter there—immediately—ran up with broom and dustpan, halted, threw one look at the black student and another at the man in the white jacket. From his glance I understood at once what had happened; he had purposely broken the glass.

My body shuddered with cold.

How much agony there was in the student's face now! Wordless pain, shuddering pain, terrifying pain which causes the blood to boil.

But he was silent, choked within himself, but silent.

He held out a dollar bill. The clerk grabbed the bill, struck the register, and I saw that instead of ".10" he had rung up ".25."

Three quarters fell on the counter.

"Twenty-five cents?" a choked voice inquired.

"Yes," the clerk in the white jacket said curtly. "Fifteen for the glass."

I felt a surge of heat along my spine. My face burned with shame. Now I could not look at the young student who was being so painfully insulted this bright, sunny day.

The black porter, having swept things up, now stood up. His glance met that of the student and—

Who, as well as I, a Jew, could feel the abysmal anguish that burned in their eyes?

The pain of innocent sufferers, of the just who have no one to whom they may complain . . . pain that fires blood, hatred, and a drive for revenge.

And should that hatred ever flow over the heads of the white-jacketed, with their light hair pressed down—who would be astonished, and who would not understand?

In the meanwhile, the young student walked unsteadily to the door. My ears were filled with cries of lamentation.

But the one in the white jacket smiled.

It was the smile of the hunting dog which has painfully bitten an innocent person for no other reason than to please its master—the boss.

A Heart Divided

PERETZ HIRSCHBEIN _____

NOW CAROLINE AND DR. ZACHARY LURIA sat side by side and, heavy at heart, observed their older brother, Daniel, who, in distraction, paced back and forth and, from time to time, wiped his eyes.

It was close to midnight. Several times the quiet was broken. At times the sister and, again, the brother sought to console and hearten him by showing that his life was not as shattered as he thought. Everything considered, he was not the only one in the new land who had wanted to live in the ways of God through observing old customs and the unity of the family.

But the troubles of others could not console Daniel. Especially since the gentle Lillian-Ruth, who was pure of heart and whose equal (not to say better) could not be found among Jews, had suddenly awakened to the non-Jew in her, and was exacting her toll of the Jew, Daniel Luria. She wanted her two children, both of whom had gone to Hebrew School, to accompany her to church from time to time and to listen to the words of the "learned" priest. It caused him anguish that, lately, to his face, she heaped words of scorn at the Jews, and that she even threw up to him his brother Asher and his underworld doings.

"Daniel"—Zachary followed him with his eyes—"you're keeping something back. Such a complete change in a woman does not come all at once. It may be that you overstepped the limit with your demands. Without even knowing it, you go and destroy a life as if to take a crystal bowl and let it fall to the stone floor. There are things in you that she

From the novel *Babel*.

will never understand because she was born a Christian. Christian blood flows in her veins. As long as she was in love with you she felt that you had lifted her up."

"What are you trying to tell me?"—Daniel came to a stop in the middle of the room. "What was it I asked of her?"

"Listen to your question—'What did I ask of her?'"

"That's when the trouble begins—precisely when you begin to ask and demand. When two people—let's say man and wife—love one another heart and soul, then neither of them keeps account of what either does for the other. Doing for the other is the same as doing for yourself. To claim, to demand, who cares for such things? However, when you begin to ask: 'What do you want?' 'What else do I owe you?'—then everything is finished."

"How true!" Caroline said quietly, as if to herself.

"Of course it's true," Daniel agreed. "In our first years, neither she nor I would have hesitated to risk life for the other. I remember all of it."

"Then you also recall that twenty-three years ago she was a poor washerwoman, in a dark hole somewhere, from which you pulled her out. And let me tell you, Daniel . . ." Dr. Luria arose from his place and looked Daniel straight in the eyes. "You should never have asked her to convert. In our free country, it would have been perfectly proper; she—a Christian, you a Jew!"

Daniel laughed bitterly: "You really mean that? That's something I'd expect to hear from Nathan but not from you, Zachary."

"Nathan isn't always wrong."

"He doesn't care anything about Judaism. He often talks like a Jew baiter."

"This has nothing to do with Judaism. Yours is a private tragedy."

"Why do you rub salt in my wounds?"

"You're not a child any longer. There was a time when you were brighter and more practical than all of us together. That's why I ask you, Daniel, about all of those who have worked themselves up, have moved out of the East Side, and find joy in their children not knowing the first thing about Judaism. Do you think they will do more to support Judaism than your Lillian?"

"May I know as little of evil as I know what you are getting at."

"Let's ask Caroline what she is doing to further Jewishness in her youngsters."

In wonder, Caroline gazed at Dr. Luria. She, too, failed to grasp his idea. In her thoughts, she was back in her own home on Fifth Avenue; she sought to find a justification for Daniel's reasoning. She, too, had moved away from the East Side. She had not done it because she wanted to flee the Jewish streets but, simply, because living on Fifth Avenue was more pleasing. Besides, if she could do it, why not? Anyway, it was her husband, Leonard Stone, who found it increasingly uncomfortable on the East Side. She realized now that in regard to her children her brother, Zachary, was right. "If anyone had suggested it, I would have sent the boy to Hebrew School."

"What did you mean, Zachary, by what you said before?" Caroline fixed a pained look upon her brother. "Did you really mean that Daniel should have lived with her as with an abandoned woman, without even marrying her? And if she wanted to become a convert, he should not have let her?"

At these words, Lillian-Ruth came into the house. Her strained look relaxed. She kissed Caroline and Dr. Luria and looked with an ironic smile, sidewise, at Daniel, who could not find a place for himself.

"I am so happy to find you here." Lillian tried to hide her excitement. "I was thinking of asking you over. Especially since you are modern beings and live in today's world, perhaps you will explain why Daniel has taken a sudden dislike to me. I am saying this in his presence. If he thinks that he made an error in letting himself be enticed by a poor washerwoman, then I am ready to step out right now. America is a free country. Twenty-three years ago I did as my heart commanded. I am prepared to act in the same way now."

"Why are you in your hat and coat, like a stranger?" Caroline asked, apprehensively.

"Do I know what I'm about? My home is no longer my home."

"Why talk that way?" Caroline approached and anxiously looked into her sister-in-law's frozen face. "I beg you to tell me the full truth. What kind of misfortune has befallen you all?"

"You see for yourself, Caroline, Daniel has come to hate me."

"Don't say what you don't believe," Daniel spoke up from his side of the room. "This is no time to talk about love."

"Why not, Daniel? Is love only for young people and not for man and wife who already have children? I ask you, what else shall I talk about?"

"Tell about your wanting the children to go away from the Jewish people."

"I don't want to take them away from anyone. Life itself has shown David where he belongs. Do you suppose that I began to love the East Side Jews and because of them I gave myself to you? When I was a little girl, like all Irish youngsters I poked fun at all the Jews who appeared in our streets. Believe me, there was no one to like among them. When I grew up and had occasion to go to the Bowery and walk through the noisy Jewish crowds, I had the feeling that I was among savages. But at that time, it was you alone I loved to the point of madness. To this day, I cannot account for what happened to me. At that time I would have embraced not only the Jewish faith but even the faith of the devil, so that I might have you."

"No, Lillian, ten times no . . ." Daniel spoke with sorrow. "You did come to love Jews! I remember well what you told me about Jews. You came into the Jewish faith wholeheartedly. Our rabbi tried to dissuade you from becoming a convert. At that time you could have changed your mind. You were happy all the time, until David grew up and opened for you a window to the non-Jewish world."

"I never promised you to break with my family. Lisbeth took me to church. I recalled those years when I would go to the priest to confess my sins."

"You even went to confession. I know that because of this you demand that I should move from the East Side. No, Lillian." Daniel began to lose his patience. "I shall not give you the children and I will not stir from the East Side."

Daniel's behavior did not make a good impression on the twins. Dr. Luria, who could not understand why Lillian was suddenly becoming estranged from her Jewish husband, now got to the roots of his brother's tragedy. It was hard for him to blame his sister-in-law. After all, her conversion to Judaism had caused no change in her blood. The Jewish customs which she had assumed were nothing more than external. No one could object to her arguing that in loving Daniel she had not undertaken to love the Jewish people. She was forthright. Dr. Luria had spoken several times with Daniel's older son and understood that Daniel's son sided with the mother. In general he regarded himself as a child of normal people. He did not comprehend the reality of Jewishness or the tragedy of Jewish nationalism in the new country.

"Stop worrying about the children," Caroline began, in a motherly manner. "They will be what they are destined to be. Think of your own life. You have loved one another so. Don't be childish, Lillian. Daniel loves you like life itself. And you, Daniel, Lillian wants to move to a nicer neighborhood—take her advice. You can afford it. Lillian deserves a prettier home. You ought to even sell your two stores. You could open a finer store on Broadway or even Fifth Avenue. Isn't that so, Zachary?"

Caroline embraced her sister-in-law and kissed her on both cheeks.

Lillian threw off her hat and, still in her coat, sat down at the table, hid her face in her arms, and began to cry aloud.

Daniel took a few steps toward his forlorn wife, as if to make his peace with her. However, he turned back and sat down beside Caroline, who was seated, with bowed head, near the window. From time to time he looked at his wife and at his silent sister. He began to feel that he was to blame, although he could not see clearly of what he was guilty. He was a Jew. He wanted his home to be Jewish. Lillian had loved to light candles on the eve of the Sabbath; with gentle piety, she would cover her eyes with her hands. Now, on the coming of Sabbath eve, she did it as if she were being forced. When he spoke the benediction, she left the room. At the last Passover, at the second seder, she went off to her sister. He suspected she had gone to church. He mulled over Zachary's words before Lillian's arrival. Zachary had said: "Church or no church, Jews, here, lose their children forever." Yes, it was true. But when was it ever known before that parents themselves should wish it?

Daniel's eyes rested on his sister, who seemed to have shriveled in the few hours' stay in his house. He regretted that the doctor had asked her to share Daniel's sorrows. However, he also knew that Caroline was perhaps the only one who, if she gave herself to it, could restore the harmony of the disturbed household. Lillian had always loved Caroline.

"Carry," Daniel, his spirit dejected, turned to his sister. "You are a woman and a sister. I will let you talk for me. Ask her in what way my ruined home can be rebuilt. Let her tell you what she requires of me. Surely, it is not only that we should move from the neighborhood. That's just a trifle. If that's what she wants, I'll agree. But what if, after we leave the Jewish streets behind us, my life in the new home becomes empty and dreary!"

Lillian raised her head and, with tear-reddened eyes, looked at

Daniel in silence, with not a trace of meanness in her face. Desolation and compassion were there. Evidently she wanted to say something, but the words evaded her and would not form on her lips.

Lillian tried to recall that gray morning of more than twenty years ago when an unknown man had knocked on the door of her damp, poor, peace-forsaken room where, day in, day out, she bent over a washtub and rubbed the wash of strangers with her worn-out hands. The man was a Jewish peddler. What had she beheld in this Jewish peddler, at that time, that the earth gave way under her feet?

Was it because her husband used to beat her black and blue and take her earnings for his sprees in the saloons on the Bowery? Was it her desolate life that had cast itself at the feet of the Jewish peddler, whose name she did not know, until much later when, in her illness, he came upon her near a hospital? It was tenderness she yearned for at the hands of a man, not blows, and it did not matter of what people or faith the man might be. She was overcome with complete exhaustion when she sensed that this unknown man, of a strange and unloved people, wanted to protect her. She was young and her emaciated body yearned to be filled with fresh strength.

She also recalled how she felt when the first child, implanted in her body by this Jew, had died in her body. She had miscarried and felt she was being punished for a sin. There would be no more happiness in life for her. The brightness of life would no longer sing in the corner of her new home, among a people she did not know.

These experiences were being relived by the two, and neither he nor she now possessed the energy to rebuild their ruined life. Her eyes strayed from her husband to his brother and to his sister. It seemed to her that, although they had always been close to her, there was now lacking in them that friendliness which might rouse her from her depression. They lacked the warm closeness which might serve to raise her from the depths. She felt that she had fallen and did not have enough strength to rise.

Dr. Luria and Caroline felt much the same way. They loved and cherished Lillian-Ruth only when she, the convert, loved and cherished not only the members of the Luria family but the race from which her husband stemmed. Now a division had arisen which separated them. At the same time, too, for both Dr. Luria and Caroline, Daniel was not the brother whom they could aid in this troubled hour.

Dr. Luria stood up, weary to exhaustion, and spoke to Caroline:

"Let us leave them to themselves, Carry. Husband and wife themselves must find the way which, at their first meeting, led them to one another. They are both sensible and wholesome human beings."

Caroline approached her sister-in-law, kissed her, and with bowed head left the house.

For a while, Dr. Luria and Caroline walked in silence. Caroline felt weariness in her limbs and held on to her brother to keep from falling.

"What do you make of this mess?" Caroline asked quietly.

"You needn't marry a Gentile wife to feel, after the children have grown up, like a tree that's been torn down—its roots having withered. Yes, Caroline, on our fat American earth our roots are withering and dying out."

My Indian Mother

SHEEN DAIXEL _____

THERE IN THE TITAN CITY from which I came not long ago—one seldom sees the true face of Heaven. More than eight million beings have crowded together in stony streets where the air, for the most part, is poisoned with the reek of gasoline and the smoke of countless chimneys from houses and factories. There, the water of the two great rivers, the Hudson and the East River, is always gray and black with waste. These rivers rarely reflect the smiling sky, the gentle flight of the rosy white clouds, the magical color display of the rising or setting sun.

Once, in the spring, I fled from there. To the blue border of sky which slumbers far off on the green prairies. I fled to the sandy desert, to the huge, stony formations and the snowy peaks of the high mountains.

For weeks on end, pack on back, I roamed the highways and byways of our beautiful, rich America, never spending the day where I had spent the night. Kindly folk would take me into their cars; unkindly or fearful ones, at the sight of my thumb, would angrily shift their eyes and swiftly step on the gas.

For the most part, poor folks would stop their automobiles, barely gasping and sun-peeled and, with a smile, move over to make a place for me.

And for their goodness I repaid them with stories of my wanderings in Asia, endless yarns of wonderful events, some true and others made up on the spot.

ऌ

It is night, a dark night, on the Arizona desert. The deep blue, almost black, sky above me is thickly covered with thousands of large, brightly flashing stars. They are so bright that when I half close my eyes it seems to me that the whole sky lifts and lowers itself in a gigantic, flaming net.

And the stillness around is equally strange; it mutes every sound that might disturb its quiet—whether it be the voices of Navahos who are close by, or the bark of coyotes, or the neighing of some horses that are grazing on a neighboring meadow.

Upon a flat stone bedded down in our blankets, I am lying with my Indian friend, the Hopi, Otaka. He is a young fellow with whom I became acquainted, and quickly made friends, two weeks ago in the Indian village, Oraibi, at the time of the Snake Dance.

Oraibi is situated on the southern part of a flat, stony mesa, over a hundred feet high, in the very heart of the Arizona desert. The village is one of the oldest and, until recently among the surrounding Hopi villages, was considered a sacred place. Understandably, for the festival of the Snake Dance, which occurs in specified, even-numbered years, there gather in this place not only Hopi Indians but Indians of other neighboring tribes, as well as a large number of white guests from nearby and distant cities.

At that time I found myself in the Indian village of Moenkopi. Learning that in two weeks' time the Snake Dance would take place in Oraibi, I set out and arrived at the mesa where Oraibi is situated, a day before the dance.

Weakened by the heat and the long trek, pack on back, I barely crawled the narrow, crooked, stony paths to the village itself, and sat down to rest on a stone between two mud huts.

In my fatigued mind only one thought stubbornly persisted: Where does one find a place to undress, wash up, and spend the night until the dance is over?

An unusually slender young man, in his early twenties, went by whistling the popular wartime melody "Over There."

After a moment's deliberation, I called to him: "Hello, brother, may I ask you something?"

He stopped, scrutinized me, his eyes resting on my pack, and came closer.

"Sure you may. What is it?"

"Tell me, do you have any kind of a house, well, anything like a hotel, where a weary devil like me can wash up, rest, and wait for tomorrow's Snake Dance?"

He smiled and looked at me again: "Where do you come from?"

"From Moenkopi. I guess it's about forty miles from here. I left it at five in the morning. Got a lift for half the distance."

"What were you doing in Moenkopi?" he said, wonderingly, as he again glanced at my pack. "Selling things?"

"No. I'm no merchant. I was there about four weeks. I have a few friends there. I stayed with one of them."

"With whom, for instance?" He questioned me with childish eagerness.

"With Neissin. I slept in his half-tumbled down old house, near his store."

He was greatly pleased.

"Oh, I know Neissin very well. But why were you staying in Moenkopi?"

"I am a writer and I got to Moenkopi direct from New York."

"From New York?" he asked quietly and wonderingly.

"Yes, from New York," I said emphatically. "I want to familiarize myself with Indian life so that I may be able, later, to write a series of stories about it. Do you understand?"

"Yes, I understand," he answered quietly and, seemingly captivated by something, leaned over very close to me: "Why do you need to do it? I mean—to write about us?"

"Because I believe a shocking injustice was committed against his native brother by the white man. And writers can sometimes be very helpful."

For a while he looked at me with widely opened eyes, then straightened up, took a deep breath, and a childish, bright pleasure suddenly flooded his face. He gave me a friendly pat on the shoulder and said:

"It's good that we met. My name is Otaka. My father's name is Lomavontiva. He is one of the priests who will perform the dance tomorrow. Now listen: Near our house there is a small, but clean, wooden hut. You will be able to stay there till after the dance and for as long as you wish, but I must have my father's permission for that. He's a wonderful man, my father, and I'm sure he'll not refuse me. As for me, I finished school in Tuba City and also in Riverside, California. And I am myself," he hesitated for a moment, "I am an artist . . . I paint various pictures and . . ." He did not finish . . . "Now wait here a while; I'll be back soon."

He again patted me on the shoulder and started off rapidly, but then came to a stop suddenly.

"What's your name?"

"Call me Brother—I'll tell you the rest later."

He was off and ten minutes later came on the run, panting and seething with joy.

"Come, Brother! Father is waiting for you . . . Mother is already laying down the blankets for you to sleep on . . . As I told you—my parents are splendid people."

And walking with me, he spoke quickly, almost feverishly: "You'll have to tell me lots about your New York and its skyscrapers, Brother, and about your writers and, especially, about your painters and art galleries."

And thus, as in a dream, two wonderful weeks went by. I would spend days with Otaka on the flat roof of their house, both of us absorbed in discussing all sorts of things, or we would dash about the desert on horseback. He would never tire of telling me of his life and the life and ways of his people. He was a born artist, and the many drawings he showed me actually breathed the life of his village. Magnificent, too, were his paintings of the desert in the spring, when the melancholy, thorny cacti bloomed in their innumerable soft colors and the entire desert was transformed, for a short time, into a blossoming garden. Lomavontiva, Otaka's father, apparently earned little as a priest, and depended for a livelihood on a plot of ground in the desert and on some ten or twelve horses, which he hired out to the villagers.

Three times in two weeks Otaka and I spent the night in the desert, looking after the horses, which were grazing on a scantily grassed plot.

This was the fourth night in the desert and also the last night we would be together: Early the next morning, by prearrangement, a neighbor was to take me in his truck and drop me off on one of the highways leading toward Los Angeles.

And so we were both lying on the customary flat stone, watching the horses, looking at the stars, while a deep sorrow filled our hearts. A sorrow of true friends who had finally found one another and must part so soon and, who knows, possibly never meet again.

"It's settled, then . . . You are really going away very early?"

"Yes, Brother. Believe me—I have no desire to go, but . . . I came here for just one day and, thanks to your friendship, stayed for two wonderful weeks."

"Yes, I know . . . I know . . . A pity . . . A great pity." He sighed deeply.

I wanted to divert him and asked: "Explain, why were you named Otaka?"

He smiled. "Because, in our language Otaka is the name of a bird—the stork—tall, with long, thin legs. That's what I was like at birth." But he would not be diverted: "Tell me, what's your next stopping place?"

"First, for just a few days, Los Angeles, where many friends have waited months for my coming. Then I mean to make my way into that rarely beautiful Yosemite Valley. I'd very much like to learn something of the life of those Indians."

"Wait a while," he said, and sat up suddenly. "If that's the case, I can help you a good deal."

I sat up, too, and eagerly looked him in the eyes: "What do you mean?"

"In school, in Riverside, my best friend was a Yosemite Indian, a fine chap named Vipayak. In his tongue that means an eagle. He once told me that his family stems from the heroic Chief Tenaya who, for many years, fought the white invaders of Yosemite Valley. He also told me about his sick mother, paralyzed, I think, who to this day remains a sworn enemy of the whites and even now refuses to speak the English language."

"Excellent," I rejoiced. "Here are pen and paper. Write me a few words to your friend Vipayak."

"Wait till it grows light." He lay down again and sighed. "It's too bad, Brother, it's too bad you're going away. Take care of the drawings I've given you. Show them to artists . . . Write me what they think of my work."

"Don't worry. I will even take them to the art museum in Los Angeles and show them to the director and I will let you know his opinion without delay. At the first opportunity, I will return here, to Oraibi."

"Remember, that's a promise."

"I'll not forget, you may rest assured."

One evening two weeks later, in the Buick of a friendly stranger, I rode past the narrow, stony, thickly overgrown mountain walls into the Yosemite Valley.

The automobile stopped at the entrance of one of the rich hotels. I leaped out first and warmly thanked the middle-aged couple who had picked me up thirty miles from the valley.

"And where will you stay?" the man wanted to know.

"In one of God's hotels," I answered with a laugh.

"We would love to hear the end of your beautiful opium tale," the woman remarked.

"That's fine! How long are you staying here?"

"Exactly two weeks tomorrow," the man replied. "If you come in time, we'll take you to Los Angeles."

"Many thanks. It's very kind of you."

"Don't you think, young fellow, a ten-dollar bill may be handy here?" the man asked me quietly.

"Oh, thank you! No, I don't need it. But it will be good to remember there are people as kind as you. Thanks, again." I picked up my knapsack and left.

In the west, behind one of the high stone walls, a blood-red sun was setting and its ruddy rays were slowly, and as if reluctantly, erasing one by one the golden flecks and stripes from off the neighboring walls and higher and lower mountain peaks. The air was saturated with odorous moisture.

Entranced, I walked slowly and finally stopped a young girl who was passing by.

"Excuse me. Perhaps you can tell me where the Indian village is?"

She looked at me closely.

"Are you an Indian yourself?" She tried to guess.

"Possibly, but where is the village?"

She pointed to the left:

"You see that big tree? Right behind it there is a narrow path which will take you straight to their tents. Tell me this," she insisted on knowing, "are you also going to take part in their dances next Friday?"

"I hope to. Thanks."

Upon a large meadow some score of canvas tents and wooden shelters were drawn up in two rows. One of the tents, much larger than the rest and round in shape, stood in the center of the meadow. Both flaps of the entrance were drawn aside, as if on purpose. A mighty oak had spread its long, thick branches both above the tent and a considerable distance around it.

Seated on the grass, their feet under them, were two couples—one middle-aged, the other young—and three small children. All of their faces were brownish-red, with sharp noses and sharp black eyes. In front of them there burned a small lively fire above which a small kettle was turning black. The sparks from the fire and the steam from the kettle rose simultaneously toward the branches and disappeared there.

I stopped at a distance, took the knapsack off my back, wiped the sweat off my face, and called out: "Greetings, friends!"

No one of them stirred from his place or answered a word, but their glances, sharp and questioning, seemed to pierce me. I waited for an answer.

From the darkness of the open tent there suddenly came the voice of an old woman, obviously with a question, in their language, about the newcomer.

Without turning her eyes from me, the younger of the two women directed a few short guttural words toward the tent.

I removed Otaka's letter from my pocket and asked: "Can you tell me where I can find Vipayak?"

They exchanged glances quickly, and the younger man stood up.

"I am Vipayak. What can I do for you?"

"I've just come from Oraibi and I have a letter for you from my friend Otaka."

Again they looked at one another quickly. A gleam of pleasure in the eyes and a smile, as of disbelief, lighted Vipayak's face at the same time. Each of us took two steps toward the other, and I gave him the letter.

Reading the letter, he glanced at me several times with looks that were still doubtful. He then went to the older man, his brother it seemed, and gave him the letter. And while the latter was reading attentively, I spoke up loudly so that their ailing mother in the tent should hear me:

"I also bring to your mother, Novim, greetings from Oraibi—from

Chief Lomavontiva and his wife. For two weeks I stayed with them. They send their best wishes for her health and happiness."

The two women looked at each other, arose at the same time, and went to their mother in the tent. Having finished reading the letter, the older brother also arose, came forward, extended his hand, and introduced himself: "My name is Leme."

He invited me to sit down and share their meager supper.

The younger pressed my two hands.

"Otaka is my best friend. Come, sit by our fire; be our guest."

Both women came out of the tent and bowed to me. The older pointed to herself and said quietly: "My name is Teveyena."

And the younger added: "And mine is Loya."

All of us sat down around the kettle and, after several minutes of eating in silence, the older brother began:

"Our friend Otaka asks in his letter that we should help you in your work. You would make us happy if you told us in what way we can help."

"We will certainly not refuse to help you," added the younger, "but explain what we are to do."

"Not a thing. You need only permit me to remain among you a few weeks, and give me a place to stay. That is all. And you need not worry about feeding me; I can easily manage that at the cafeteria of one of the hotels."

Again the voice of the old woman issued from the tent. But now the sentences were more sustained and the tone one of command.

Vipayak translated his mother's words:

"Mother said that a friend of Lomavontiva's is a friend of ours, and we do not send them to our enemies for any reason, least of all for food. We share with our guests whatever we possess." Quietly he added: "Mother knows English well, but will not use the language . . . she won't make peace with them—the whites." He was silent a while, then added: "She wants to see you after we've eaten."

A number of neighbors, men, women, and children, came out of their tents, observed me from a distance, and spoke quietly among themselves.

"Just what's the matter with your mother?" I quietly asked the older brother a little later. "Is she paralyzed? How long has she been bedridden? Has she been seen by a doctor?"

"It is now six months that she has not left her bed. She is not para-lyzed, but she suffers severe pains in the back and the legs. About a month ago, after a great to-do, I got a doctor from one of the hotels to see her. He merely looked at her, asked how old she was, then touched her back with his hand, and pulled a face when his hand apparently became moist with her sweat. Three days later, by a messenger from the hotel, he sent her a box of pills. As you probably understand yourself, she threw away those pills and her hatred for them" (he omitted the word "whites") "became even stronger."

"What do you say, Leme? Would your mother permit me to examine her?"

"Are you a doctor?"

"No, not in the ordinary sense of the term. I do not write prescriptions, but I have studied and learned how to manipulate ailing muscles of the human body. It's possible I may be able to ease her pain. But I can assure you of one thing—I will not make her worse. Rest assured of that."

"I don't know." Vipayak shrugged his shoulders. "Come, let's introduce you to Mother and you will ask her yourself."

All of us went into the old woman's tent. Loya, lantern in hand, went ahead and remained standing near the head of her mother-in-law. The aged woman, lying on her cot, was covered with a blanket. Her face, a net of wrinkles from which her nose protruded sharply. Her eyes, unnaturally large and deep black, seemed to pierce my face.

My heart was filled with pain, mixed with a strange feeling of fear and pity.

She reached out her hand, which I took in both of mine, brought to my lips, and kissed. A smile seemed to flow over her lips and a gentle light issued from her eyes and was reflected on the wrinkles of her face. She stroked my hand and began to talk to me in her own language.

Leme quickly began to translate her words:

"Mother welcomes your coming to us and thanks you for the greetings you have brought her. She hopes you will find rest here and will also be able to do the work you have come to do here."

I spoke directly to her:

"Thank you, dear friend. I am sure the time I shall spend here will prove the best time of my life. But I want to take up with you something that may result, if not in your complete recovery, at least in a slight easing of your pain. I should like . . ."

She halted me with a wave of her hand and said something to her older son. With a faint smile, the latter informed me that his mother had heard my suggestion that I examine her and was willing. It was agreed that I would see her about ten the next morning.

That evening we, together with a few neighbors, sat around a fire. At first I told them about life in New York. Next, a group of men, divided into two sets, engaged in a game that involved songs and the tossing of pieces of bone. Even later, try as hard as I could, I was unable to make anything of their game.

The next morning, I went into the old woman's tent, together with her sons and their wives. I bought, in a nearby store, a bottle of rubbing alcohol, a jar of vaseline, and a pound of cotton wadding.

"Good morning, Mother Novim! What kind of night did you have?"

Teveyena, the older daughter-in-law, replied, saying that the invalid had had severe pain and had not slept a wink.

Following my directions, the two brothers raised their groaning mother and then turned her over, face down. With alcohol, mixed with warm water, I washed her back thoroughly and, at the same time, felt several places where the muscles were bunched and stiff. These parts I smeared with vaseline, massaged them gently for about twenty minutes, and tried to relax the stiffened muscles to their normal place. The old woman groaned and spoke to herself. Maybe she was praying to the Great Spirit.

Suddenly Loya touched my shoulder, pointed to the old woman, and said quietly: "Sh . . . sh . . . she has fallen asleep."

All of them repeated: "Sh . . . sh . . . she has fallen asleep."

After that morning, twice a day for two weeks, I washed her back and massaged the stiffened muscles. Her pains were eased somewhat and slowly she began sleeping through the nights. At the end of the third week, both sons, holding their mother under the arms, led her out, and seated her on a soft, worn-out hotel chair beside the fire where supper was cooking.

I spent entire days with Vipayak, admiring the enchanted valley. We climbed all the mountains, did not overlook a waterfall, paced around and around the gigantic sequoias, and raced three times through the ten-foot auto road cut through the very heart of the titanic tree, Vivian.

"It's a great pity that our friend Otaka is not with us," Vipayak said several times. And once, looking down from a hill into the long valley, a painful cry escaped from his lips: "It's enough to drive one crazy—to see what they have stolen from us! The loveliest valley in the world! And take my word, if they still allow us to breathe in this region, in our poor village, it certainly is not out of their humanness but merely to advertise the dances with which we entertain their guests every Friday."

The days sped.

The pains in the back and legs from which the mother suffered grew fainter, and I taught both daughters-in-law to do what I had done, now needed only once a day, and also the light physical exercises which they were to have her perform.

It was now the sixth week of my stay and I had finally decided on the morning of my departure. On my last night there I, the mother, both sons, and their wives gathered on a high, flat-topped hill behind the village—a hill before which there unrolled a magnificent view of a large portion of the valley. The mother was seated in her upholstered chair and we, around her, were seated on boxes.

The sun was setting and, as on the evening of my arrival, the golden red rays were still resting on the topmost portions of the rocky walls and peaks of the surrounding mountains, and the gathering shadows summoned all their powers to drive them off. And, at that time, too, the air was soft and cool and filled with the most delicate perfumes.

For a long time all of us were silent. Sadness oppressed each of us and there was no desire to speak. The mother looked straight ahead thoughtfully, and once, quickly, wiped away her tears. All of us pretended not to see. And soon she began to talk quietly and, to everyone's astonishment, in English, in very fluent English, at that. We understood this was for my benefit. And as she spoke, her eyes looked directly at me.

"You came to us a stranger, a strange white man, but I am sure you were sent here by the Great Spirit who, apparently, could no longer bear to see my suffering, and would not allow my hatred of them to consume me, to poison me.

"I have thought a great deal and cannot understand why he selected you in particular . . ." She scrutinized my face: "I don't know . . . there is something in your face . . . something of our own . . . maybe you yourself also descend from one of our remote ancestors . . . who knows?"

She took a deep breath: "Every winter I read many books in English, yes, English"—she emphasized the word as if to spite herself—"As yet there are none in Indian. Well, one time a Bible came to hand, with its story of the creation in six days and of God's resting on the seventh . . . and of the way He later settled Adam and Eve in the Garden of Eden, of how, after that, they sinned and He sent an angel with a sword to drive them out. A very fine story, and a just one, too: Sin should be punished.

"But we, Yosemite Indians, have not sinned in any way. Why has the God of the white man sent against us—not only no angels but bloodthirsty gold prospectors who have driven us from our Paradise? And later, when under the leadership of our great chief, Tenaya, we began to oppose them, they dressed in military uniform, slaughtered thousands of us, and confined the survivors, like wild beasts, in a reservation on the Fresno River. Now, I ask you, where is the justice in this?

"True, your God is stronger, but only because He is more terrible. Our Great Spirit is more just, more humane." She was wrapped in thought for a while and then said, quietly: "Our family, I think, is the one that stems directly from Chief Tenaya."

From the direction of the hotels there suddenly came a burst of licentious music and the sound of wild singing.

She nodded her head in that direction:

"Hear that? They've turned our peaceful, sacred valley into a marketplace, and just as in the time of the early miners, they are still looking for gold here, but no longer in the earth. Instead, they seek it in everyone's pockets."

With a gesture of the hand, she indicated the wide prospect around us:

"Tell me, where else in the world, in the span of some dozen miles, can one see so much grandeur, so many places made holy by the beauty of nature? Where does one find such magnificent hills as El Captain, Cathedral Spires, Glacier, and Inspiration Point? Such monuments as the Three Brothers, Cloud Rest, and Watkins Mountain? Where else will one see such indescribable waterfalls as Vernal, Yosemite, Nevada, and others? And the oldest, tallest, thickest trees in the world, the sequoias, grow only in our valley, and why should the two most remarkable of them bear the names of American generals—Grant and Sherman—and not those of two of our Indian chiefs?"

She wiped her tears.

"I beg you, Mother, calm yourself!" Teveyena, the older daughter-in-law, pleaded.

"You must not excite yourself," added Loya.

Their mother nodded her head toward me:

"But he is going away early tomorrow morning and I have borne these words in silence for so long . . ." She suddenly clenched her fists and a thick stream of curses in her own tongue poured from her mouth.

Both sons put their hands on her shoulders, at the same time.

"Easy, Mother!" Leme said firmly.

"Enough, I beg you!" Vipayak added.

I took both her hands in mine:

"Enough has been said about all that, Mother. No words and nothing at all can be of any help. Life often moves in terrible ways and your only hope, like that of all who have been wronged, is that the future will alter circumstances and the whole of life will take on a new aspect. A wholly new world will come into being, a beautiful, brotherly world, and the devil, gold, will lose all his glamour. I am happy that I was able to lessen your pains a little and I hope to get word that you have recovered completely.

"When I arrived among you, I looked only for some friendship, but I have received more, much more. Many, many years ago, in my childhood, I lost my mother. But even the strongest and bravest man from time to time needs the help of a mother, of a simple, loving mother, and I found this help. I found here, my mother, in you."

I was suddenly out of breath and tears burned my eyes. I pressed her hands to my face.

And Mother Novim, the wife of a chief of the Yosemite Indians, bent over and kissed me on the head.

"Thank you, my son, for everything! Take me away in your heart, as your face will remain in mine. And may good fortune and peace attend your ways. And see that you do not forget us."

The Authors

B. Applebaum (1887–1945). Born in Vovkin, Poland, he began writing in 1912. He lived in Lodz and, later, in Odessa, where he experienced the civil war about which he wrote several novels. He came to this country in 1922. He wrote on many aspects of American life, including the difficulties and problems of greenhorns from many walks of life.

Sholem Aleichem (1859–1916). Born in Pereyaslev (Poltova Province). He wrote his first literary work in 1885. In 1888–89, he published the *Yiddish People's Library,* establishing a significant trend in new Yiddish writing. He quickly became one of the most loved and popular writers, taking his place, along with Mendele Mocher Seforim and I. L. Peretz, as one of the three pillars of modern Yiddish literature. He visited the United States in 1906, and in 1914 settled in New York City, where he died in May 1916. His works are most widely read in Yiddish and Hebrew, but have been translated into many other languages. His characters Menachem Mendel, Tevye the Dairyman, and Mottel, the Cantor's Son, are world famous. His plays are still performed throughout the world. Sholem Aleichem's popularity was expressed by the worldwide celebration, in 1959, of the one hundredth anniversary of his birth.

Sholem Asch (1880–1957). Born in Poland. He won early recognition among Polish-Yiddish writers under the influence of I. L. Peretz. Asch wrote scores of novels, plays, and short stories. Through translation into English and most European languages, he reached vast audiences. He came to the United States in 1909, where he wrote as extensively about American Jewish life as he had about Jewish life in Europe. He also wrote many historical novels. His best-known works are the play *God of Vengeance* and the novels *Salvation, Uncle Moses, Motke the Thief, Three Cities, East River,* and *The Nazarene.* Asch spent the last years of his life in Israel and died while visiting London.

Sheen Daixel (1884–?). Born in Russia. He came to the United States in 1911, after years of roaming across Asiatic Russia. His stories about that experience form a body of writing unique in Yiddish. Similarly, his writings about Native American life bring an element of the exotic to Yiddish readers. His later works dealt with paratroopers in World War II. His one-act plays have been performed by Yiddish groups in the United States and abroad. Like many other Yiddish writers, Daixel was a teacher in secular schools for many years.

Borech Glassman (1893–1945). Came to the United States in 1911 and was a housepainter for many years. He received his B.A. degree in Columbus, Ohio. He served in the U.S. Army in 1918–19. Some of his stories, in English, appeared in the *Menorah Journal, Jewish Sentinel,* and the *Jewish Spectator.* He wrote many novels and hundreds of short stories, which were published in Yiddish newspapers all over the world. His sustained interest in American life resulted in vivid stories about Jews and non-Jews, African-American and white workers, and the unemployed.

Jacob Gordin (1853–1909). Well-known playwright. He was born in Mirgorad, Russia. He began his literary career by writing in Russian, about 1870. He came to the United States in 1891 where he began writing for the stage, and became an innovator and reformer of the Yiddish theater. His works include some sixty plays, originals and adaptations, which enabled many actors to attain great prominence. His plays have been translated into many languages. Some of them are performed to this day in Yiddish, Hebrew, and other stages. He also wrote short stories and humorous pieces.

Chone Gottesfeld (1890–1964). Born in Galicia. He came to the United States in 1908, and worked in many shops and on Yiddish newspapers in Cleveland, Chicago, and Philadelphia. His literary activity was primarily linked with the Yiddish theater. He is the author of many comedies, most of which have been presented in the Yiddish theaters of the United States and abroad. Among his better-known plays are *Parnosse (Making a Living)*, *Malochim Oif Der Erd (Angels on Earth)*, and *Gvald, Ven Sharbt Er (Will He Never Die)*.

Peretz Hirschbein (1880–1948). Born in Russia. He wrote his first play in 1907 and a year later organized a theatrical group in Odessa. This group became the vanguard of the modern Yiddish theater. Hirschbein wrote more than a score of Yiddish plays and one-acters. He was a dramatist of distinction whose work resulted in the refinement of the Yiddish theater. His plays include *Di Puste Kretchme (The Idle Inn)* and *Grinne Felder (Green Fields)*, which have sustained their popularity over the years. His trilogy of novels, *Bovel (Babel)*, is an absorbing story of Jewish experience in the United States. He died in Los Angeles.

Leon Kobrin (1872–1946). Born in Russia. He came to this country in 1892 and wrote for the Yiddish Socialist press of the day. His first story was published in 1894 and his first play (written in collaboration with Jacob Gordin) appeared in 1899. Kobrin was a member of the group of writers who pioneered Yiddish literature in the United States. He wrote many stories and a large number of plays. He introduced new aspects of life to his vast audience of readers and theater-goers. Among his early novels was *Fun a Litvish Shtetl Biz a Tenement Hoiz*, which appeared in English in 1920 under the name *A Lithuanian Village* in a translation by Isaac Goldberg. Among Kobrin's best-known plays are *Sonim (Enemies)*, *Yankel Boile*, *Tzurik Tzum Folk (Return to the People)*, and *Riverside Drive*. Kobrin died in New York.

Zalmon Libin (1872–1955). One of the best-known Yiddish writers in America, Libin came to the United States in 1892. He worked in shops and was a peddler. He published hundreds of short stories about the hard life of the immigrant. His plays received frequent performances in the Yiddish theaters in the United States. His popular stories have been published in several volumes.

Aaron Maizel (1890–1936). Born in Berezin, Russia. He came to America in 1911 and began his literary career ten years later and in 1927 published his first collection of stories. In 1939 and 1953, posthumous volumes of his work appeared, the latter issued by YKUF. Maizel's work is marked by simplicity and clarity, his characters being drawn from humble Jewish men and women here and in Europe. Maizel was one of the most prominent teachers in progressive Yiddish secular schools. In 1929 he wrote what was then a pioneer work, *Jews in the United States.*

Sheen Miller (1895–1958). Born in Russia. He came to this country in 1913 and began writing in 1917. Miller is the author of several books. His short stories dealing with the Yiddish intelligentsia are notable for their psychological insights. Miller lived in Los Angeles for a considerable time.

Moishe Nadir (1885–1943). Born in Naraiav, Galicia. He came to the United States in 1898 and made his literary debut in 1902. He wrote poems, short stories, essays, and humorous sketches of a unique and biting character; he was also the author of a number of plays. His work, revealing a virtuosity of expression and sustained satire, is contained in several volumes.

Joseph Opatoshu (1887–1954). Born in Mlava, Poland. He took part in the Russian Revolution of 1905, after which he went to France and studied engineering. Opatoshu came to the United States in 1907. After trying various occupations, including newspaper carrying and teaching Hebrew, he attended evening classes at Cooper Union and received a degree in civil engineering in 1914. He began to write in 1910. In 1912, he won immediate recognition with his novel *Der Roman fun a Ferd Ganev.* He wrote many novels and hundreds of short stories. He was one of the creators of the historical novel in Yiddish. His trilogy *In Polish Woods,* a monumental work on Jewish life and the degeneracy of Chasidism, brought him world renown. His last works, *Rabbi Akiba* and *Bar Kochba,* depict the Jewish uprising against Rome. Opatoshu died in New York.

Chaver Paver (1901–1964). Born in Bershad (Podolia). He came to America in 1923 and wrote extensively for young people. Among his novels about Jewish life in America are *Clinton Street* and *Tzen Landsleit (Ten Fellow Townsmen).*

Isaac Raboy (1882–1944). Born in Bessarabia and came to the United States in 1904. After graduation from an agricultural school, he spent several years on a horse farm in North Dakota. In 1913 Raboy returned to New York where he worked as a furrier. He made his literary debut in 1914 and was included in the collections published by Di Yunge. He became a prominent member of that group. He wrote several novels and numerous short stories, many of them dealing with life in the West. His novels *Der Yiddisher Cowboy (The Jewish Cowboy)*, *Nine Bridder (Nine Brothers)*, and *Beim Poss fun Yom (The Edge of the Sea)* established him as one of the most accomplished authors of fiction among Yiddish writers in America.

Abraham Raisin (1875–1953). Born in Russia, served in the czarist army. He began to write in the early 1890s. He came to the United States in 1908. Next to the Yiddish classicists, he was one of the most popular and beloved writers among readers of Yiddish in Europe and this country. His works run to more than a score of volumes of prose and poetry. His poems have the simplicity and lucidity of the folk song, and many of them were set to music. His stories depict the everyday life of the Jewish people in a period of transition in the old country and in a difficult period of adaptation to the new. Raisin died in New York.

Tashrak (1872–1926). Born in Harki, province of Mohilev. He came to America in 1889 where he became a peddler. In 1893, he began his writing career on Yiddish newspapers. His stories and humorous sketches about Jewish immigrant life became very popular in his time.